LEAVING BARNEY

LEAVING BARNEY

BETTE ANN MOSKOWITZ

Thorndike Press • Thorndike, Maine

Library of Congress Cataloging in Publication Data:

Moskowitz, Bette Ann.
  Leaving Barney.

    Large print ed.
    1. Large type books. I. Title.
  [PS3563.088445L43 1988b] 813'.54— 88-24807
  ISBN 0-89621-186-X (lg. print : alk. paper)

Grateful acknowledgement is given for use of lyrics
from the following:
"Buckle Down Winsocki" by Ralph Blane and Hugh Martin.
Copyright © 1941 by Chappell & Co., Inc.
Copyright renewed. International copyright secured.
All rights reserved. Used by permission.
"I Get Ideas" by D. Cochran and J. Sanders.
Copyright © 1951 by Hill & Range Songs Inc.
Copyright renewed and assigned to Unichappell Music, Inc.
International copyright secured.
"When You Were Sweet Sixteen" by Delores Williams.
Copyright © 1975 by Southfield Music Inc., Detroit (ASCAP).
All rights reserved. Used by permission.

Large Print edition available by arrangement with
Henry Holt and Company, Inc.

Cover design by Michael Anderson.

TO
MARVIN, LYNN, AND MICHAEL
WITH ALL MY LOVE

ACKNOWLEDGMENTS

I want to thank Janet Jurist and Evelyn Diaz for sharing their knowledge with me; Genevieve Kazdin for her numerous acts of kind and tactful assistance; and some great, fighting women I have known—my mother, Mary Solomon, among them.

Most especially, I want to thank Sandra Taub, without whose intelligent, loving, and liberating encouragement I could not have written this book.

MYSTERY

REVISIONIST HISTORY

FANTASY

The customer was standing in the recessed doorway when the owner came. The owner nodded and turned his attention to opening the locks on the door. It was an old bookstore, the door wood with a glass panel. Steel covered the glass from the inside. The customer said it sure was cold out, and shook his shoulders, but the owner seemed not to hear. The alarm above the door screamed briefly as the owner hurried behind the counter to trip it. The customer followed the owner in and stood just inside the door. The owner looked up, uneasy, looked at the cash drawer, but the customer didn't move, just held up his hand, said take your time. The owner shrugged and went to the basement, locking the door behind him.

He changed his hiding place for the previous day's cash receipts at least once a week. In the old days, when his wife had worked there with him, she had, without telling him, changed it again sometimes, as if he might be likely to rob himself. When hiding money he favored

11

the *Purloined Letter* approach, rolling the cash in a display poster and placing it with other posters on the floor in plain sight, or in a gift box with other gift boxes stacked against the wall; his wife had tended toward *Treasure Island*, leaving a book in the upper-left-hand drawer of the desk, the title of which led him to the receipts (*The Sacred Fount* – to the toilet tank, money wrapped in plastic – was his favorite). Thought of his wife made him edgy. He had something to tell her. Soon, but not yet. He turned his attention away from her, to the customer upstairs, scraping his feet, pacing. He didn't like to bring up the cash while someone was there. He decided to wait until the customer was gone. He felt around in his pants pocket for cash, to make change. Then he went upstairs.

The customer was standing in the center aisle, looking at the top shelf of books. He held one in his hand. Ah, he said, proffering the book. I'll take this, and do you by any chance have – his expression was wistful, expecting a negative answer – a copy of *The Man Who Died?* D. H. Lawrence? The owner smiled. He liked surprising people, having what no one expected him to have. But more important, being able to provide the unexpected justified collecting what his wife called flotsam and jetsam. She had never grasped the possibilities. Rare isn't valuable, she would say, thinking that ended it. That rare might *become* valuable was only part of it, he knew, though that was the part he told her. The other part — having what no one else had — was fine in itself.

I think I might, he told the customer, and was rewarded with that look of surprise, skepticism, as if he might be lying. But I'll have to look around for it, he said, and I really can't do that now. If you could come back, say this afternoon?

The customer said that would be inconvenient. But I'll look after the store, he said. If someone comes in, I'll call you. Where are you, down there? He pointed to the basement door. I'll leave the door open a crack, the owner said. Just shout if someone needs me.

He kept the rare books in a common carton. He had always done that. Once the carton had been no bigger than what would hold a small shipment of paperbacks, maybe twenty-five or fifty. Now there was a carton big enough to hold a store, or a man. He tipped it on its side, pulled the step stool he kept for this purpose over to him, and began to go through the books. The king is in his countinghouse, he thought, and smiled.

The elevated train rumbled, and as always,

the ceiling-high metal bookshelves wobbled on their stilted legs. It always alarmed his wife. Although it didn't bother him, he waited until the sound of the train receded before he went on with his search. But the bookshelves seemed to rock more, and in the moment of confusion, he thought it might be a dizzy spell, and then the giant, skeletal structure made a cracking sound and began to come apart on him, throwing books, bolts, small boxes, hitting him with sharp corners, hitting him flat, crushing him. The cash receipts, which were in a box marked "Buttons," landed on his face.

Someone is following old persons and putting hand-held knives to their necks and taking their cash, watches, and jewelry. Someone is breaking into their shops. Someone is walking precisely in the sound of their footsteps, picking out the deaf ones, tiptoeing, wearing sneakers, coming along-side — at an alleyway, or through an open door — and with quick, young movements taking what is waiting for him. He calls the men Jakie; women are all Sadies. They always carry some-thing for him, not to make him mad, they say. If he finds you with nothing he gets mad, they say, and beats you badly. If you have something for him, he takes it and beats you up good. I carry nothing. I carry what I mean to keep. I listen as I

14

walk, I turn around quickly when he is not expecting, and hold up my turkey fork, strong, tempered steel which used to lift a fourteen-pound bird heavy with juice, and transfer him to a platter. After the fork if it goes any further, I use my legs. My legs are the strongest part of me. I lie down on the ground (I never wear my good coat) and kick up at him, getting him with the heels of my shoes on the shins, in the privates, and if he bends down to stab me, if he goes that far, I just lift my left leg (which is stronger than my right one) and kick him in the chin, on the cheeks. If he does not run away then, if it goes that far, I just grab the turkey fork which he has pulled out of his stomach and thrown close to me, and aim for the eyes. My eyes are protected by my glasses, but he could pull them off and see in them that I am not afraid of him.

She translated her shock at Barney's death into certainty that a crime had been committed. At first she suspected he had been killed.

Confronted by a robber, she told the police, and killed.

For what? the sergeant asked patiently, pointing out the petty-cash-covered body, to show her no crime had been committed. The customer who had been there had behaved properly if not heroically, running downstairs (*too late* was her comment) to see if he could help Barney, calling the police, staying until they came. He had been there all the time, had heard the rumbling of the train and the crash of the shelves. No one had come in, no one had run out. There was no reason not to trust what he said.

The police told her all this several times: in her apartment when they came to give her the news, getting her in the middle of cleaning (she buried her face in the dust rag she held, then lifted it, smudged, as if the news had mottled her skin); they told her in the store, where she insisted on being taken, to see for herself; they told her again and again on the telephone each time she called.

"There was no motivation or evidence we can find," the pleasant sergeant repeated.

"In this neighborhood who needs a reason," she argued. "Around here they do it for fun."

And because in a way he agreed with her, he didn't hang up right away.

"You ought to move out of here, Mrs. Goodman," he said, kindly.

They call it the Wilds. "I live way up in the Wilds of the Bronx," people once said, meaning the outermost boundaries of the city, where farmland still existed, and dirt roads, in the twenties and early thirties, and Jewish and Irish couples from Manhattan and New Jersey came to raise families. They bought white clapboard houses and later row or stoop houses of red brick, or they rented apartments, like Tessie and Barney Goodman did. The buildings were red brick, with ornate cornices and fancy courtyards, wrought-iron filigree on double-door entrances, hallways of marble. Somewhat later came the yellow brick buildings, with Art Deco façades, swooping mosaic patterns above the entrances, mirrored lobbies, fanlike designs in carpet or tile floors.

When the elevated train came, living conditions got more crowded, but even then it was a starting-off place full of young and hopeful people who looked forward to getting rich and moving on, to Queens, north to Westchester, or east to Long Island. Now there is no one left, the place is overrun with old people, the ones who never left (out of inertia or lack of money), and a lot of what Tessie's son-in-law likes to call "ethnics." Spanish. Now when politicians or policemen call it the Wilds, they mean where the animals live.

The nice sergeant was young and wanted to help. "It can be a dangerous place for an elderly woman, Mrs. Goodman. Because of the element."

And although Tessie didn't like the Spanish

any more than the nice sergeant did, and despite the fact that he was just repeating what she herself had just said a minute ago, she couldn't stand those mealymouthed *e* words: *ethnic* and *element* — like saying "passed on" when you meant "dropped dead" — so she gave him a little zinger. My husband, who just dropped dead, *loved* the element, she told him. He played cards with them. He joined their committees. He said you couldn't find a phony among them.

The nice sergeant got a little flustered. "Well, just be careful, then," he said.

And although Tessie had been after Barney to sell the store for years, had said at least once a day, "What are we still *doing* here?" she disliked the idea that this young fellow thought she was weak. Elderly, my ass. "I'm not afraid," she said. "And I'm not going anywhere. I have a business to run."

The business, Barney's Books, was a landmark in the Wilds, though not one many people frequented anymore. Once it had belonged to two elderly sisters, Nellie and Fritzie O'Neill, who lived in the basement of the store, and died there. Tessie and Barney had bought it in 1949, from the old girls' nephew. Barney had been instantly delighted with the old stock, the clutter, the charm of the downstairs living quarters; Tessie with the possibility of what she could turn it into. They had borrowed the money from Tessie's father, and business was so good in the beginning that by the end of two years they had paid everything back, owned it free and clear, and were able to move to a large apartment in one of the best houses in the neighborhood.

The house, in walking distance of the store, sat on top of a hill. The only apartment house on that block, it towered over the one- and two-family houses that clustered at the bottom as if they had slid down. The hill itself was famous in the western part of the borough for its fine sledding, and because at its foot stood a billboard, where every two months crowds of people came to watch the men mount scaffolds and lay the big Camels sign on in wet strips. It is said that these people were among the first in the world to see the Coppertone dog snag his teeth on the bathing-suited bottom of the Coppertone baby. No one seems to go sledding anymore, and the billboard space hasn't been rented in decades. Winters of exposure on the windy corner have eaten through the wood; the platform that ran like a small boardwalk along the base of the billboard, from which adventurous children jumped, was torn away in chunks and set on fire one winter by another generation's adventurous children.

The granite front on Tessie and Barney's house bore the words "The Jefferson" cut in bold gothic. One of only two such titled buildings in the neighborhood (the other, "The Washington," was two blocks away), it was rumored to have once housed the great Babe Ruth, on the second floor, front. A black limousine was supposed to have picked him up and taken him to Yankee Stadium. Later, some people said it hadn't been Babe Ruth at all, but Joe DiMaggio who had lived there, third floor front, and the car had been gray, but the point was still that a great Yankee had forgone the grandeur of the Concourse Plaza Hotel, where run-of-the-mill baseball stars stayed, for the greater grandeur of the Jefferson. A band of fieldstone wrapped the building from the sidewalk to the first-floor sills, and then it rose six stories in red brick, with cornices around the roof. The double doors were glass, covered by floridly worked, black-lacquered iron, dusted every morning by the super's wife; they opened onto wide gray marble steps, double-tiered, six and six, with brass banisters that curled into thumbless fists at top and bottom. Here the building's children used to spend rainy days playing Palace. The second set of doors, at the top of the marble steps, were stained glass:

gold, purples, reds, greens, framed in golden oak; the glass is gone now, gaps and opaque bathroom panes making another kind of crazy pattern. Mothers do not let their children loiter in the halls for fear of what will happen to them. The Jefferson, someone said, had the first incinerators in the entire borough. Now the garbage cannot be contained. It comes out of the windows, in the front, or into the back alley, where once children learned to ride bicycles in safety, and the old peddler stood calling "I cash clothes" and could be assured that all that would be thrown at him were soft bundles of worn but clean aprons, jackets, and dresses. Now it rains garbage, single pieces or whole bags.

Once, before the Major Deegan Expressway was built and blocked the view, Tessie used to sit at her window and watch small, slow boats moving up the East River on summer nights, when fireflies lit the sky, and she would think about redecorating her apartment, or dream of bookstores with his and her name on them all across the Bronx. Sometimes she would lean out and call to her friend one floor below, and they would talk, or meet downstairs to sit on the front steps until midnight, or walk slowly down the hill to the candy store for a pint of vanilla and chocolate. Breyers. Her friend doesn't live there anymore, there is no one to meet; and if you lean out, you will get hit by garbage. The candy store is a crack store now. The streetlight outside her window has been out for a year. She hasn't seen a firefly in many years, as if even the bugs knew enough to leave, and leave such a mess under cover of darkness. What, Barney, what are we still doing here, she used to say.

It had been easy to do well in the early years. They had the college trade, from New York University's campus, right up the street; the people in the neighborhood were good readers, a lot of schoolteachers, some lawyers, obedient children. And Tessie and Barney were a change from the O'Neill sisters, who had been nice enough, but quiet, and too devoutly bookish to be successful merchants. Tessie, as she herself said, had Personality with a capital *P*-plus, and she handled the customers. Barney knew his books from A to Z, she said, and he took care of the stock. And then, when Louise was born, people would stop in just to coo to her, or shake the handle of her carriage, which was always parked in the sun that poured in the front window in the morning. When Tessie noticed this, she began to put little piles of books, as if just by accident, right there in front of the carriage, with the covers facing out, so people

22

would notice them. Barney smiled, or shook his head, but Tessie tossed hers, saying no one should walk out of the store empty-handed. They hardly ever did, in those days. Yet, though life and work were ideal, they were by no means peaceful. Sometimes I think, Tessie would say, people come in here just to see the "Tessie and Barney Show," the way we fight. Barney would frown then, in puzzlement, and say, Fight? This would make Tessie fume and exaggerate and say, Yes, fight, fight, always, every day, to which Barney would lower his eyes, close them, and say in the same puzzled way, Always?

Yet it was true. Conflict, sweet and unvengeful as a taffy pull at first, was a big part of Tessie and Barney's life together. From the start, the separation of power — Tessie the customers, Barney the books — was also a difference of opinion. (Barney would have denied this.) Barney was a saver — he held a book, as he did his thoughts, quietly and for a long time. He saw the store as a place for his collections, only incidentally of interest to others, who now and then might become *customers* for a short time, but were always people either to be ignored — "Barney," she would scream, "how can you treat a customer that way?" — or lavished with conversation far too rich to be justified by a two-dollar purchase. Tessie, on the other hand, was a practical, hard-nosed kind of dreamer, with visions of a book-store so clean and dust-free you hardly noticed the books – and those that were there were glossy-covered best-sellers that caught sparks off the waxed floors as they sailed out the door on the wings of commerce. She saw bright, legible signs that pointed the customers' way to exactly what they wanted, and business was a prompt and profitable divestiture of stock in exchange for cash, no discount.

Tessie was generally believed to be the victor in these conflicts, since she always had the last word; yet Barney's Books somehow continued to be a dusty, serendipitous place and Barney continued at his whim, silent or talkative, and casual about profit and loss. For this reason, when business was so good that Barney took a lease on a second store, although it pleased Tessie, she also felt a certain spite in it. As if, in his quiet way, he was telling her, I told you so.

The new store was in the up-and-coming section of the Bronx called Riverdale. From the start, Tessie thought of it as hers. The floors were asphalt tile in black and green squares, which she chose; the fixtures were modern, and she saw to it, with little notes on the floor plan, that there was more space between the shelves

24

for customers (though less for books). She loved the new place. Don't you love it? she kept asking Barney. He never answered, that she can recall. Each morning, as Barney dawdled over breakfast, Tessie got into the green DeSoto and drove up to Riverdale to open the new store. At first they had planned to alternate — Monday and Wednesday Barney would be in the new store, Tessie in the old; Tuesday, Thursday, and Friday the other way around — but something always came up, and soon, without anything said, it was understood that "Barney's Too" belonged to Tessie. At first the place did well: people were drawn to the newness of it, and Tessie put up red, white, and blue bunting across the front window to call attention to it, although Barney said mildly that it hid all the books she had on display. Sometimes she stole books from the old store, or whole boxes of books she had not foreseen the demand for. Then she called Barney's attention to how much more of this and that she had sold than he. The worst of it was, Barney didn't seem to mind. They were like rival businessmen with only Tessie acknowledging the rivalry. He would shrug and say, What difference did it make who sold more of such and such a book this week? It was all their money, anyway, wasn't it? But Tessie wouldn't

25

let it rest. She brought it home.

"Just listen to me," she would say, putting her small, dainty hands with the very long, red nails on his arm. Then he would get up and go to the bathroom, or into the kitchen, or his eyes would close and he would fall asleep sitting in the living room chair. She looked upon these actions as ultimate weapons, and got angry. And then, when the Riverdale store needed refinancing, and Tessie wanted to sell the old store to feed the new one, and Barney refused, she got more than angry. A fury took her in hand. "The Bronx is going down," she screamed. "It's going down, and you are going to get stuck if you don't listen to me." Though Barney might have argued that it was her store that was going down, he didn't; and when it finally closed, there was never a word of reproach. He claimed it was his fault, it had been a poor location to begin with. "Not enough traffic," he said; "there wasn't enough parking." Or, "There weren't enough readers. What they needed was a delicatessen, not a bookstore. If we had put in a deli, we would have made out."

But the more Barney took the blame, the more she blamed him. "I'll never forgive you," she had said with satisfaction, the rage making a pretty flush on her cheeks. And she never had, though often through the years she forgot what it was she did not forgive. And though she had been right about the Bronx going down, she had been wrong about Barney ending up stuck there; it was she, after all, who was stuck. That is why Tessie is still in the Wilds, and the wild rage that had become the fabric of life with Barney is something she cannot part with.

She didn't have to, as it turned out. Not only had Barney sneaked out on her, abandoned ship, so to speak, he had also left her with her ass in the water. She was in a terrible financial fix.

Fishman, the accountant, did a complete review of their accounts.

"Ahem," he said, warming up, walking his pencil toward and away from her on the kitchen table, tip, eraser, tip, eraser. "As your accountant, as your C.P.A.," he clarified, "I must be frank. As your friend" — he sang the word, raising his eyes from the depths of sincerity to the ceiling — "I am appalled."

You're appalled, she thought, running hot water over the dishes in the sink, I'm exhausted.

She had given him dinner (low-sodium hot pastrami because of the blood pressure, lean because of the heart, seedless rye bread because of – excuse the expression – the colon, Cel-Ray Tonic because of its magical properties). After dinner she gave him tea in a glass and listened to his *mayse* about Harriet (on her second master's, asking for a divorce because she had just learned that what was going on all those years was called premature ejaculation – "this God help me she learned in school which I am paying for, and now she's blaming me because once in a while I tell her to hurry up, *herst*, and it gave her some kind of complex" – and she was threatening to write it down like that on the filing papers – Insufficient Sex – when she knew he had a prostate problem and what did she expect him to do, risk his life?), and now she was exhausted.

"Get to the point," she said.

He flushed, and Tessie realized that the words must have reminded him of his sexual problem. Then he told her the bad news. Barney had kept very sketchy records, very sketchy. But one thing was clear. Six months before he died, he converted his life insurance policy into cash. He did not pay his bills with the cash, as evidenced by those still outstanding. Fishman shook his head and clicked his tongue. There was one twenty-thousand-dollar expenditure in the ledger, made in September, but Fishman didn't know what it was; did she?

He turned the book around for her to see. Under "Purchases/September," Barney had entered: "Item, G.d.B." That was all. What "G.d.B." stood for was a mystery, as whether it signified the item itself, or the seller.

After taxes, accountant's fees (he flushed again), and all the bills were paid, the bookstore was Tessie's only asset.

"Asset," she screamed. "What kind of asset?"

A questionable one, Fishman agreed. Although, Barney had often said the store held something of value, he said hopefully.

When she didn't answer, Fishman said, "No, really."

"Fishman," she said, "it's late. Go home."

He pressed her hand. "If there's anything you need . . . ," he said, his eyes watering.

"I know," she said. "Now go home."

Dear Mrs. Goodman:

I understand that you are interested in selling your bookstore. For reasons which I prefer to keep mum, I am interested in buying it. This is by way of a preliminary feeler, to feel you out. Please think about this proposition, and be assured that I will be in touch with you in the near future.

Very truly yours,
M. H. Ross

P.S. Though you don't know me, I am well acquainted with you and have been in your charming bookstore many times. I will see you again soon.

M.H.R.

On the same day that Tessie contemplated suicide, someone offered to buy the dilapidated, debt-ridden bookstore she owned, which no one in his right mind would want.

This needs some elucidation.

"Contemplated suicide" does not mean Tessie considered killing herself in any decisive way. She was thinking about suicide as a theme for the day, as a solution (in the abstract) for the problems she noticed around her. For instance: Miss Carter on the sixth floor, who had never been married, who had been hated by generations of schoolchildren for her teaching methods at P.S. 31, and who now had a debilitating disease. Or: Victory Schrier (named for the disposition of World War I), who had been mugged four times and could not find a satisfactory compromise between her desire to show off and her desire to live. She *would* wear the gold chains and diamonds that drew the thieves. So they approached her in broad daylight, when she was coming from the beauty parlor, or at night, as she was returning from dinner with friends, stripped her of all precious metals and stones, and beat her up. She wore the bruises until they were gone, and then more gold and diamonds from the seemingly endless supply that her late husband, George, had given her over a lifetime of reconciliations and commemorations. This supply was not limitless, Tessie knew.

Tessie had these thoughts early in the morning, after she found the hallway outside her door strewn with garbage again. Mr. Hirsch. There were squeezed orange quarters, empty cans, a milk container, grains of rice, a large clump of something covered with blue mold which might have been a cat-food casserole, forgotten in the back of Mr. Hirsch's refrigerator for a month. Mr. Hirsch, who stole cat food (he had no cats) would have meant to return and clean up his mess, but since his memory was extremely short, would have forgotten as soon as he closed his door. When Gonzalez, the super, found the mess, he would bang on Mr. Hirsch's door, cursing and muttering in Spanglish, "*Coño*, look at this, *mira, eso es una* goddamn pig hole," but when Mr. Hirsch opened the door, he would simply rub his head and say, "Ay ay ay, Mr. Hirsch," his face would turn all red and he would look away from the

31

old man. Hirsch would look surprised, then ashamed, and he would come out and clean the garbage. Gonzalez would help him, and pat him on the shoulder when he apologized. If Mr. Hirsch's memory didn't blot this out quickly, he might have been a good candidate for suicide, too.

Every morning for the first few weeks after Barney's death, Tessie came out of sleep abruptly, with a single shudder — she felt her cheeks shake — reminding her of the old air conditioner in what used to be her daughter's room, which, whenever you turned it on shook so hard you thought it would jump right out of the window. Barney had said it needed that much juice to get going. More than once it blew a fuse. Poor old thing, she would think, and then remember she had had another bad dream which she couldn't recall but which would stick to her for the rest of the day.

Everyone wanted to know how the new widow was doing.

Louise called every morning, just as Tessie was trying to get food down. "Fine, dear," Tessie said.

Russell, her son-in-law, took the afternoon shift, saying in that false, jollying tone he used on all his elderly patients, "What's shakin'?" and sometimes she wanted to say "Me," but always said, "Everything's fine."

Worst of all was Victory, her best friend. She showed up at Tessie's early in the morning, or sometimes late at night, with her killer smile, her martyr smile, or her sad-sad smile. "How *are* you?" she said, and there was no way in the world Tessie could pawn off a "Fine" on her.

"Fine."

"No, really."

"Fine."

"You don't *look* fine. Now tell me the truth. I want to know."

She had a shoppingbagful of little sayings to comfort Tessie, and she would pull one or another out like pieces of clothing, unmindful that they didn't fit: "Buy yourself a new dress." *For chrissakes, Victory.* "Never mind. Look on the bright side." *Which side is that, Barney's dead or I'm in debt?* "Everything always turns out for the best." "If it is meant to be, it is meant to be." "Get up, get dressed, and face the world with a smile." *What good is that if my best friends don't believe it?* "What is, is" (a variation of, "What is meant to be is meant to be"). When she began repeating herself, Tessie tuned her out.

Victory herself, once bereft of a child, once widowed, had a closetful of new dresses bought in grief, and each morning she got up and dressed, put one on and all her jewels, and went to work as a bookkeeper for her brother's sporting-goods concern (*concern* the operative word here, and she frowned a bit when she said it). A tall, dignified woman, she had an incongruously childlike voice, like Baby Snooks or the boop-boop-e-doop girl, so everything she said came out as though it wasn't to be taken seriously.

"When I lost my Mindy . . . ," she said, and Tessie wondered if she knew she was smiling.

When she had lost her daughter, Mindy, that terrible year of the polio epidemic, she had been, everyone said, magnificent. Tower of strength, holding up George, taking care of the boy, Mark, no one had ever seen her shed a tear.

Where, Tessie wondered, had she put all the grief? Stuffed up, like cotton wadding, somewhere in the upper throat, so she couldn't talk in a normal voice?

As to Tessie, she thought she herself might be having some kind of a breakdown, or a physical collapse. She was seeing things: a dead gray cat lying on the street corner, its yellow eyes accusing her, which turned out to be a pile of dirty snow with lemon rinds; a bloody arm in a ragged sleeve on the highway, which a moment later was a rag; a dead bird which was a discarded rolled-up magazine. Once it was a dead body behind the driver's seat of a parked car, and she walked three blocks, her heart pounding painfully, trying to find a policeman to tell, and when she finally did she knew at once the body was laundry, though she did not go back to make sure. She began to squint, not to sharpen her vision but to limit it, and ward off sights the reality of which she might have to question. She walked looking at the ground, which did not help at all, because most of the corpse visions were at ground level. One morning in the bank, she killed an old woman for pushing ahead of her: murdered her with eyes, pushed her with thoughts to a bloody death on the cold floor, fingernails dug into palms as she strangled her, foot cramped with the effort of kicking her to death. The exertions were beginning to tell. She had frequent indigestion. She became afraid to drive and spent much of her time at home. Though she had often told Barney that their apartment was too big since Louise had gotten married and moved out, now she could hardly walk from the bedroom to the living room without bumping into things. Every day she dusted the furniture, a Louis Quatorze suite she and Barney had bought at Macy's in '45. It had cost them a lot in those days — it would make the apartment elegant,

35

she had promised. It died trying, she thought, dusting the thighs of overstuffed chairs and in between the toes of claw-and-ball feet. It was like having a roomful of stuffed animals. She tripped on the leg of the Queen Anne chair and fell flat on her face, knocking the wind out of herself and scaring herself so badly that she had crawled to the phone and called Russell. He had sent her to his colleague, Goffstein, a psychiatrist masquerading as an internist. Goffstein examined her and asked personal questions.

Did she miss seck sewal relations?

"Not since 1953," she had said, staring at him until he turned red.

Did she do much crying?

She had not cried at Barney's funeral, she could not. Too mad. Yet, a woman of her age, in her position, if she knew what was good for her, better cry when it is expected of her, since sympathy is about the sexiest emotion she is likely to get.

Everyone had been waiting for her to cry. Louise was looking over at her from where she was sitting. Victory, Mrs. Face-the-World-with-a-Smile, kept patting her hand, comforting her, even encouraging her, you might say, to break down (this is the right time and place for it). She had tried to prime the pump, saying phrases like, "Oh Barney, my Barney" and "Thirty-five years of marriage" to herself, but nothing helped. All she kept thinking was, "You son of a bitch" and having the useless impulse to kill him. So she sat there, poking a tissue at her eyes, which nothing short of an onion would draw tears from. Then the rabbi had said, "If the widow could speak at this moment, she would say . . . ," and Tessie thought, "Up the creek without a paddle," and the thought of his sabotage, dying like that, made her choke with anger, and the mint she was sucking got caught in her throat, and the coughing that ensued brought tears to her eyes, nice fat ones that rolled down her cheeks and splashed onto the collar of her dress and puckered the silk. So, after all, and for the record, you could say she shed tears at Barney's funeral. But she hadn't cried.

Now, the things that brought tears — moving vans, parades, Bell Telephone and "Coke Is It" commercials — embarrass her. Pictures of Barney, Barney's old clothes and golf clubs (still sitting in the foyer waiting for Goodwill to pick them up), the word *Barney* drove the tears straight to the back of her head, where they made her scalp tingle.

After the funeral, back at her apartment, they had put Tessie and Louise on crates sent over from the funeral parlor to serve as mourners' benches. They were supposed to symbolize the hardness of the situation. Louise took to it, but Tessie kept getting pains in the backs of her knees crouching there, and didn't see why they had to make it worse than it was, so she kept moving over to the couch, and the damned rabbi kept coming over and gently moving her back, as if she was out of her mind with grief and didn't know what she was doing. She kept thinking, I shouldn't have married him in the first place, it was Mama's fault, she kept telling me how wonderful he was, and saying, "Yes, thank you, yes," when people told her how wonderful he was.

Barney's only living brother, with whom Barney had been in an on-and-off feud for the last twenty years, sat in the corner, threatening to become the best mourner, crying his eyes out, shaking his head, blowing his nose into a large, wrinkled, grayish-white handkerchief. His two daughters, who had brought him from Philadelphia for the funeral, were in a huddle with Louise, telling her, Tessie was sure, what to expect from a widowed parent. Their kids, whom someone had told to call her Nanny Tess, kept running back and forth down the long foyer of the apartment. The little boy had dust in his hair, so Tessie guessed he had been under the bed. Her own grandchildren were better behaved: the baby because he was too young to do anything but lie there and sleep or gurgle, and Sibboan (God, Tessie wondered, where had they come up with a name like that, Sibboan Kaplan) because she was such a quiet one.

Victory was bustling around, having a good time showing off her funeral smarts, since she had been through this so recently when George died. Every few minutes she would grip Tessie by the wrist, and sigh loudly and smile her sad smile, or shake her head and squeeze her eyes shut. She was clearly glad to have Tessie as a fellow widow, and Tessie didn't hold it against her.

Gonzalez, the super, came, carrying a dish of pork, rice, and beans that his wife had made (Victory wrinkled her nose), explaining that he was there not only as a representative of the Local Action Committee (of which Barney had been one of only two non-P.R. members) but as Barney's friend. He adjusted the steam heat twice, and Tessie was glad to have him. Two other members of the committee came as well, and Russell made an idiot of himself, holding up the mass card they had brought as if it were made out of diamonds and had come just in time, shouting at them as if their accents made them deaf. Then, when he found out that one of them was a lawyer, he made a fuss about that, saying *"abogado"* and ushering him around, introducing him to everyone as his friend, until Tessie had to turn away in disgust.

This went on all day and into the evening. Everyone was there, Louise said with satisfaction, everyone: friends, relatives, and even forgetful Mr. Hirsch, who had left a cake outside the door, with Barney's name on the box (had he forgotten whether it was Barney's birthday or funeral?).

The envelope containing M. H. Ross's letter was lying outside the door, and at first Tessie squinted, thinking it was another illusion, and would presently decompose into grains of rice, more of Mr. Hirsch's mess. But when she opened it and read it, she got scared. She didn't believe in magic. Had she finally gone crazy, her unremembered dreams taking tangible form?

She kept staring at it, as if focus would prove reality. It was an oddly shaped envelope, not the oblong, business kind, but something a greeting card might come in. When she looked, there was the imprint of Hallmark on the flap. The paper was oddly shaped, too, folded (she could see the fold) and torn imperfectly, to conform to the shape of the envelope. The message was strange: "I understand that you ..." From whom did he get this understanding? It was true she had wanted to sell (though *want* was less the word than *dreamed*, and she was not one to mention her dreams to anyone). "For reasons which I prefer to keep mum ..." That sounded like something out of the Hampstead Heath mysteries. Who keeps "mum" anymore? "A preliminary feeler, to feel you out ..." Redundant; a little feeble, she thought. And she didn't like the sound of the postscript at all: it was ominous. There was no return address or phone number.

He must have known Barney was dead. Had he known Barney? Had Barney told him he wanted to sell? Was it possible that M. H. Ross knew something about the store that Tessie didn't? Fishman had said Barney claimed there was something of value in the store. "I thought you knew," he had said. Had M. H. Ross known, too?

She walked the four blocks to the store slowly. She hadn't been there in a while, and everything looked both strange and familiar. It was like coming into your own home after a day in the fresh air and smelling camphor, or Wednesday's fish supper, and realizing it had been there all the time but you needed to be

41

away to notice it. The apartment house on the corner of University Avenue was gutted by fire, with charred window sashes and no windows, scrawled sayings in red paint on the old brick front, the wrought iron painted an ugly light brown. How long had it been like that? A large sign on the corner, announcing "Urban Renewal Project #33," was illegible with graffiti and dirt, and someone had scratched away the *Ur* in *Urban*. She felt that all these things had taken place a long time ago, but she had only just seen them. She felt she might have walked past people she knew just now and never noticed them. Wake up, she told herself. The garbage on the corner overflowed the rusty basket. Barney's latest project on the Local Action Committee had been to persuade the sanitation department to pick up the garbage; they hadn't made regular runs in years. She had laughed at him, told him it was futile, trying to fight City Hall.

The bookstore was there — *there it is* came into her mind, as if she had somehow expected that with the cessation of Barney the store might disappear — between Hum's Chinese and Durite Cleaners, where it had always been, in the middle of the long hill that stopped at the elevated train. In the old days, there had been fruit stands in the shade of the trains, a bank on the corner, a carpet store, a cigar factory. Now there was nothing but decay, one or two stores, and the after-hours clubs where the shootings took place every month or so.

Hum's Chinese, once a dark, fragrant place where she and Barney had gone on Sunday nights for vegetable chop suey, was now a narrow space with a bright orange sign and sheets of paper Scotch taped to its window, advertising take-out specials. Hum was Joe Figueroa, "Joe Fig" to his friends, a former toll-booth operator who put *salsa* in the Bok Choy Beef and ran numbers from the kitchen. Durite was dark, and a shirt cardboard in the window said, "Closed Due to Illness," which Tessie suspected meant that Charlie Hoffman, the owner, had finally decided to sell.

Once a customer had complained to Tessie that the books had smelled like dry-cleaned chow mein. "Sure," she had said. "And I should charge you extra for it, but I won't."

She stood there, thinking of that, the smell, not wanting to go in, letting her eyes pull her mind away.

"How many of us are left?" Durite (maybe on the way out), the hardware store, Billy's Lunch-eonette, maybe a few more. Nobody. The drug-store, Kelly and Kavashefsky, hadn't changed the window in thirty years: how was it she never noticed that before? The truss, its elastic curling, hugged a legless torso framed by a chrome walker. A hardwood cane with black rubber tip was hooked onto the walker, and crutches (she had always pictured someone flinging them aside, crying dramatically, Oh Lord, it's a miracle, I can walk) lay on the battleship linoleum floor, their inner boundaries marking a wide avenue covered with the bodies of roaches, ants, flies, and waterbugs. On a platform above this scene reigned two immense apothecary jars filled with liquid, evaporated some inches since the day Louise had called the red liquid Kool-Aid, and Tessie told her the yellow liquid was the urine sample of a giant. Louise uses this as an example of her mother's warped sense of humor these days.

The sign, "Barney's Books," jutted out from the brick on a rusted iron arm and swung in the March wind. The old sign, "Bronx Bookstore," was there too, on the wall above the door and so faded now it was indistinguishable from the brick itself and hardly legible. Renaming the store had been Tessie's idea; Barney had never liked his name hanging out there like that.

Joe Fig rapped on the window and motioned for Tessie to come in. She shook her head no; she didn't want to talk to

44

anyone. He came to the door.

"You wanna egg roll?" he said.

"Maybe later," she said.

A bag of garbage was lying in the recessed doorway. When Tessie tried to pick up the bag the bottom fell out, and garbage spilled all over the ground.

She couldn't open the door. The key didn't work at first, and then the tongue hasp jammed and finally, as it gave, the door shook so badly Tessie thought it would unhinge. Talk about smells. She had to prop the door open with a carton, the smell was so bad: dampness and dust, and a kind of rancid nut-smell of old paper, but then something else, like spoiled food. Just inside the doorway was a saucer of dried milk, but she didn't think such a small amount could account for such a pervasively rotten odor. She picked up the saucer, wondering suddenly what had happened to the cat, the latest in a succession of strays Barney had fed through the years.

When she reached for the broom near the doorway, she realized that the alarm had not gone off. She supposed in all the confusion after Barney's death, she had forgotten to set it. She swept the garbage into an empty carton, dumped the saucer in, but left it propping the door open. The sunlight stopped inside the door, and the rest of the place was dark. She stood there for a minute, to let her eyes adjust, and to calm her suddenly upset stomach. She turned on the lights and heat. The light was dim (she would have to replace some bulbs) and the place was a wreck. There were cartons of books everywhere, stacks of books lying in the aisles, some knocked over and sprawled across the floor, some piled across the tops of shelves. Was this the way Barney had left the store? She had been here the day he died; why couldn't she recall?

She tried to concentrate, to remember the last time she had been with him in the store. Two weeks before his death? A month? Less and less frequently in recent years. She recognized one stack of swollen, misshapen books from the flood they had had last August. She took the yardstick from behind the counter and slid it under the nearest shelf, pushing out more books, dust, pennies, a candy wrapper. She bent, grunting, and collected the pennies: "See, we took in a profit already today," she said out loud, and slid the rest over to the water-damaged books. To Barney she said, "There is no point in trying to reclaim any money for these now; let's just get rid of them."

Barney would have disagreed. He would have spent all morning making space, rearranging the shelves, writing the sign, "Hurt Books – Drastically Reduced." Then he would have waited six months (no sales) before taking them down again, re-rearranging the shelves, putting the sign in the basement (never throw a sign away, you might need it) or somewhere on top of his desk where it would join other signs and be forgotten. It wasn't that he was cheap, or even mindful of money, that was for sure. It was just that once he felt there was value in something he couldn't part with it. He would put the books in a pile on the floor. Tessie would say, "*Now* get rid of them," and he would answer, "Well, just leave them there just for now," and there they would stay until he died.

"Leave them," Tessie said now. Maybe M. H. Ross was another Barney and would appreciate a pile of rotting books.

The smell had begun to fade (or maybe she was in it and couldn't smell it anymore). When she turned to close the door, there was a man standing at the curb, looking in. He was hatless (in this weather) and the wind blew his wispy gray hair (Barney's had been strong as coiled wires, and thick) and he was altogether so thin he looked as if he would go over in a strong gust. But he stood his ground, clasped his hands behind his back, and – this was odd – bent his knees slightly, as though about to

47

spring, which for some reason made Tessie feel he was going to speak.

Nu? she thought. Spit it out.

But he stepped backward, off the curb, and she got the impression if she had stepped out he would have stepped back, and if she had advanced he would have retreated. Yet she felt he wanted to come in. She closed the door and turned her back. Then she rummaged under the counter until she found the old Store Open/ Store Closed sign. She adjusted the paper clock and slipped the paper tongue through until the sign said, "Closed. Will Reopen at 10:00, Wednesday." She hung it on the nail at the top of the door.

I didn't want to do that, she thought. She supposed, though, it was easier than pulling the clock hands off, or making a new sign. What would a new sign say? "Almost Sold"? "Maybe Under New Management"? No, it would be better to leave things as they were until she knew what was what. And she thought again about M. H. Ross.

The heat had begun to work. She took off her coat, reset the wall clock, which was running slow again, to 11:00, and looked around. She would have to get the place into shape if someone was going to buy it. And reminded herself she had to find out *why*, why in the world someone would want to buy it. What was it worth? She decided to start in the basement.

The light was out on the stairway and she had to go down slowly, groping along the wall until her hand contacted the basement light switch. There were twisted bodies all over the floor — no, no, not bodies, books, signs, Barney's old chair pad lying in the center of it all. The source of the spoiled-food smell was there, too, on the floor, cottage cheese covered with pink and green mold, an open carton of milk, a black banana.

"Oh God," she said, and a wave of fear or the bad smell pushed her down, and she sat on the floor, not crying though thinking she was crying, wishing silently though thinking she was shouting, for an answer to this, and a window to clear out the smell.

She called the police. The same police sergeant came who had been there when Barney died. He tried the cellar door. It was bolted, gray paint still sealing the opening.

"No one came in this way," he said. "Does anyone else have a key?"

She said no, and he nodded, as if it was something he suspected all along.

She showed him the scratched, distressed metal near the opening of the front door, and told him the trouble she had had opening it.

He followed her back downstairs. "It's an old door," he said.

"Maybe it was forced," she said.

"Is anything missing?" He held the pencil above his pad, as if ready to record a long list of missing items. She didn't think so, no. That is, although . . .

He shook his finger at her, as if she might be making things up. "Now, Mrs. Goodman . . ."

Damn, she wouldn't be patronized. "What about the food?" she insisted. "And the chair on the floor, and the chair pad? You listen, sonny, someone's been in here." She heard herself, and the Little Golden *The Three Bears* picture book came into her head — "Whooo's been leaving cottage cheese on my basement floor?" said Mama Bear — and made her feel silly.

Soothingly, the policeman suggested that this was the way the basement had been left on the day Barney died. Maybe, he said, apologetically, one of his people had knocked the chair down before leaving. Tentatively, he offered the idea that the food had been her late husband's lunch.

Oh. Oh God. Oh yes. It had been Barney's lunch, and the shock of that, the *spoilage* of it made her think of Barney down there in his blue suit inside a wooden box. She had to sit down again.

"All right, now," the policeman said, quietly. "You had a bad day, a bad shock." He patted her shoulder. His indulgence brought her back to herself, made her angry. All right, it was his lunch, but she still wouldn't let herself believe the rest.

"I still think someone was here," she said.

"Is anything missing?" he said again, this time with an edge.

That's more like it, she thought. "Yes, yes," she said. Definitely. Only she didn't know what.

The policeman smiled. "Well, when you find out, you let me know," he said, and took his leave.

"Do you want me to close the door up here?" he called to her from upstairs. "You'll feel safer if I do."

I won't, she thought. "All right, close it," she told him.

She scooped the garbage (yes, all right, Barney's lunch) into a large bag. She used cleanser on the desk top, sprayed it with Lysol, and dried it, using half a roll of paper towels on it. She took the chair upstairs with her, but left the piles of books and posters where they were, staring at them hard, so she would remember what they were and not mistake them for bodies

51

again. The collapsed shelves, under which Barney had been buried and had died, were still as they were on the day it had happened. She pretended not to notice. She swept the rest of the floor, and scoured the bathroom tile and toilet. By the time she finished, it was almost three o'clock and she was tired. The garbage pickup might not be along until next week. She stuffed the trash into a Macy's shopping bag and took it with her, to put in the incinerator at home. She switched on the alarm, turned off the lights and heat and went to the door. The small carton of trash in the doorway had been overturned, probably by strays rummaging for food. She added it to her shopping bag and closed the door behind her.

She walked up the hill slowly, partly because the garbage was heavy and she was tired, partly because the sudden, assaulting cold was welcome to her. Impulsively, she decided on the long way home, and turned left.

P.S. 31 was just releasing its charges. Louise had gone to this same school when it went all the way through the sixth grade. Nowadays, the neighborhood was so overrun with children that they had to put the overflow, the bigger ones, into the Flambeau Garden, an old wedding hall a block away. The iron gate, which had once protected neat rows of flowers, planted by the second-grade garden squad each spring, now seemed a pen to contain the most junior members of an unruly and dangerous population. Yet it occurred to her that they looked, as they filed out, just like the little ones who had come out those gates in the forties and fifties, holding hands, hatted and gloved, as Louise once had. She tried to imagine exactly when and how they turned dangerous, became toughs, then druggies, muggers, murderers. She knew, of course, that it was gradual, and had to do with such things as poverty, bad influences, and the proximity to all that garbage; yet she occupied herself thinking about an exact instant when one turned into the other, like Gonzalez's little girl, Modesta: one day little Dessie in a yellow-and-white lace party dress, the next a haggard woman of seventeen, letting herself into tenants' apartments with the passkey, stealing to pay for drugs; the last day a body in the entrance under the mailboxes. Mrs. Gonzalez had screamed for a week, and then gone really nuts.

Two older boys jostled Tessie. She looked at them: this was the day, she thought, between yesterday when they were children, and tomorrow when they would be killers. There was a young mustache on one, tender baby hairs above the puffy lip set in a dreamy smile, under sleepy eyes of a baby who had just sucked. She sensed the danger, but, like the cold, it was welcome, and she let them trail along after her for one minute or two. Then she seemed to wake up, and looked for somewhere safe.

Above the storefront, which had once been Sam's Fish, was the sign, "Local Action Committee (Acción Locale)." She left the bag of garbage outside and went in. This was where Barney used to come to meetings, to talk about such impossibilities as getting the sanitation men to come, and saving the community. The room was bare, except for an old Formica kitchen table, with some leaflets on it, and a desk in the corner. The floor was scarred where Sam's counter had been pulled out, and Tessie thought she could still smell fish. A fat young woman sat behind the desk, knitting. When Tessie came in she looked up briefly, didn't smile. Tessie thought, She must know I laughed at Barney, yet knew she couldn't have. The woman asked if she might help Tessie. Tessie didn't know what to say. She certainly wasn't going to say she had been frightened off the street by two babies. She said the wind had taken her breath and she needed to rest for a minute. The woman looked toward the window, then back to Tessie, but she didn't say anything, just shrugged, and went back to her knitting. Tessie waited until she saw the boys leave. She thanked the woman and left. She went cautiously, looking to the left and to the right (as she had once taught Louise to cross streets) to make sure the boys were gone, and was relieved to see there was no sign of them. Then she noticed there was no sign of her Macy's bag of garbage. They had taken it. The two little bastards had stolen her garbage.

She smiled all the way home, thinking about the smile on the face of the baby-faced boy, which — long distance, single-handedly — she would soon wipe away. But then her smile too went away, because would he remember her, come back and find her? Was her face as sharp in his mind as his face was to her?

They ran, laughing, until Mateo got a stitch in his side, and doubled over from the pain.

"Wait, man," he said, but Bobby, the big one, kept on for another half a block. When he turned back, Mateo was gone. He went back looking for him, and when he couldn't find him, he stopped thinking how for once he had outsmarted Mateo, and started thinking how Mateo had probably meant to do this, to leave him holding the old lady's bag. If Mateo had taken it, Bobby would have wanted it, but Mateo had let him hold it, which made him suspect it was not good to have. Like, if the cops came or something, who was going to get picked up?

Mateo was smart like that; Mateo was tricky.

He went back to where Mateo had stopped, and leaned against the building. He went up that block, looking in every alleyway. Finally, he went over to Mateo's house, mad now, because he didn't want the old lady's bag anymore, and when he went into the hallway, Mateo grabbed him from behind and started laughing and jabbing. Bobby couldn't get his hands on him, and Mateo kept laughing and slap boxing, saying *"Bap, bap"* every time he caught him one; finally, Bobby backed away and leaned against the radiator and just let Mateo *bap bap* until he wore out.

"Maricón," he said. *"Qué carajo te pasa?* What's the matter with your head?" but Mateo just laughed at him, and feinted a couple more times, and then someone yelled from inside to get outa the hallway or she would call the cops, and Bobby said he was going to split. He left the bag and said he didn't want it.

"Come on, man," Mateo said. "Come up." Bobby said no, at first, but Mateo gave him a push and said, "Come *on*," and finally Bobby followed him upstairs. Mateo's mother was at work, Bobby knew, but Mateo went in, pre-

56

tending she was home, saying, *"Eh, chica,"* like he wasn't afraid of her. They went into the kitchen, and Mateo gave Bobby a beer and took one, and lit up a cigarette, and put the bag on the kitchen table.

When Mateo put his hand in, deep inside the bag, and it came out dripping, like of puke or something like that, Bobby couldn't help it, he started to laugh, he just cracked up, and Mateo went nuts: threw the bag on the floor, kicked it around, and then went for Bobby, not kidding, like before, but hard, beating on him hard, and Bobby had to pin him to stop him. He pressed down on Mateo's stomach until he screamed *"Basta!"* and then Bobby let him up and let him take a swing to get even, so he wouldn't hold it against him later; Mateo said he would kill Bobby if he ever told any of the others. *"Te mato* if you say anything, bro," and Bobby had to swear on his mother, and then Mateo told him to get the fuck out, and he took his beer and went.

Mateo turned on Channel 5, and half-watched "He-Man and the Masters of the Universe" and some other cartoons. When his mother came home, she gave him a hard time because he had fallen asleep and didn't get milk like she told him to, and she wouldn't send the little *muchacho* to the store, she kept him too close to her, like a mama's boy, like to protect him from the 'vironment, Mateo said to himself in disgust; so *he* had to go get it.

He remembered the old woman's eyes. In the night, in his sleep, they stared into his eyes, and he stared back so hard and mean that his eyes teared and teared and dripped and dripped, and he woke up all wet and had to pull off the sheet in the middle of the night and hide it under the bed.

There is a group of women who cook dinner for one another once a week. Tonight it is Pearl. They have known each other since they were young wives, when they all lived on the same street. Pearl and Helen have long ago moved up, to Riverdale, but keep in touch with Tessie and Victory, who remain.

Tessie takes two buses, since she has recently become afraid to drive. She calls the women the Black Widows and comes home in a terrible state, but goes nevertheless. At least they don't think she is imagining things when she talks about someone (or some*thing*, Victory says, and shivers) lurking in the basement of her store. They also know about her financial troubles.

"It could be worse," Helen consoles her. "You could be totally broke. At least you have what to live on."

"Never mind that," Victory says. "You had (God rest him) thirty-five beautiful years to remember. I know a woman, her husband left her two million and she hanged herself in the basement."

"I'll try to figure that one out," Tessie says.

"She didn't have anything to look back on and cherish," Helen explains, giving *cherish* a twist. "Well, never mind cherish, I'll take cash," she says. Helen's husband left her nothing and she has to work in a girdle shop. Helen working in a girdle shop is like a colored man working in a coal mine, Tessie thinks. How much blacker can you get? Helen is so thin, she is all hollows: cheeks, eyes, midriff, even her palms. Her legs are so thin in shoes she looks like Olive Oyl. They worry about her, tell her she never eats. She says she does, but no one has ever seen it.

They talk about husbands.

"When George died . . . ," Victory says.

"He just wouldn't slow down; I said, Irwin, slow down," Helen sighs, gazing dreamily past Victory's head at the mirror over the sideboard.

Pearl enters, bearing crudités. "He killed himself," she says, setting the platter down. Tessie asks who.

"Mel," Pearl says.

59

"George," Victory says, at the same time. "When my George died he weighed two hundred and forty pounds."

"Oh, Victory," Tessie says. "You don't mean it. George wasn't that overweight."

"He weighed two hundred and forty pounds," Victory says, in her high-pitched voice, her chin puckering. "I should know. I weighed him."

This is greeted by silence, as if Victory is passing around a picture of herself, lifting a floatlike George onto a scale and everyone is looking.

"Well . . . ," Helen says, finally, "Irwin was trim. But the stress . . . the stress that man put himself under . . ." There is wonder in her voice.

"I know, I know," Pearl says. "Right before Mel died I said to him, Why? Do I need all this? Did I ask for all this?" She waves her hand at the fabric-covered walls.

"It's beautiful," Helen says.

"Thank you," Pearl murmurs.

Victory is sulking.

Pearl bustles around, getting dip, getting drinks. *Bustle* is the right word, Tessie thinks. She is short, as short as Tessie herself, and as fat as Helen is thin, especially in the caboose. She is a plump bird, her hair lacquered into

60

permanent auburn wings. Fluffy bustle, fluffle, Tessie thinks, and a giggle escapes. They all look at her. Victory frowns.

They are drinking white wine, except for Helen, who drinks straight vodka, explaining that white wine gives her a headache. She brings her own lime, in case the hostess forgets, cuts it into wedges and squeezes a wedge into each glassful she drinks. She eats the pulp after each glass and finishes a lime each time they meet.

Tessie looks around the bright California room which Pearl had been three-quarters finished decorating when her husband died. It is like sitting in a basket of fruit. Pearl is a decorator, though the only customer she has had so far is herself. She has "done" her house three times.

"Finishing it saved my life," she says, running her hand over the white lacquer sideboard. Her eyes fill as she looks at the little white wicker chair covered in the same yellow-and-green grapevine print that covers the walls. "Lemon and lime," she calls it. There are lemon-and-lime pillows thrown everywhere, mirrors filled with lemon-and-lime reflections, yellow and green flowers wherever you turn. She holds a pillow against her breast, picks a piece of thread from it.

"This is my tribute to Mel," she says.

Mostly, Tessie listens.

Their late husbands, men Tessie knew, are hardly recognizable these days from what their widows say. Not that they lie, Tessie thinks. They don't lie. It isn't lying, exactly.

For instance, Victory on George:

"That George" (ruefully): "That George was one man in a million."

That George, Tessie could say, was a lunatic who beat you up once in 1952 and you ran to my apartment, crying. *Then* you said, "Of all the millions of Jewish lawyers in the world, I had to get the only one who beats his wife. All the others litigate. George beats."

This George is a myth.

"What did you say?" Victory asks.

"I said you miss him," Tessie says.

Pearl, who is still on Mel's uncalled-for generosity, says, "What can I say?" and sighs. "The man thought with his heart, not with his head." That is, if his heart was just below his belt buckle, Tessie thinks.

What can I say? she tries, silently. Barney talked with his nose, not with his mouth. He sniffed when he was angry, he rubbed his nose when he was annoyed or puzzled, he sneezed when he was sick, his sinuses got stuffed up when he was sexually aroused, once a year.

It's the little things, you know, the little endearing things that you miss the most.

There is a delicate technique to being a good wife after the body is buried. No lies; you get caught. But take the facts and rearrange, slipcover them, and maybe you have something left to live with. She sips her wine and prepares a glossary:

OBSTINATE Knew what he wanted
HYSTERICAL High-strung, sensitive
MEAN Hot-tempered
PHILANDERING So so *so* full of life
LAZY Relaxed
STINGY Careful

Why do they bother? Don't be a fool. Think of Eleanor Roosevelt. Weren't you an Eleanor Roosevelt, the *old* Eleanor Roosevelt fan? What happened when it all came out the way Franklin treated her? Didn't it make you think more about how poor Eleanor looked, how ugly she was, than how rotten Franklin had been? Protect yourself.

"Your Barney," Victory was saying, "was a man of few words."

Mum? Dumb? Once, sitting in his chair, not answering her, she swears she thought he was dead.

"He never talked unless he had something important to say," Tessie says.

She had hated it.

"I never minded it, though, because behind that faraway look were brilliant thoughts."

They all seem to believe each other. More than that, they seem to believe themselves. Tessie doesn't; Tessie can't. It occurs to her that she might have done things backwards regarding Barney. Instead of saving the illusions for last, like dessert, like the rest of the widows had, she had kept the illusions all of their married life, and now, with him gone, she can hardly recall his face, much less his habits or the things he liked to do. She hears women say, "Oh, my husband always liked to do that" or "always liked blue suits" and she gets scared because it seems more knowledge than she has ever had. It makes her wonder who Barney was, and if they ever had a life together.

It is the result of living with a silent man, she tells herself. It was the only way, with a silent man: a blank sheet, an empty slate, a what-have-you. What else can you do but keep the illusion? I made the illusion, she thinks. I made it heat, anger, manliness, anything I wanted. Now I wonder if it was anything.

Conversation with Barney:

TESSIE: *Momser*, son of a bitch, what did you do to me?

BARNEY: . . .

TESSIE: To die is bad enough, but like this, without a will, suddenly, cashing in your life insurance and spending it on a secret. What were you thinking? Why did you do this to me?

BARNEY: . . .

TESSIE: What kind of answer is . . .

Maybe that was what she really wanted.

Esther (Tessie) née Fox was born beautiful and adored. She teethed, you might say, on gold lockets. By the time she was five, like Cleopatra, all she had to say was "Give me," and it was hers. At Spring Street Elementary School, her life was a round of tributes — bouquets of multiflavored lollipops with soft chocolate centers, large (128-color) boxes of crayons, vases made from H-O Quick Oats Cereal boxes wound in twine carrying roses made of tinted Kleenex, Teaberry gum — from little boys captured as much by her certitude as by her blond curls. Yet, and even then, at the beginning, all the getting in the world did not satisfy her. By the age of ten, her secret wish was to be bested, or at least equaled. Then, when she was thirteen, she met Arnold Barnett. He was as handsome as she was pretty, as tall and manly as she was short and girlish, as sought after as she was. And, best of all, he said he loved her only after she admitted it first.

Arnold and Tessie remained sweethearts all through high school, and Arnold always said that as soon as he became a pharmacist they would be married. He sealed the promise from time to time with extravagant gifts: a gold necklace, a delicate ankle bracelet with twin hearts, earrings with red stones in them, and a lavaliere of marcasite and onyx. In exchange, Tessie allowed certain liberties, and gave him her heart.

Then, one Friday afternoon, two weeks before the senior high school prom, they met to walk home from school together, as always. Arnold seemed pensive, and Tessie assumed he was composing an inscription for the inside of a ring she had been hinting she wanted for graduation. When he stopped walking she put her face up to his, and closed her eyes.

"Uh . . . ," he began, instead of kissing her, and in the voice which she admitted years later was feeble and piping but at the time called light and gentle, told her that he did not love her anymore, would not be marrying her someday, and (worst of all) would not be taking her to the senior prom (wasted dress already bought, no corsage to set off her eyes). In fact, he told her, he was now in love with Rose Grubman (big breasts, little eyes), and he wondered if Tessie would be kind enough to give back the expensive gifts he had given her, since they had actually been only borrowed from his grandmother and he wanted to keep them in the family.

Her heart died. How could she have been so betrayed? How could she have betrayed herself by believing him?

Although she was a great girl, always would be, he said.

In anger, she rallied. (Didn't she always?) Not a great enough girl to give back the jewelry, she had said. No. No.

That night, her mother pleaded with her. "The family will sue us, God knows," she said, wringing her hands.

Arnold wrote her a note, full of compliments and flowery language, calling on their long relationship, ending with a plea for the return of his grandmother's jewelry. "At least some of it," he wrote. She didn't answer.

In the next note, he assured her that he had no intention of giving any of it to Rose Grubman if that was what Tessie was worried about, because in his heart he would always have a little place for Tessie Fox, but the jewelry's rightful place was back in the Barnett jewelry box. After this letter, Tessie dropped the earrings down the sewer.

After the next letter, which hinted that Tessie had no right to keep the jewelry, she flushed both necklace and ankle bracelet down the toilet. They slid down easily. Then she wrote Arnold a letter telling him she had lost them.

Two weeks later, she received a beautifully wrapped box, and in it was a carefully folded, stinking pair of sweat socks, which, the enclosed note explained, came directly from Arnold's sweaty feet to Tessie's door. Tessie sent them back with a note: "Stick this in your grandmother's jewelry box."

Rose Grubman called her once. "Tessie?" she said, to which Tessie replied, "You have the wrong number, Rose."

The summer after graduation, Tessie worked at the *Bayonne News*, taking classified ads and going to the movies with her friends, who were always running into Arnold Barnett and his new romance. By midsummer, she no longer felt a sad pulling inside her when she heard his name. By summer's end she no longer cared about Arnold at all; but she also no longer believed that the world was on deposit in her account, either. Her hair, which had been gradually darkening through the years, slipped quietly out of the blond category and into a drab, intolerable, light brown.

She enrolled in Teachers College, in New York City; Arnold, she had heard, was at Rutgers University. She began coloring her hair a wild, honey shade, and dating young college men. There was one fellow; but he was too worshipful by far, and she sent him away.

In the spring of that year, Tessie began having uninvited late-night visits from a succession of young men. A knock would come at the door. "Western Union," someone would say, or "Meter man," but once the door was open, there was one of Arnold's fraternity brothers demanding the return of his grandmother's jewelry. The fourth time this happened, Tessie opened the door to find a tall, embarrassed youth standing there. She got so mad, before he could state his business, she placed her two small hands against his chest and pushed, and then watched, surprised, as he tumbled down the stairs. She hadn't really meant for him to go down the whole flight, she said later, although he said mildly (not complaining), she had pushed hard enough for him to have been propelled clear to Diner Street if the downstairs door had not been there to stop him. He lay so still that Tessie ran down to see if he was breathing. She put her face close to his. She helped him up, sat him in her parlor, put a cold cloth on his head, and gave him iced tea and a sugar bun. He really was a Fuller Brush man, and had never heard of Arnold Barnett. His name was Barney Goodman. He had a handsome face, dominated by fierce, bushy eyebrows and a sweet smile.

What he was to others didn't count; to Tessie he was Arnold's opposite: undemonstrative, noncommittal, unflashy. There is no way to tell whether Barney would have been exactly the same man if he had been seen by Tessie as himself, rather than as Arnold inside out. He was her savior. He made no declarations for her to disbelieve. He did not ply her with danger-ous gifts. He gave only himself, which was silent as a brick wall, quiet as a man at the altar, mild as an elder, or reverently struck dumb with love. When he said nothing, she invested it with import beyond words.

"He never gave me diamonds," she says, draining her glass, her voice trailing, as if to imply, "but his love was as brilliant as dia-monds themselves."

Helen refills her vodka and sighs.

Eventually Tessie and Barney married.

"Not that I'll ever trust you," she had warned him. "Men are not to be trusted."

The day of their wedding she sent Arnold Barnett his grandmother's lavaliere.

70

Their first apartment was in the East Bronx, on Bouck Avenue. Tessie got a job teaching in the nearby elementary school and Barney worked in a men's store in lower Manhattan, selling hats.

"Remember what a lousy cook I used to be?"

Helen looks at Pearl who looks at Victory who looks down.

"All right, still am, but at least now I know it," Tessie says.

She had made her mother's stuffed cabbage, and to keep the meat inside the leaves she had neatly hemmed each cabbage roll from end to end. Barney spent the night picking threads from his teeth, and never said a word.

"But he was so patient, so understanding. Understated, but understanding."

They were having trouble making ends meet, because Tessie had insisted on this particular apartment, which was more expensive than the others they had looked at. It had a southern exposure, she had said, not quite sure what that meant, but very sure that if it cost more it was better. But it had not been. From the beginning they had been plagued by plumbing problems, little gray mice (which made Tessie cry, and blame Barney for bringing her there), and, worst of all, roaches.

One morning, on a school holiday, after

Barney had gone to work, Tessie went into the bathroom to brush her long blond hair and there, caught in the bristles of the silver-backed hairbrush was a large roach. She went crazy, and after throwing the brush away, roach and all (she would never be able to use it again), she slammed out of the apartment and went looking for a new place to live. Two hours later she was home with the lease on an apartment two blocks away. By promising the landlord an extra three dollars a month rent she had gotten leave to move that same day. She called a moving company, and the last truckload of furniture was just leaving the curb in front of the old building when Barney arrived home from work. In her excitement, she had forgotten to tell Barney about the move, yet he hardly even looked surprised. What kind of lox wouldn't blow his stack at something like that?

"A saint. He never said a word, just picked up a lamp that still had to be loaded in the truck and walked with me over to the new place."

She sometimes wondered, if he had come home and found her gone, would he have bothered to look for her?

In the evenings, after dinner, he would settle himself in the chair by the window, and open a book.

72

"He always dreamed of owning a little book-store of his own."

Had he ever dreamed of anything? Had he even connected his love of reading with selling books? Once, maybe. While he was selling *Encyclopaedia Britannica* door to door, he said, in passing, "I think I like selling books more than hats." But it had been Tessie who had the bookstore idea.

"Books were his life," Victory agrees, drinking more wine.

He turned into a monster.

In all the years, Barney surprised Tessie only twice, that she can recall right now. The first time was an afternoon in 1945. They were in the bookstore.

"I'll redo the window," Tessie had said.

"No," he had said, firmly.

Louise, who was barely two at the time, and was playing on a blue blanket spread on the basement floor of the store, stopped banging her rattle long enough to honor this remarkable exchange with complete silence.

"He might have seemed mild-mannered to you," Tessie says, holding out her glass, "but inside him was a tiger."

He hadn't growled, but he had frowned. It had frightened her. Since she had closed her eyes for Arnold's kiss and gotten something else, surprises frightened her.

Still, she had fought with him.

Still, Barney had said no.

She persisted. Just listen, she said. "No."

"Let's make it modern," she said. "Fill the window with new books, the latest." The book company had sent them a display for nothing. Why not use it?

But Barney continued to refuse. He wanted the rocking chair, the old, battered cabinet, the pipe, and the antique volume of something in the window.

"Everyone thinks we're a used-furniture store," she complained.

But Barney wouldn't listen.

I will make him listen, she thought. I will show him. And the next morning, while he was downstairs doing inventory, she rearranged the window her way, with stacks of the latest books in their shiny covers, and a life-sized, brightly colored cardboard author pointing to his own chin. Something new in displays, the salesman had said.

When Barney came upstairs and saw what she had done, he went crazy, crawling into the window on all fours, tossing the books out at her. He punched the cardboard author in half. She had never seen him like that. When he tried to put the rocking chair back in the window, she had gripped one arm of it, and that is the picture that is frozen in her mind now: she and Barney pulling opposite ways with the old chair between them. Had he let go, given up, or had the chair slipped from her grasp? She fell back. You attacked me, she had said, from that day on.

"We had very different ideas about running the store throughout the years, but it never *really* came between us," Tessie says. "Just a little touch more, or I'll be drunk."

After he had attacked her and she lay (half dead almost) on the floor among the books, he had arranged the window his way (as if nothing had happened), went out to lunch, and came back (as if nothing had happened). He went downstairs to finish his inventory, leaving a sandwich on the counter for her (aha, no mustard on the pastrami, don't tell me you aren't mad, that's a deliberate act, who eats pastrami dry?). But he did not come home that night or the night after. The third night he came home, just like himself, sleepy and mild. She never asked where he had been, and he never told her. Maybe he had stayed downstairs in the little room the O'Neill sisters had lived in. Maybe he sat in the rocking chair in the window and put himself to sleep reading those leather books in the dark.

75

The window is still the same after all these years, except now and then he added a volume to the old books, so today there is a stack of them. She had never tried to change it.

"He liked an old-fashioned kind of place," she says.

That clutter everywhere, and the old argument grabbing her by the throat, making her cough as if she had breathed a lungful of book dust. Pearl fills her glass.

Mr. Keep-It-You-Never-Know. Old books. Paperbacks with fifty-cent prices on the cover, which he could have returned to the publisher for the same titles with new, higher prices and bright new covers, but no, he had to keep the old ones. Why? So people could discover a bargain. Because he liked the old covers. Because, who knows, one day they might be worth something. Books no one read, Mr. Businessman, were going to turn into Cinderellas and make our fortune? Books so expensive no one could afford them, and when their bindings dried and eventually fell off you put the covers in one place and the naked books in another? He had an old copy of a mystery novel by Gypsy Rose Lee, the pages so brown they looked toasted. This would be a collector's item, Mr. Crazy?

"She didn't even write it," Tessie had said.

"That's the whole point," Barney had said. Crazy.

"We may not have agreed," Tessie says, "but we understood each other."

And the other surprise, in two parts.

Tessie sighs and touches her breast, as if feeling for her heart.

"I'll never forget the day he died."

She woke cranky, as if the morning were a moment after the night, when Barney had said something to irritate her. What had it been? Or had it been his saying nothing at all? Or was it his smugness, when by all rights he should have been as worried as she? Business was down, way down.

In the clear morning light she had said it again. "Barney, business is down."

He had rubbed his hand across his face as if what she said was a strand of hair that had brushed him.

"True," he said, sleepily. "True and true."

She had sat bolt upright, then eased the slight twinge in her lower back by leaning all the way forward, head to feet. She could feel her stomach flab fold over. Three tires. She ran her hand through her pink-gold (Champagne #31) hair.

Barney had closed his eyes again.

She reached across him to turn on the radio

and held her face above his for a minute, until he exhaled. Sweet, she thought with fury. His breath was always sweet, even in the morning, before he brushed. He sensed her above him, and puckered up.

Sometimes she thought the one reason she had never left him was this nutmeg smell of his breath, living proof he was sweet to the core.

"You want to, maybe?" she said, feeling the vague desire slip away as she spoke.

Barney rubbed his nose again and reached over, groping, and patted her hair. "Nah," he said. "I'm not up yet."

And though she was relieved, she said tartly, "You never are."

Instead of getting mad, though, Barney had laughed.

"Tessie, I'm an old man. What do you want?"

"Nothing," she had said, lying back down. "Just nothing." Then — "Barney, I had another dream."

He hadn't answered.

"Are you up?" she had said. *"Are you up?"*

He had shaken his head groggily.

"I had another dream."

Nothing.

"Say *some*thing," Tessie had said, shaking him.

"What do you want me to say?"

"Say, 'What was the dream about?' or 'Was it a bad dream?' or 'Gee, Tess, I'm sorry,' or just put your arms around me."

He had put his arms around her and said, "What was the dream about?" and she had pushed him away.

"Now it's too late," she had said.

Barney had sighed.

"I saw Papa," she had told him. "He was waving at me. He was getting smaller and smaller and when I woke up I felt like I was a grape in the middle of the bed."

Barney had lifted himself up.

"A grape?"

"No, a prune, then, all right?" she had said, and begun to cry.

Victory rubs Tessie's back soothingly.

"It must have been a terrible shock," Helen says.

Tessie sighs. "Oh, yes, of course," she says, "but at least that last morning we were . . . together."

The widows look into their laps.

"So hard," Helen murmurs.

"Yes," Tessie says. "But then I think how so many people suffer long, painful times in the hospital, such a drain, and I'm grateful. At least he died quickly, without pain, doing what made him happy to the last."

Intestate. Son of a bitch. I could cut them off.

Fishman had laid it all out. She kept coming back to it. She hadn't been able to get back to herself since it happened.

"I haven't been able to get back to myself since it happened."

"Grief," Pearl says, her eyes filling, thinking of Mel.

Victory and Helen take Tessie home, right to the door, because she can't walk straight. Victory says she has never seen Tessie drunk before.

"Grief," Helen says.

"Shit," Tessie groans.

Memories are a pain in the ass, a burden. Memories, the sound of the word, smooth, like an old song, or nice mahogany, should soothe me. I want to say, "This was my husband and I definitely loved him and it tore my heart right out of my chest when he left me," and then forget it. Instead I am confused, I contradict myself, as if I'm not even sure who he was, and then I have these insulting, disparaging thoughts about him which I don't want to have, which are not fair to someone who is dead and can't defend himself: at the dinner table, barricading his peas against the meat juices with a potato-wall; picking radishes out of his salad; picking his nose in front of the television set. And humming. He hummed incessantly while he ate, denied he did it, hummed in the act, too, right when I was getting in the mood, like an old refrigerator, or like he was davening, he would crank up and start to hum, and then I couldn't go on with it, it would cool me right down. Oh, Barney was all right, wasn't so bad. Wasn't mean, certainly. Didn't philander. Wasn't the type. (Wouldn't undress in front of a stranger. Didn't want anyone to see his bony knees.) Yet there were times, he was so sexy. I wanted him to come up behind me in the kitchen and slap my behind, or put his hands over my eyes or around my waist and turn me around roughly to face him, grab me at the back of my neck, and pull me close to his face, to kiss me inconsiderately hard, and longer than my breath could last, letting me go to come at me again, and again, until I was down, helpless on the kitchen floor. Bruising kisses. Of course he never dared. But he vacuumed every Sunday morning and he wasn't mean. Grab me, I once said to him, and he made believe he didn't hear me. Or maybe he didn't.

She replayed days, weeks, months.

I could have left him.

One spring night, in the first year of their marriage, Tessie packed a bag.

The evening before, Barney had come home

to their apartment with the news that he had lost his job.

"Again?" she had said.

In answer he had breathed in through his nostrils the longest stream of air known to man, which lasted, she swore, a full half minute during which she held her breath, too, and then exploded, saying again, "Again?"

He had let his shoulders down and answered "Yes" in such a piteous way that the rawness of her anger was instantly boiled down to irritation swimming in a broth of sympathy and affection. She had led him to a chair (their only one, currently, since furnishing kept being interrupted by the downswings of his fortunes) and made him put his feet up (as if bringing the news had tired him) and recline (it was one of the first recliner models, with three positions) while she went into the kitchen to fix him a cold ginger ale with a scoop of ice cream in it. But then, coming back to the living room with his float, she had walked behind the chair and accidentally glimpsed the top of his head, seeing, to her horror, pink scalp showing through the hair she had always thought of as thick enough to last a lifetime. All her anger came flooding back with a suddenness which caused her to bump into the leg of the chair. When she bumped into the chair some of the soda sloshed out of the glass and onto Barney's head, dripping down and off his nose. The surprised look on his face was so comical that she couldn't help laughing, and she wasn't mad anymore.

Later that night, lying by his side in the double bed with the fruitwood headboard, she said to herself, if he touches me tonight I will turn away, not in anger but in sorrow. When he hadn't touched her by 3:00 A.M. (she knew he was awake because she heard the long whistle of his sighs), she grabbed him, but not without a little reserve, she told herself.

The next morning, rising for work in the early chill, and seeing him still fast asleep, she decided definitely she would leave him. But then he turned and she saw in the corner of each slightly slanted eye, a moistness which brought tears to hers. She kissed him bravely, and then dressed for work, not noisily, but humming, as Norma Shearer might have. She wrapped her beautiful blond hair tightly in a bun so she would look older to her students. She stood at the foot of the bed and gazed at him, but her bravery and beauty went unnoticed as Barney slept on. I will leave him, she said to herself, and went into the kitchen to make an egg-salad sandwich for her lunch. But then it was time for work at the small corner school where kindergarteners fought to sit on her lap, and touch her earrings, and it would have been a shame to disappoint them. I will leave later, she said.

At lunchtime, in the teachers' room, through smoke from her English Ovals, she listened to Patsy and Lenore, two daring young unmarried teachers, talk about going to Paris in the summertime. I'll go with you, she thought.

But in the middle of the afternoon, Rita DeLorraine, the new assistant principal with the mannish shoes and the little mustache over her upper lip, came into Tessie's classroom. "Your husband called," she said, and Tessie felt superior for having one. *Spinster*, she said to herself. A good man nowadays.

She came home late, having stopped at the fish store for something for supper. She had pictured him all the way home, pitiful in his robe. Wistful at the window, waiting for her. Hopeful at the kitchen table, looking through the classifieds. Grateful as she swept in through the front door, flushed and wifely.

He didn't hear her when she came in; he was recaulking the tile in the bathroom tub.

She slammed the fish down on the commode and said,

"This is how you look for a job?"

"I got one," he said, not turning around,

concentrating on his work.

"You got one?" she said, unwilling to stop in the middle of her indignation. "Again? Doing what?" When he told her selling encyclopedias door to door, she felt justified in getting indignant after all. "Selling *what?*" she said. "That settles it. I'm leaving," and she stormed out of the bathroom. She came back for the fish. "Right after dinner," she said, because she wanted him to be good and sure she wasn't walking out in anger, but only after careful consideration, on a full stomach, and she wouldn't be back.

He wouldn't be shocked. He wouldn't beg her to stay. He wouldn't do *anything*. He didn't look at her through the whole meal, and when she couldn't catch his eye, she finally had to speak.

"I suppose you want to know why," she said.

He sighed. "I know. You told me."

"Really? Why?" she challenged.

"Because I lost my job again."

"It certainly is *not* why," she said. What kind of woman would abandon her husband just like that? When the ship was sinking? "What kind of woman do you think I am?"

He didn't say.

"If you don't want me to go why don't you try to stop me?" she said. "Not that you could."

"I don't want to force you," he said.

"But Barney," she said, exasperated. "You wouldn't be forcing me if you told me you loved me and you wouldn't let me leave."

"But you know I love you, Tessie, and you know I don't want you to leave," he said. He was picking at the fish.

"Don't you like the salmon?" she said.

"It's a little overcooked," he said.

She slammed her fork down. "Don't you know anything about human nature?" she said. "Is this the time to tell me I'm a lousy cook? Is this the time to complain about the fish?"

"I'm not complaining," he said. "You asked."

"Don't try to twist things around," she said. "What kind of job is door to door? You were moving up to manager in a retail store. Why go backward?"

"We need the money," Barney said.

And there was something so stubborn, and distasteful and needlessly truthful in what he said that it flooded Tessie with deep tenderness that made her feel she would drown, and terror, too. Removing her plate to the sink, she went into the bedroom to pack.

Barney didn't follow. He did the dishes instead.

As she packed, she kept thinking he was standing there in the doorway watching her, so she flung her clothes into the tan valise emphatically, dramatically. Each time she turned and didn't catch him standing there, his eyes pleading for mercy, she thought he had just moved away. Finally, she was packed.

"I'm leaving in the morning," she told him. Because by this time it was too late, and already dark.

But then in the morning she remembered that the piano they had ordered was being delivered on that very day, and if she left there would be no one to sign for it. And that evening there was so much to do, and hear, with the new piano, and Barney's new job, that somehow she forgot all about leaving until she went into the bedroom late that night and couldn't find a nightgown until she recalled they were all packed away. And although she put her arms around him that night, she didn't unpack for a week, and sometimes she thought she had unpacked never.

A thousand times, a million times was it? she had said to him, "I should have left you that time when you lost your job, remember?" and he always claimed not to remember and she always said to him, "Sure you remember. I would have, too, except you wouldn't let me go."

Could she have gone to Paris, with Patsy and

Lenore? Gotten a job teaching the ambassador's children? The ambassador, a widower and handsome, wanting her? But then, Barney turned up, and a lucky thing, because the ambassador turned out a bastard, and Barney, who was a success in the encyclopedia business, rescued her from him and his miserable and demanding children.

Could she have gone on to a career, like Rita DeLorraine, except maybe in the journalism field, and become the first woman to win the whatchamacallit prize, and Barney was there in the audience when she came to the podium, and she thanked one and all for the honor, but she set everyone straight on one thing: she could do without the prize, as long as she had her darling, and she walked off the podium into Barney's waiting arms.

Or she could have become a brilliant lady lawyer who made a million bucks and won case after case but always came home to Barney, and never, never threw it up to him that she made millions more than he.

Only she could never have left him.

She wished she had never said she would.

She went to the piano and played the only fast song she knew by heart, "Buckle Down Winsocki" ("You can win Winsocki if you knuckle down/If you break their necks/If you make them wrecks") and then called Louise. "The piano is yours," she said.

I could have gone with him.

He went to California once, to visit dying Cousin Hesh. It was when Louise was about nine.

Tessie had hated the way his family all called on him. It made her feel tucked to the side, not even in their sight. As if *he* were the important one. She had once heard them call her *the wife.* Oh, she had hated that. After the first few years of marriage, she always tried to find a reason not to visit them. When Louise was old enough, she sent her along in her place, each time secretly worried that Barney might object, and secretly angry when he didn't. Louise loved going, and became friendly with all her cousins and uncles and aunts on Barney's side of the family. Tessie said, "Isn't that lovely dear," and turned aside quickly which made Louise ask the routine question, "Why are you mad at me?" to which Tessie responded with the usual lie, "I'm not."

It was a big family; Tessie used to say they traveled in packs. One night, Miriam, Irving, and Sylvia (the ones Tessie called "the enforcers") came unannounced, to ask Barney to go to California to represent the family at Hesh's bedside. Tessie thought it was a morbid thing to do, and would tip Heshie off he was dying.

"You think maybe he doesn't know?" Miriam said, smiling sourly and shaking her head.

If they had called on the telephone, Tessie would have stood by Barney's side and written "No" on the little pad beside the phone. But they were there in person, so she had to make coffee, and pretend to agree finally, and when that didn't get their attention she had gone overboard and said, "I'll go with him."

Then, the next day, when Barney was making arrangements, he said, "We" and she said, "We?" and he said he thought she was coming with him. And she had said of course, she was, but did he really think she should? What about Louise? Miriam and Sylvia had both offered to look after her, he said. Who would mind the store, though? Victory and George, or we could close up for a week, he said. So she had to say yes.

All night she hid on her side of the bed, trying to figure out how she could get out of it. She faced (if only because she had to, and only for that moment) that she was afraid: of his family, of flying in an airplane, of strange places, strange beds; she was afraid to be even for one moment unanchored to the places she knew.

In the morning she said, "I had a bad night. I

didn't feel well all night. Did you hear me tossing and turning?"

He said no. As if he didn't know she was leading up to something.

"I think I might be getting sick," she said.

"So should I still get two tickets, or one?" he said. The arrow struck home too accurately. Was he being sarcastic?

"Of course get two," she said. "Did I say anything?"

"I just wondered," he said. "If you aren't feeling well . . ."

He was making it too easy, making her feel guilty. So she escalated. Would he still go, she demanded, if she was sick? Would he just walk off and leave a sick wife, not knowing what was wrong with her? She was not separate from the question then, as she was now, in memory. She had meant it. She had believed. Indignation was there, real. Would he take an airplane while she lay in bed? Go off to a cousin whom he hadn't seen in thirteen years and who had not even come to their wedding?

"He was sick then, too," Barney had said.

You see, she had said, he didn't die then and he probably won't die now either, so what was the point of the trip? But if you want to go and leave a wife who is coming down with god knows what to visit a cousin who might or might not die . . . She left it to him.

"Get your ticket, go," she had said. "I'll be all right."

"You're not going?" he had said.

She gave him a dirty look. "Do you think I should, in my condition? I'll leave it up to you."

"Better not, Tessie," he had said.

Was it the "Tessie" at the end of the other two words, which she remembered so well, that had made her feel so bad, like a last caress, or regret?

When she didn't come into the kitchen by five o'clock, he made scrambled eggs for supper and brought it to her on a tray.

"I'll eat at the table," she said. "I'm not dying, you know." To remind him that he was choosing his cousin Hesh over her, and to take his mind off what came closer and closer to hers: *once* he asks me to go with him and I don't.

Which, as soon as he was airborne, tormented her. So, when he called from California, she said, her voice husky with tears, "I miss you already, my darling. Forgive me. Forgive me." But Barney, who might never have attached the importance she had to her coming along, said "For what? Forgive you for what?" which made her feel silly.

"Do you miss me?" she said.

"Tessie, I just saw you a few hours ago," he

said, quite sensibly. And though she didn't really miss him either, the truth seemed terrible to her, like a betrayal, and in the end she said, Dammit, Barney, and hung up on him. Of course the clatter was all on her end, Barney just heard the click, and being Barney, and having said all he needed to say (which was, he had arrived safely and a letter would follow), he didn't bother to reestablish the connection.

Tessie waited in agony for the black receiver to jump off its cradle, smoking with urgency, passion, remorse. Drama.

After an hour, the telephone melted, and became part of the dark mahogany table stand, hardly noticeable. The crack of lightning drew her to the window, where she stood most of the night, waiting for the airplane that carried Barney (urgently remorseful and passionate as he sat in the cockpit) as he tried to make his way through the storm. And he would, he wouldn't, he would, he wouldn't, she pinched her face with tired, tense hands, rubbed her eyes red, watched the spot there, on Burnside Avenue, where he would, he wouldn't land safely.

She threw herself across the width of the double bed that night, her feet hanging over the side, saying to herself as she would say to him at some future time, "I can't even sleep in our bed without you, my darling." But she awoke on her own side with her head on her own pillow, so she must have moved in the night.

The long vigil, Waiting for His Letter, came next. She reminded Louise he was gone by saying, "Don't you miss Daddy?" and pursing her lips when Louise answered, "Not yet, Mama."

I'll shop for his favorite foods, she said, so they will be waiting for him when he comes home. But then, there in the supermarket she stood, stumped, because she didn't know what his favorites were, he always said "I like everything" and his appetite was so good she assumed it was true. So she bought her favorites instead.

The mailman told her she was making him put the wrong letters in the wrong boxes because she got him so nervous standing behind him waiting for What? What was so important? and she told him, I'm not worrying about you, so don't you worry about me.

The letter came. Dear Tess, it said. Everything fine. Hesh very weak but holding on. We are visiting some bookstores to see how the other half does it. Be home end of next week. Love, Barney.

Who is "We," she said. I let him go off by

94

himself, I disappoint him, and now I am faced with the crucial question, who is "We?" Is "We" a woman? What to do? Call him and demand to know? Bring on the crisis that way? What if he told her yes, "We" is a woman, a woman? What turn would her life take then? Would she suffer, lose weight, lose Barney? Or should she do what her friend Pearl did and swallow the needle of knowledge, which would circulate dangerously inside the system of their marriage possibly forever?

She couldn't stand it. She called him that night, screaming the question, screaming it ten times before he could understand what she was saying; he had thought she was saying, "Who is Louise," and he couldn't figure out why she was asking who her own daughter was. She demanded he come home at once. He did, and his cousin died three days later. He never said a word about it.

Who is "We," she thought now in disgust. Who you always knew it was: cousin Fanny, Hymie, maybe Rose, his wife. And how much of my life did I carry on like that, to hide how scared I was, making Barney act according to the way I acted, creating fictions into which I fit him without telling him. Who was I?

"Wait," she wished she might have said the night he made arrangements to go. "Wait. I changed my mind. I am coming with you."

I could have danced all night.

She loved to dance (cha-cha-cha). But dancing, like certain foods, was too spicy, too zingy, too everything. So she said. And she liked it much too much. So she felt she could not stop.

A good occasion, according to her (take your bride, take your groom, take your flowers, take your food, take your Johnnie Walker Red), depended completely on the music. The music. The mambo, the samba, ay ay ay. If the music was good, the party was good. But the next day, the morning after, although she hadn't had a drop to drink she couldn't remember anything. And she wondered with an uneasy itch inside if she had imagined that inability to stop swinging her hips and feeling the flow and going around the room with her hands raised high above her head, knowing her breasts shook and her ass shook, and her hair tickled the middle of her back as she tossed her head, and she wondered if she had stuck her tongue out of her mouth and pointed it, if her teeth had shown, and if a sound had come out of her throat. She felt ashamed, as if she had let everyone see something they weren't supposed to see. And dancing destroyed her balance, it took her two or three days to straighten herself out, she felt turned inside out, and impractical and immature when she danced, thrilled and filled with only the desire to dance some more. It turned a key.

Barney didn't know step one. Barney couldn't dance for beans. He wouldn't go to Fred Astaire or Arthur Murray. Tessie counted in his ear and still he put in extra steps. He didn't feel the rhythm and then he sat down. He didn't get up at all for fast dances or Latin ones. She estimated she must have thrown him daggers and dirty looks across ten thousand centerpieces of blue-tinted flowers at ten thousand weddings or bar mitzvahs or engagement parties, where they were left at the table while everybody else danced. She refused to be like those women who take another woman for a partner, broadcasting to everyone in the room that she couldn't get a man to dance with, not even her own husband. Widows did this, and spinsters, and younger men and women laughed at them behind their backs. She wouldn't dance with another man because you never knew what to say and you couldn't let yourself go, and you could never be sure he wouldn't step on your feet. The only one she took a chance with was George Schrier if he and Victory were at the same party, and then only twice a night, when Victory unhooked the leash. So she would sit there, at first coaxing Barney, then arguing with him or silently pitching fury at him, and then finally, as if he had driven her to it, saying the hell with you I'll dance by myself.

The week before Louise's wedding she said to him I'll be goddamned if I'm going to dance by myself at my own daughter's wedding, and she put Perez Prado on the phonograph and pulled Barney out of the reclining chair, and made him cha-cha with her until he was counting to himself correctly, and she could see him in the hall mirror and he looked good even from the back. *Olé, señor*, she said to him, and kissed him, and he bowed like he had just done the minuet, which was the wrong style but the right spirit, she said.

Louise's wedding dawned gray, and by noon weather reports were calling it the coldest day in six winters and the coldest December 30 in fifty years, five degrees below zero. They had to leave for the wedding hall early, while it was still light out, since the photographer expected them there for family shots. They carried Louise's gown, since she was going to dress in the bridal dressing room; but Tessie wore hers, not wanting to put her clothes on in a strange place. A bitter gust of wind whipped the flared bottom of her dress around her, skimming a puddle, wrapping her an involuntary column of peach silk, and Barney had to take her shoulders and turn her the opposite way before she could move. Pewter icicles, which clung to the hem of her dress, clicked like castinets as she alit from the car under the canopied entrance of the wedding hall.

"Something is wrong," she said. It was freezing in the wedding hall. She sent Barney to find out what was wrong. The heating system had broken down, the manager said, but now it was fixed. It would take an hour or so for the place to warm up. Louise shrugged and closed her coat, Barney shrugged and said he would have a little something to warm up his insides, and Tessie said, Am I the only one who thinks it is outrageous that a thing like this should happen? We should at least get a partial refund, she said. Louise walked away. The manager politely promised to see what he could do. Tessie looked at Barney as if to say, See? and went off with Louise to help her dress.

"I'll be at the bar," Barney said.

The photographer photographed all of them standing at the bar, holding up their glasses for a toast. He took six variations of the shot, rearranging them each time, both families, then each family alone, bride and groom, all the women, all the men, both families again, and each time Barney drained his toast and refilled his glass.

It was the fashion in those days to heighten the drama of the moment. Brides in wedding halls emerged from behind velvet curtains, or rose from sunken pits like the Rockettes at Radio City Music Hall, or, as Louise did that day, floated behind frosted shower-glass panels along a pathway (which was cinderblock and covered with frost from the record cold), to appear with the swell of the organ, at the top of the aisle where her father was waiting to walk her down it. But Barney was not waiting, and Tessie had to go and get him. She walked right into the men's room, where he was sitting, holding his handkerchief open in his hands, as if he were reading it. Are you drunk? she said. Don't worry about a thing, he said, and between Tessie and Russell, they got him to the head of the aisle where Louise was waiting. He escorted her down the aisle soberly enough, swaying just slightly when she let go of his arm, and bowing as Russell reached for her. And then they had the ceremony, the breaking of the glass, the party, and Tessie lost sight of him, except for a glimpse now and then, as he wandered about with a box of cigars in his hand and a smile on his face.

"I'm too busy to dance," she told anyone who asked her, but she had her hands above her head, and her hips swaying, her fingers snapping as she moved around, nodding absent-mindedly if people talked to her, listening to the music. She hardly realized she had come full circle when she reached the head table, and there was Barney, sitting alone, looking at her, smiling.

"What?" she said, as he stared.

But Barney didn't answer (which in itself was not unusual) except that he raised his face to hers, and put his big hands, first his left, very deliberately on her right cheek, she could feel every finger, warm, and then his right hand on her left cheek, and held her face like that and just stared at her, and then lifted her, by the face, and rocking her face back and forth between his hands, told her she was the most, the most, the most beautiful mother of the bride, the most beautiful woman in the world. Then he raised his arms, everyone was watching and listening, and proposed a toast to her, the most beautiful woman in the world, the most beautiful mother of the bride, the most beautiful bride, he said, and she flushed at the mistake and pulled his hands down. And though her eyes watered, she pulled away from him.

"Ah, Tessie," he said, and pursued her, caught her by the shoulders. "My beautiful Tessie, dance with me, my love," he said, and counting to himself, began to cha-cha. She turned away, pretending someone had called her. But he followed behind, cha-cha-ing and making kissing sounds to her back, and when the band switched to a mambo he tried to do that, too, although that was the dance he never caught on to. Then he stopped, and went to the bandstand, and the leader announced that Mr. Goodman had made a request, and the band played "When You Were Sweet Sixteen." Barney stood there while they played, swaying, and when they got to the words "I loved you as I never loved before/When first I saw you on the village green," he grabbed the microphone and sang it straight to Tessie. Then the bandleader shouted "Mother and father of the bride" and started off the applause as he led Barney over to Tessie to dance, and Barney put his arms around her, and she threw her head back in a proud gesture, as though she went along with it, but she had whispered in his ear, "Stop making such a goddamn fool of yourself, Barney, you're drunk." Though he had not sobered up instantly, he had kissed her cheek soberly enough, dryly, and straightened his back, and she felt such relief and such regret, it had been repeating on her ever since.

I could have taken his long face in my hands, rubbed the five o'clock shadow that has already grown there through the long night, kissed him, and said, "Ah, Barney, now I know your price — for one whole bottle of Johnnie Walker Red you will dance all the fast dances and make love to your wife in public to boot," and then to hell with everyone else put my arms around him and danced with him until 3:00 A.M., until the band went into overtime.

Or did she not want anyone to hold her?

We could have lived another life.

Every spring from 1954 through 1958, Tessie and Barney spent Sunday afternoons house-hunting in the northern suburbs. Tessie packed a picnic lunch of peanut-butter-and-jelly sand-wiches (always the same, it was the only thing she would trust not to spoil), or sometimes in the coolest, earliest spring, cream cheese and jelly or olives (even then pressing her nose close to the cream-cheesed side of the sandwich before letting Louise eat it, to make sure it hadn't "turned"), and they bundled Louise (later she would object, and sometimes be allowed to bring a friend, though never to stay at home) into the back of the car, and set off. They went to Ardsley, Dobbs Ferry, Nyack, Peekskill, Suffern, Spring Valley, Monsey, along the pretty, green-flanked narrow high-ways which preceded the Thruway.

They never said explicitly why they were going, either to their neighbors or to each other. They always called the trip "a ride into the country, we'll see, maybe we'll stop, maybe we won't, a family outing." They never once said, "We're thinking of buying a house."

The postwar building boom was at its height then, and they didn't even have to plan a route, they just headed north and eventually they passed signs advertising new housing developments.

"Let's just take a look," Tessie might say then, or Barney might just take a turn. Then they would find themselves in a horseshoe or a circle of houses (like a wagon train ready to fight off the Indians, Barney once said) decorated by bunting and colored plastic flags.

Whatever Barney liked, Tessie didn't. Whatever Tessie liked, Barney was not so sure about.

TESSIE: Not enough closets.

BARNEY (knocking on the wall): Solid construction.

TESSIE: Small rooms, though.

BARNEY: Built forever.

TESSIE: This little kitchen?

BARNEY: Look at the backyard.

TESSIE: Who's going to mow it?

BARNEY: Nice and close to the city.

TESSIE: Too close to the hustle and bustle.

BARNEY: Countryish.

TESSIE: Too far from the city.

104

Same house, another time another plot.

BARNEY: Cheesy construction.

TESSIE: Look at the closets.

BARNEY: Collapsible.

TESSIE: Roomy rooms, though.

BARNEY: No backyard, though.

TESSIE: Nothing to mow, though.

BARNEY: Too close to the city.

TESSIE: What a kitchen.

They were afraid: to take on a mortgage, though they had the money; of being home-owners, or suburbanites, as if it were a religion and they would have to convert; of owning land. So they protected one another from it. But then, there was a house. The Heritage model. Tessie had strolled through, from roped-off room to roped-off room, thinking how the dark, colonial furniture was so sweet and polished and unreal, like chocolate pieces, good enough to eat, skirted and ruffled appetizingly, and she loved the fake colonial pillars in the front of the house. Barney knocked on the side of the wall with his knuckles and said solid, solid. But then, because it was habit, or to protect themselves from change, Tessie found something to counter "solid." "Not enough closets," it was. "Built to last forever," Barney said, and she said, "Small rooms." And before she could change her mind, or say "Barney, wait," they drove away from the house and never saw it again. She thought about it on and off for years.

"Sometimes I think of the Heritage model," she had said to Barney one Indian-summer day a long time later, and he hadn't said, as she had expected him to, "What?" "So do I," he had said.

The sun would have slid sideways into the yard through the fence, making a plaid of light and shadow, and that Indian-summer day Barney and she would have occupied opposing sections, though close together, he in the shade, Tessie in the sun.

Remnants of an outdoor breakfast (which Tessie had prepared without complaint because she loved her big, bright kitchen and large pantry) would have been on the picnic table and as she reached for her cup she remarked to him that the sun was so strong the coffee was still hot. He would have smiled his vague smile and held up one finger, reading, don't disturb, and so she would have leafed through the *Times* and leaned back to watch two sweet nestlings, sparrows, hop in the low branches of her own little peach tree. Then Barney would have gone upstairs to watch the ball game on television, and she would have fallen into a snooze outside and dreamed vaguely of the outdoor things that surrounded her, birds and harmless insects, butterflies and tangy, sweet-smelling grass. When she would have awakened, the *Times* would have been burned yellow and she could feel the sting of sunburn across her nose. She would yawn and reach across to Barney's watch, which was strapped to the arm of the lounge chair. It would be after four, the day burned down like a good cigar, and, stretching, she would go into the house, leaving Barney's watch strapped where it was, because there were no thieves to worry about where they were. Then she would call a good Chinese take-out place, which would come in a clean little truck at exactly the time she told them, with piping hot dishes of Sweet and Sour Chicken, and Beef Chow Fun, which she would put in the special part of the oven just for warming. Then she would go upstairs, where Barney was dozing in front of the television, and she would unfold her arms and drape them over him, standing behind the chair, stroking his hair, not one bit annoyed about anything, because here where they lived it was so safe, and pretty, and easy.

And after she cried about this, she pictured the last scene with Barney not waking up, the last loving scene turning into the way he died, with his face the way it had been in the basement of the store, and her shaking him and telling him to wake up and he wouldn't, and she ended by saying what the hell's the difference. House or no house, he died and that's that.

She could have gone with him, part two.

Simon and Anna came from the other side.

She told the story this way to Louise. Sometimes she would get confused, starting the story with "Grandma and Grandpa," and then halfway through switching to "Mama and Papa," so Louise would interrupt and say "you mean my grandma and grandpa," so finally she changed it altogether, and told the story from the beginning using their names, which made her feel strange.

Simon and Anna came from the other side, from the farm (the land, she said, because it sounded like a grand novel plot that way) into trade. It doesn't matter, she would say, if Louise asked what kind of trade, pretending she only wanted to skim the surface of the story. But then she would relent quickly and tell her millinery, because really she didn't want to leave out a single thing. Hats. Simon could (and did, to his dying day, she said, her voice thickening with tears) take a hat in his hand and feel the brim and run his hands inside where the sizing band and the sweat band was, and without looking or even feeling the label (someone had once accused him of feeling the stitched lettering of the label) could tell you without a doubt who made the hat. He could tell you who invented the skimmer and who the boater, and what happened the year W. C. Fields made the derby so popular you couldn't keep it in stock. He himself had once taken out a patent on an adjustable baseball cap, but it ran out before he could figure out what he wanted to do with it, or find the time for it, and then someone reinvented it and made a million dollars. Which bothered Simon and didn't bother Simon. It bothered him because it did not allow him to fulfill his one life's wish, as he told it, which was to put down before his Anna, on the kitchen table, like a piece of sturgeon, one hundred thousand dollars, and say "Here, *katzele,* enjoy." He, himself, he often said, had no need of such things. Not getting his life's wish was thoroughly consistent with his view of life. He harbored a free-floating cynicism which posited that good deeds reap bad, the good die young, and to be generous is to be a fool. To illustrate the truth of this he told the story of how, when he came over on the boat, he had shared what little money he had with a fellow of his own age, who had promised to take Simon to live with his rich relatives when they landed, only to disappear once they went through immigration. The man's name changed, from one telling to the next, and once Tessie had angered her father by suggesting that maybe the man had *lost* Simon and not run away from him. His face had reddened, his fists clenched, and he had turned away in silence, pretending for a week he did not even see her. A hard man, she told Louise. His one exception, his one weakness was Anna, his wife. There is a picture of Simon — the mad Russian, they used to call him in the family — taken on a cousin's farm upstate, beside a workhorse and a plow, next to a slouched hat that hung, like a territorial flag, on a staff stuck in the ground. There is another of him, naked to the waist, wielding a large hammer over a pile of rocks, a stone fence in the background, a satisfied look on his face. His hair was thick and curly, and his head was a little large for his body. A stern mustache canceled the comic effect of his large, jutting ears. There was none of the famous explosiveness, the fierce temper, or the family strain of melancholy. Anna, who stands behind him, wears a big sun hat and looks at him with pride.

"Why was he so mean?" Louise said.

It wasn't that he was mean, Tessie thought. It was that he was so afraid of getting slammed down that he couldn't let down his guard. Better assume everything is bad than get caught off guard.

"What was Anna like?"

"Oh, Mama, Anna, she was sweet, she went along with Simon on everything."

"Was she afraid of him?"

Yes. But she wouldn't have known what to do without him, how to live, anything. He gave her everything. And Simon, he could never have found another woman like Anna. She seemed to know exactly what he wanted before he asked for it. And it was there, ready for him. *Sha*, quiet, she would say to Tessie, even before he came through the front door, Papa's tired, Papa's had a hard day, *sha, sha*.

Tessie sighed. Without Simon's strength, Mama would have been in bed all the time.

"Was she sick?"

Oh, she was just . . . a worrier. She used to get blue. She got blue all the time. And when she got blue she had to lie down in bed.

"Then who took care of you?"

Tessie shook her head impatiently. That wasn't part of this story.

The only one who could make Anna happy was Simon.

"From the sound of it, maybe he was the one who was making her blue," Louise said, when she was thirteen. Maybe you aren't ready to appreciate this story, Tessie said.

Everything Simon wanted to do, the family did. And if Simon wanted it, Anna did, too. One day, in 1913, they went to visit Anna's brother at the beach, and from then on they never summered in the country again. Simon loved the beach. He loved the toughness of the waves. There was something strong, he said, and nature was never on show at the beach, it just did what it had to do. (To this day Tessie loves the beach.)

At first Anna did not like the sand, and was constantly afraid of drownings. Simon bought her a pair of binoculars, and she sat on the porch from early morning to late at night whenever Tessie or any of the cousins went to the beach. Once she got a sunburn everywhere but around her eyes, and she looked like a raccoon.

Tessie doesn't remember how the business of the lucky stone started. Sometimes she thinks Simon instigated it. She does remember that one summer Anna stopped watching through the binoculars, and started believing that a wish made on the right beach stone would save everyone from drowning.

"What made it the right beach stone?"

Oh, it had to be smooth, perfectly round or

oval, and either completely white or a nice combination of colors, black, gray and white, veined in purple or marrow red. At the beginning of every summer she would choose just one, testing it for size and quality in the palm of her hand, and then when she was satisfied she had the right one, closing it in her fist and never mentioning it again. She moved it from the pocket of her apron to her change purse to the corner of her night table. And if it ever got misplaced, well, the whole house was in a tizzy, and no one was allowed to go swimming until it was found.

"Did you believe in it, too?" Louise asked.

Tessie shook her head impatiently. That wasn't part of this story.

When Tessie married Barney, Simon and Anna moved from New Jersey into the little bungalow at the beach, all year round. By this time Anna said she liked the beach, too. Though, as Tessie thinks back now, she can't remember ever seeing Mama's feet touch the sand. After a while, when they got old, crippling arthritis forced Simon into a wheelchair permanently. Anna, weakened by multiple ailments, grew vaguer and vaguer.

"What happened to them? Who took care of them?"

Here was the good part. They took care of

each other. It was remarkable, inspiring. They were such a perfect couple. Of course, the family was very concerned as they got on, especially as their ailments got more severe. Cousin Dave, the doctor, tried for a time to talk to them about going into a home. They refused.

Anna was cute. Tessie would ask her something and she would stop her with her hands. *Sha, sha,* she would say, you need to be quiet when the bread is rising. (You see, she had gotten very vague.) Yet, when it came to Simon, if she had to remember what time he took a pill, she was sharp as a tack. And Simon, in such pain all the time he never wanted visitors, growled at everyone, always had a smile and a good word for his Anna.

Once, at this point in the story, when Louise was nineteen, she expressed skepticism, said it sounded too good to be true, and Tessie got so angry she pretended for a week she did not see Louise.

But finally, Anna's forgetfulness led to . . .

She left the front door wide open all night one night, and they almost froze to death, and Anna got a bad case of the flu. Or pneumonia; they never knew which.

By this time Simon, too, was becoming vague. Halfway through his cereal he would stop, milk brimming over his slack lower lip, while he thought about something, still as a beachbird, and then catch milk at his chin, take in his lower lip in little tucks, come back to the present. Sometimes he would break into an argument he had left off thirty years ago, with Ray Hanschal, who was dead.

Anna, on the other hand, seemed to Tessie more alert, though more restless.

One day, Tessie brought her soup, and found her crying.

"No," she said, when Tessie tried to comfort her. Only Simon.

"I'm afraid," she had told him. "I woke up and didn't know where I was."

"Ahh," he said. "Pish tosh."

She told him not to smooth it over this time. "I'm afraid."

He asked of what.

Of death, she said.

He snapped his fingers. Easy, he said. Living was hard.

She said she didn't want to go to the hospital.

I won't let them take you, he said.

She said she kept thinking about the funeral parlor.

He told her to think of it as a beauty parlor, where they fix you up for the last time.

Weak as a kitten, she was, Tessie said, yet she

laughed. It sounded like meowing.

"I'll go with you," he promised.

She sent Tessie to the beach to get her a stone. Be careful, she called. At first Tessie didn't go, thinking Anna would forget about it, but in the morning she asked again, so Tessie walked down to the shore and gathered a handful of small beach stones.

Anna chose a flat, marbled oval.

As soon as she had it in her hand, Tessie told Louise, she seemed to sleep better, to be at peace.

Simon sat beside her during the day, reading the newspaper, or dozing. His gray sweater vest gave his thin body a bulky look, so when Tessie brought in a cut-up orange for him, for an instant he looked like papa of old, a much younger man. She bent to kiss his forehead (I had never done that before, she told Louise in a Twilight Zone voice that told Louise the story was reaching its climax) and felt it cold to her lips. Simon had died peacefully in his sleep. Anna slept on, and Tessie quickly called the doctor cousin to know what to do.

The cousin came, examined Simon, and confirmed his death, and then they whispered about how to remove his body to another room before Anna woke. She opened her eyes.

"Leave him there," she said clearly.

116

Tessie tried to intervene.

"No," Anna said. "Simon stays with me and we go to the beauty parlor together."

Tessie swears this is true.

The cousin said to leave him until Anna slept again, or until she would listen to reason. Instead, she died that night. And so Anna and Simon were buried the same day, in the adjoining plots they had purchased the first year of their long, very beautiful, very perfect marriage.

Isn't that a beautiful story, Tessie used to say to Louise.

Tessie had tried rubbing the stone, though she was the first one to say she does not believe in magic.

The night Barney died, when she was alone, she took the stone and placed it in her palm and arranged herself on the bed, and at first a color plate of Juliet from *The Picture Book of Shakespeare* flashed in her mind, and she tried to blank it out, or replace it with the mind-picture she had always thought she carried, of Anna on her deathbed. She just saw worms of light behind her lids, from squeezing her eyes shut so tightly. She uncrossed her arms, which had been laid across her chest, and placed them at her sides. *The human cannon,* she thought, from a sepia print on the cover of a book about carnival daredevils, in which the human in question stuck out of the mouth of the cannon like a wick, his arms pressed against his sides as hers were, his hands unseen. She flung her arms above her head, *I give up*, and whispered, "I don't want to live without you," but the tears that followed came because she suspected this was not true.

A terrible lethargy came over Tessie. Her eyes were always closing, but never closed. Russell said maybe it was viral, which proved that Russell sat on his brains. She knew better.

She felt all her life had taken place in one careless moment, when she wasn't looking, and the rest had only been waiting: for Barney to change, for her life to change, for Louise to grow up, for retirement; for wealth, for the snow to stop and spring to come; for Thanksgiving to be over so she could go on a diet, or Barney to get the hell out of the house so she could wax the floor without him underfoot. Now she only waited to go to sleep at night, and when she couldn't, for the night to go away.

She was stricken with an intermittent amnesia, which came in the middle of a memory and wiped it clean. She felt both unwritten and used up.

118

You know the story of the three old ladies in Miami Beach?

LADY ONE: I don't know what's happening to my memory. I got up this morning, got all dressed, put on my good hat, my coat, and when I got to the door, I forgot where I was going.

LADY TWO: Oy, me also. I got out of bed, went to the refrigerator, and stood there with the door open, wondering what I was there for.

LADY THREE: Not me. My mine is poifect. I remember everyting. Knock wood (*she knocks wood*) I . . . Who's there?

Victory did not get it, but she diagnosed it, anyway. You aren't sleeping good, she said. She left Tessie some Valium for her nerves, some Dalmane to sleep, and Fiorinal for her headaches. I don't have headaches, Tessie said. Never mind, Victory said, implying, *You will.*

Unable to sleep, yet asleep when she was awake, Tessie sensed that she could break bones, lose balance, or trip on the edge of the rug if she wasn't careful. So she moved with exceeding care, and one morning, shortly after she gave Louise the piano, she rolled the rug up and gave that away, too. She was careful where her mind stepped, as well, avoiding what she began to think of as potholes of thought, preventing her eyes from slipping back into some deep part of her mind by staring hard at something close by. Victory noticed this and told Louise, who told Russell.

"Now she's not only squinting, she's staring. She looks crazy."

She was crazy now, she felt, but that wasn't the worst. The worst was the boredom.

She refused to meet with Fishman to go over the books again.

She refused to talk to Louise and Russell about selling the store.

She refused to think any more about what Barney had done with the insurance money.

And finally, the effort of her refusals, and the boredom at having nothing she was willing to think about, exhausted her and she fell asleep.

When she woke it was Thursday.

"I'm as likely to die in my sleep as any other way," she said to Barney, who, being a picture, continued to smile at this remark.

This is not a suicidal thought, she told him. She only admitted overnight, sudden death to her thoughts as a decoy, to deflect the boredom and inject some feeling of gladness into the occasion of getting up. But lately, she had become interested in endings.

Barney, hadn't he always read beginnings? Sometimes, hadn't it taken him days to check in a shipment of books, because he read the first paragraph of everything before he put it on the shelf?

Tessie liked stories with bullet endings, where you knew for sure something had happened. It didn't matter if they were happy or not, though she believed the miserable ones more easily. She wanted, most of all, a satisfying finality and something that throbbed. Her favorites included Graham Greene ("Poor Crabbin . . . Poor all of us when you come to think of it."); old Charlotte Brontë ("Madame Beck prospered all the days of her life. . . . Farewell."); and Gypsy's last words. " 'Hold onto your hats, boys, . . . here we go again.' "

She tried out her ending: One day the bookstore didn't open and everyone knew she was dead. She tried out two more: *The cancer went quickly. She did not last a year, but did not suffer one bit*; and, *The Florida sun dried her to dust and one day a mild breeze blew her in the direction of the Fountainebleau, saving her daughter the cost of a funeral.*

The phone rang.

"Tessie? Are you there? Are you all right?"

She held the receiver away from her. Annoyance roused her now. "Of course I'm all right, Victory. I was sleeping."

"It's after ten o'clock."

Tessie looked at the clock. "I know," she said.

"I'm opening late today."

"Oh?" Victory was suspicious. "Is everything all right?"

"I've got a checkup with Goffstein."

"Oh. But it's your regular checkup, right? You're feeling fine?"

Am I? Tessie thought, suddenly nervous.

"Leave it to Victory," she said to Barney, after she had hung up.

He smiled tolerantly. His smile had gained variety since his death. In fact, Barney had changed. For one thing, he was shorter. The top of his head came to Tessie's chin these days, and the clasped hands hiding his belt — which was as far as the picture went — were level with the small night table. Tessie had done this one morning, leaving the slightest scar of spackle on the wall, like a dot of styptic, four inches above. Now she was taller than he.

She put the coffee on and while it brewed, she sipped hot water to get her plumbing started. She took a container of cottage cheese out of the refrigerator, and spooned some on a leftover quarter of a bagel, tapping her finger on the table as she chewed, impatient for her teeth to finish the job. When she was done she nodded in approval and swept the crumbs off the table with the side of her hand, onto the floor. She reached for the broom and duster, and got ready to tidy the apartment. She wondered what Victory would think if she knew her best friend dusted every morning without any clothes on. Tessie had always liked feeling her breasts flop and her behind quiver and the dust cloth brush her skin. Now, even that pleasure was gone. Victory wore her underwear uplifted beyond comfort, permanent notches in the cushions of her shoulders and striations from an undersized panty-girdle ringing her waist.

"Don't ask, I just know," Tessie said.

She waved the dust cloth in Barney's face.

"What am I going to do, Barney? Whether I blame you or not doesn't matter, just what am I going to do? It's dangerous out there. The baby-faced boy is everywhere, I feel him; and now I'm afraid to stay in. Where am I going to go? How is it going to end?"

Dead silence was not different from Barney's previous kind. Tessie nodded and assumed his taciturn reply.

On the way to Goffstein's, she stopped at the drugstore to check her blood pressure, but the blood pressure machine was badly mangled. It had been vandalized, along with the bridge chair, which was smashed into a legless mass of metal, and the phone booth, its phone dial strangled with its own eviscerated cord. Had some old person done this, with her last strength, sick of warnings, Salutensin, banana a day for potassium? Did the empty chair finally get to be too much, snidely inviting a weak, high-blood-pressured oldster to collapse after reading the bobbing needle? Did the phone booth go too far, smugly waiting to be used for the emergency medical call?

She took her pulse: nice and regular. She guessed at her blood pressure: 140 over 90 sounded good, but not good enough to make Goffstein frown and check again to be sure.

The doctor's waiting room was crowded. Opposite Tessie sat a couple, the man with one leg straight out. He seemed to be in pain, and his wife got up frequently to question the nurse. Tessie thought she was trying to get her husband in before his turn, but the nurse sent her back (don't think pain gives you privileges in *this* office).

A woman knitted, and the room was filled with clicking, from the knitting needles and the woman's dentures, which she dislodged every other stitch. She was a customer of Tessie's. She nodded.

"And how are you?" Tessie said.

The woman nodded again, encouraging herself, and said, "So far." Went back to her knitting.

"I'm just here for a checkup myself," Tessie

said. And thought of books in which this dialogue was a setup, heavy foreshadowing. Heroine has endings on her mind but never suspects; the routine visit takes place, the doctor makes the professionally reassuring disclosure of disquieting content: the smallest tumor to be sure ... but it took care of plot and ending.

She picked up *The New Yorker. So, I'll die.* The cartoons looked familiar. *So who doesn't?* The prints on the wall, rabbis on roofs with fiddles in their hands, looked familiar. *So what else do I have to do?* The man with the stiff leg looked familiar. He looked familiar. Tessie got up and walked around to stop herself from looking at him. He was wearing a brown shirt. The thick lenses of his eyeglasses blurred his eyes, was he winking at her? Who did he remind her of? She went to the bathroom, and when she came back he had gone into the examining room. With him gone, she could look at him more clearly. Had he been the mysterious M. H. Ross who wanted to buy the store?

"Well, Tessie," Goffstein said heartily, and patted her arm. She came back to him because he was Russell's friend, which was also why she disliked him. Whenever her son-in-law asked her how she was, she had the feeling he already knew, and whenever Goffstein asked, she had the feeling *he* already knew. She didn't like being called by her first name, her children's friends should always call her Mrs. Goodman; she evened the score by calling him Goffstein instead of Harold.

His hands were cold as he examined her, yet she didn't mind. It was a relief to be touched, and to feel it.

"You're looking better," he said, enthusiastically. "Great, great," he beamed.

And although she was relieved that she was not going to die, and *that* was settled, she was annoyed that he should be the one to give her the good news. So she said testily, "Don't take any credit, Goffstein. You're just watching."

He looked puzzled, and his smile strained. As he stood there, facing her, his hand on the examining-room doorknob, as she sat on the edge of the paper-lined table, hands on hips, the motes of time stopped drifting. They began to collect, to draw into a scene, and the scene was there, in the present.

Tessie dressed slowly, thinking, and knowing why she was thinking of the end of *Roses Tell No Tales*: "Rose watched as the door closed behind Franklin." Or something like that. "Silence replaced the silence"—no, that was "music" – "of his voice, and emptiness filled the room. She called to him but he did not return." Come back, appear. "She would have to go on without him."

The bus was empty; Tessie could choose any seat she wanted. She skipped the first few, leaving them for the elderly and infirm, neither of which, she noted with satisfaction, she was.

When the bus stopped at the next corner, there was a burst of noise at the rear door, like someone had hit it, or was trying to open it; then there was laughing, and three boys clambered aboard the front of the bus. One of them threw money into the box, but the other two didn't. The bus driver glanced back, but didn't say anything. The three took seats behind Tessie. Tessie automatically avoided looking at them, and kept her eyes on the advertisement for a business school, reading the word *Institute* so many times that it didn't look like itself anymore; it had crumbled into meaningless letters. She knew she could not look at those boys; yet she could hardly stop herself from just stealing a glance, just to see if any one of them was the one she was sure had it in for her, the one who had stolen her garbage. She lowered her eyes carefully, leaving her chin pointed up at the ad. Oh, oh, god, it was him. She was sure of it. She looked away quickly. But then, she couldn't help it, she had to look again, and this time she was not sure. The third time she looked, he nailed her, held her eyes hard with a mean stare.

"Whatsa matter, Sadie?" he said.

She wasn't sure it was the one. She didn't think he knew her. She wasn't going to wait around to find out. This is not for me, she said to herself. Her face was numb, her legs weak when she stood up, and heavy when she tried to walk.

"Getting off," she called to the driver.

"Getting off," they mimicked her. They got up and stood in the aisle behind her.

She faltered as the bus hit a bump, and she caught the metal pole. Then the driver stopped short, and she was thrown back against the boy, and he said, "Whoa!" and gave her a rough push into his friend, who pushed her back, and they volleyed her back and forth between them, firm-footed and not even holding on, while she flailed for balance and tried to ward off their blows. She covered her face. They seemed careless of where they pushed her, or even whether they were hurting her or not, as if she really were just a toy to them. She went blind for a moment, realization of her helplessness (or the bulk of their bodies) blotting out all the light in the bus. She took a deep breath and pulled as hard as she could, and made a grab for the pole. She pulled herself out of their grasp so forcefully that she was jerked forward, and felt the quick, cold bump of metal as her cheek made contact with it. She caught sight of an old woman in the metal reflector, fattened and flattened by the distortion of the mirrored surface. Before she looked away, she saw behind her the reflection of the three boys, having a conference about what to do to her next.

Not me, she thought. She went to the front door; they went to the rear. She tried pretending to step off the bus; they only pretended to step off, too. Then she did get off, and after a moment's hesitation, so did they, jumping down almost on top of one another, in high spirits. Tessie quickly got back on the bus.

"Hurry up, close the door," she said to the driver, and he did, and took off. They chased for a while, she guessed, from the sound of it; one might even have hitched on to the back fender for a block, but at last, they were gone. Tessie sank down on the seat. She was shaking, her whole body was shaking so hard she felt all the loose parts, and she was as tired as if she had run up a hill, or vacuumed a ten-room house; the little nerve in her eyelid had begun to twitch. She wanted to say something to the driver: "You see?" although she didn't know whether she meant, "You see how dangerous it is around here?" or "You see how I can take care of myself?"

"You gonna report this?" the bus driver wanted to know.

Am *I* going to report it? Sure as hell *you* aren't, sitting there shaking in your boots while you let an old lady save your life, she thought. "What for?" she said.

At first she thought she wanted to report it to someone, tell someone what she had done, how she had outsmarted them. Yet, later on, when Louise called, she found she could hardly speak, and when Victory called, she knew immediately she would miss the point, which was, the more Tessie thought about it, similar to the Grimms' fairy tale about the little tailor and his "seven at one blow," only this was three. Victory would only want Tessie to count her bruises. She went through the adjoining basement door into Hum's Chinese, intending to say to Joe, "You want to hear what three little sons of bitches tried to do to me on the bus but I fixed them?" but ordering a pint of chow mein instead. "Go ahead, Spanish it up," she told him. She felt like something spicy.

By dying intestate, Barney had provided an

ironbound link between Tessie and her daughter, Louise, since without a will everything was divided equally between mother and daughter. Which meant that Louise was half owner of the store, which meant she had every right in the world to nag Tessie about making the decision to sell, which made Tessie want to think about it just a little bit more.

"If you really want to sell the store . . . ," Russell said.

"What do you mean, 'really,'" she said, indignantly.

There were things to be done, he said. Inventories to take. A fair price to establish. An ad to write up, and so forth. To place in the *Times*. *The Bookseller. Publishers Monthly.*

"*Weekly,*" Tessie said. Weakly, because she had no strength for this.

"We aren't going to get rid of it by magic," he said.

Tessie walked to the window and opened it so she could breathe. I wish I could rid of you by magic, she thought.

"Mother, it's cold in here," Louise said. "The baby." And closed the window.

The baby was still in his snowsuit, a lump of blue. They were all in their jackets, to prove, Tessie assumed, that the visit would be short. The baby hadn't made a peep since they had walked in the door. "Is he all right?" Tessie asked.

"He doesn't like it here," Sebby said.

Louise stepped over to Sebby and shook her shoulder, and said, "Now, Seb."

It was ten-thirty on Saturday morning; they had arrived at ten, with a bagful of bagels, lox, and cream cheese.

"Surprise," Russell had said.

It's a raid, Tessie thought.

Louise had said nothing at first, but her eyes cased the joint. Then she said, "Where's the rug?"

"I gave it away," Tessie said.

"Gave it away?"

"To Gonzalez."

"To the super? Gonzalez?"

"Louise, are you having trouble hearing?" Tessie said. "To Gonzalez."

Russell and Louise traded one of their she's-crazy looks.

"Mother," Louise said, patiently, "that was not just carpeting, that was Karastan."

"And who are you, Einstein and Moomjy? I know what it was. I didn't want it. Did you want it?"

"No, I didn't want it, that isn't the point," Louise said.

Russell was looking in the refrigerator.

"Are you eating, Tessie?" he said.

"No, Russell, I'm standing here being interrogated by your wife about my pedigree rug. Are you eating?"

Sebby giggled.

"Are you eating, Sebbeleh?" Tessie said.

"No, Gram, I'm sitting on a chair," she said.

"Smart girl," Tessie said. "See how she catches on?"

"And Pookie is sleeping in his car seat."

"Pookie? You call that baby Pookie? Oh my God," Tessie said, and slumped into a kitchen chair. "Spread me a bagel, I think I am going to faint."

Sebby laughed some more, her pale, serious face for once bright.

"Come to Grandma," Tessie said. The little girl put herself in the circle of Tessie's arms, and Tessie hugged her hard.

"Sebby, you're hurting Gram," Russell said.

"You'll get overheated," Louise said.

"So the baby doesn't like it here. You like it here, Sebbeleh?" Tessie said. "You want to stay here with Grandma?"

"*No,*" Louise and Russell said at the same time.

"You'll come with Grandma to Poppy's store, and help me fix up the books and we'll order in Chinese. . . ."

"She doesn't eat Chinese," Louise said.

"Can I get free books, Gram?"

"Sure, sweetheart, I'll give you all the books you want. You like books? What kind of books do you like?"

"I don't know," Sebby said, serious once again.

"Maybe some other time," Louise said.

"We have history books and picture books and story books, pop-ups, you want to give a pop-up to the baby? A nice name like Peter, you call him Pookie. You want to give a pop-up to Pookie?" She exaggerated the *p*'s to make Sebby smile again. "How about magic books, we have a book that shows how to do magic tricks." Because she still had magic on her mind. "You believe in magic?"

"No," Louise and Russell said at the same time.

"I don't know," Sebby said.

"Bring me my pocketbook," Tessie said, pointing to the old black bag hanging on the doorknob of the hall closet.

"Don't run," Louise said.

Tessie shook her head.

"You ought to keep your bag closed," Louise said. "You shouldn't leave it hanging open in plain sight. You should put it away."

It was too full to close. She carried every-

134

thing in it: pins she found on the floor while she was cleaning, all her cash, a rain bonnet, her good earrings, pictures she had cut out of magazines of hairdos she was going to try, expired twenty-five-cent coupons for coffee, toilet paper; Barney's obituary notice from *The New York Times*, the letter from M. H. Ross, offering to buy the store. Her wallet fell out.

"Where did you get all this cash?" Louise said. "You shouldn't walk around with all this cash."

"Here," Tessie said to Sebby, rummaging in her change purse. "You know what this is?"

Sebby didn't.

"It's a lucky stone," Tessie said. "It belonged to your great-grandma, and I'm giving it to you."

"I wouldn't encourage this," Russell said.

"Three hundred dollars," Louise said. "Why are you walking around with three hundred dollars?"

"What does it do?" Sebby asked.

"You make a wish and rub it hard," Tessie said.

"And your wish comes true?"

"No," Russell said.

"Maybe," Tessie said.

"Tessie, you don't really believe that," Russell said.

"I do." She didn't. Not in lucky stones. The stone was a harmless toy, to let the child dream. But wasn't it magic how time went by, how you lose a husband in the blink of an eye, how one minute you are young and the next you are someone's grandmother?

The Spanish, they believed in magic. They had spirits. They played the numbers like it was magic, and when they lost it was magic, and when they won. Your bird dies, you count the feathers and play that number, you win, the spirit of your dead bird gave you the money.

"Where did you get this money?" Louise demanded.

"From Gonzalez," Tessie said.

"From Gonzalez?"

He had come to the door last night and handed her three hundred dollars. Money. Like magic.

"What is this?" she had said.

"For you," he had said. "For your troubles."

She had started to shake, with rage, with shame. Is this what I have come to? she had thought.

"I don't want it," she had said, handing it back.

He had put his hands behind his back. He said he couldn't take it. He had played the number of Barney's date of death, and the number had won. The spirit of Barney was giving it to her. She had a suspicion. Had Barney lent Gonzalez money, by any chance?

Gonzalez looked at the floor. "When I had my troubles," he said. "When my little girl died."

"How much?" Tessie had said.

"Three hundred," Gonzalez had said.

"I'll take it," she had said.

"He paid me for the carpeting," she told Louise.

"He got a bargain," Louise said. "That was Karastan."

After Louise and Russell and the children had gone, she said to Barney again, as she had said last night, Why, why didn't you tell me? but of course she knew. She would have objected, given him a hard time about it, wouldn't she?

She went through every checkbook, bankbook, every scrap of paper she could find. She spread them on the kitchen table and tried to find correlations between withdrawals and little notes and reminders she found in the pockets of his pants. She found a note in the pocket of his pants that said, "committee meeting, 23rd" and she called the lawyer from the Local Action Committee, saying she believed her husband had made some sort of contribution? But the lawyer sounded so puzzled that Tessie knew he was telling the truth.

She followed Gonzalez as he mopped the hallways, asking again and again if he was sure all Barney had given him was three hundred, asking if he knew anyone else Barney had given money to. At first Gonzalez looked miserable, but then he got angry. When he got angry, she believed him and left him alone.

She had another idea. She went to Hum's Chinese, and ordered an expensive take-out, shrimp in lobster sauce, lobster in shrimp sauce, the works, and then casually asked Joe Fig if Barney had ever played the numbers. "Not that I would have minded," she lied. But Joe said that Barney never had. She threw the food away when she got home.

She no longer walked the streets looking down, but as if she were searching, which she was, and she gave passersby dirty looks, because you never knew which one of them Barney had given his money to.

And finally, she was left with two choices. Either the money was gone, or it was somewhere in the store. And because she did not want it to be gone, she decided it was somewhere in the store. She would not sell the store until she found it.

So one March morning, she locked her apartment, and with a small suitcase and her G.E. coffeepot, she moved into the store, into the room downstairs in the back, where the O'Neill sisters used to live.

She had often wondered how the two of them had managed back there. Now the cramped space felt just right, just the size for her, and her one thought. The little room had only one bed (what happened to . . . had there been another?) in it, and a small chest of drawers in a dark, chipped green enamel. She looked inside the chest and even read the newspapers lining the empty drawers before she threw them away. There were two pictures, a dark, brandy-colored portrait of a stone house with curtained windows etched in black, and a framed greeting card picturing Jesus, "For Your Ordination" lettered in strokes of gold which tapered daggerlike at the bottom of each letter (hadn't the nephew become a priest?). She looked behind the pictures for hidden safes, dollar bills stuffed behind the cardboard matting.

She still felt a presence in the store: a feeling someone had just been there or would come in a moment. She talked Joe into unsealing the basement door between them, and left it open during the day, which made her feel safer. Then she decided that the presence she felt was welcome: it was the buyer who would be there any day, to take this dump off her hands as soon as she found Barney's treasure; the letter or the person of M. H. Ross was waiting in the wings and she had to get ready for him. She listened for him, opened the store promptly for him, and the longer she waited, the more she felt he was the buyer waiting for her.

After two weeks, she decided he was on vacation, and would not be back from Boca before the following Sunday. That's okay, she said. I'm not ready. He was holding off until she had found what she was looking for. His lack of presence became stronger with each day. Sometimes she thought he would come through the basement door and surprise her. Sometimes, when Joe tapped on the adjoining door, she forgot about Joe and thought it was M. H. Ross. She tiptoed upstairs in the morning and looked in the display case and for an instant saw him there, laid out like Barney, in his blue suit, the keys to the store in his pocket.

She stopped seeing her friends. Discouraged Louise and Victory from coming by. But sometimes they did.

"What are you doing?" they asked her then.

"Keeping busy," was all she would say.

At night, downstairs, she removed every book from every shelf and made stacks on the floor that no one could understand and she would not explain, but no one was allowed to disturb. With her own hands she dismantled the enormous, toppled metal bookshelves, and put the bones in a carton across which she scrawled in red Magic Marker TO GO. Her appearance was altered. She had lost weight, she wore blue jeans and Barney's old shirts, bright scarves about her hair, which was half dyed blond and half gray, and had grown long enough for her to toss out of her eyes with a girlish motion of her head. She had always been small; now, as if she were afraid she were shrinking, she augmented her height with high wooden clogs without backs, on which she seemed to rock all the time. "She looks European," Victory told the others, wrinkling her nose.

She looked as if she had been digging in the ground. Her fingernails were chipped and unpolished, and her hands covered with scrapes. The knees of her pants were soiled. She wore a turkey fork around her neck on a string, like a lavaliere. The sharp ends were wrapped with adhesive tape, like practice fencing foils. ("Thank God," Louise said. "It's a sign she isn't self-destructive, at least.")

Starting with the basement walls, she worked her way down to the floor, clearing everything out of her way. She tore old posters from the walls, reading each one carefully before she discarded it; old calendars came down, obsolete price-change notices. She spent one whole evening prying tacks and nails off the wall with a dime. Getting ready for M. H. Ross, she told herself.

She tackled Barney's desk, which was covered with catalogs, letters, small wire book racks, and cardboard sleeve boxes for books; paper clips and dried-out Bic Clics filled the tray in the top drawer so the drawer didn't close. She discarded everything but the letters. She read them all. Every Tuesday and Thursday morning, the back of the store was lined with cartons of trash for the sanitation pickup. One morning early a woman came in, holding a wire rack which Tessie had thrown away.

"Por favor?" the woman said, and through her overwhelming desire to say "No, you may not," Tessie learned of her feelings that things were going to the place they belonged. This rack must not be separated from its garbage mates. This interested her so much that she began to subdivide the trash according to its materials, wire to wire, cardboard to cardboard, dust to dust.

Often during the day she read, picking up books, opening them anywhere, feeling interchangeable with their characters. Sometimes she even felt she could slip into the body of an object or be a process. From "How Iron Is Produced from Iron Ore": "The limestone flux floats on top of the molten iron, where its lightness draws the impurities to the surface. . . ." She could be the flux.

As easily as she slipped in and out of books, one of her customers sometimes emerged from a book she had in her hand; out of a gothic fog, investigating some crime. Sometimes, when she was not feeling well, this customer also seemed a manifestation of the high blood pressure she suspected was making her head spin. Sometimes she thought of him as Barney's ghost. He came almost every day, spent a long time looking, and always bought something. She waited for him to speak, as everyone else was waiting for her to speak. In this she felt he was her mate. He was tall, like Barney, with soft gray hair. He was tanned, and she imagined he sat in the park in good weather playing championship chess. Or had just come back from a Florida vacation. He was a widower, she felt, and an only daughter lived far away, in Los Angeles or Santa Fe. He was grandfather to little girls, as well. The older girl, the one he bought *The Little Princess* for last week, received it on Friday, when she came home from school, with an indulgent groan, "Oh,

Grandpa" at his having selected such an old-fashioned book. Her mother had made her sit down at once and write a thank-you note to him, and accompanied it with her own long, newsy letter—"Father dear, are you taking care of yourself?" and "Have you met any nice people in your new apartment house?"—and so on. He wrote back, saying he was healthy as could be and that as far as meeting people, he was quite content with his own company, his books, and his memories. He had found a delightful bookshop not far from where he lived and a sensitive and quite beautiful proprietor who made him feel welcome. With the letter he sent *Brian Wildsmith's ABC* for the younger granddaughter, its clear and rich illustrations striking just the right note for her. Tessie had made the recommendation.

An aroma came from him and seemed to linger for hours after he was gone. Tessie went into the drugstore across the street and sniffed men's lotions but she couldn't find the right one. Once, in the morning, before she opened the store, she thought she smelled it near the front window. Louise was there.

"Come here. What do you smell?" Tessie had said.

"Nothing," Louise said.

"Your nose is blind," Tessie said in disgust.

"Don't you smell it?" Which caused Louise concern, since she had read somewhere that hallucinating smells is a sign of insanity.

The next time she came she gave Tessie a little test, but Tessie was ready.

"What smells in here?" Louise said, as she walked in.

"Lysol," Tessie said. "I cleaned the toilet."

The browser's head floated toward them over the top of the shelves.

"Oh," Louise said, when she saw him. "May I help you?" She gave Tessie a look as if to say, See, this is the way to be gracious.

Don't answer, Tessie thought.

The browser shook his head and drifted away.

One day he tripped over a box of books lying in the aisle. If he had fallen she would have caught him, cradled his head in her lap, lifted the books from his fallen body. He was dying of something slow and irrevocable having to do with loss of muscle tone. She looked it up in *Webster's Medical Dictionary:* Amand Duchenne muscular dystrophy. She could not cure him, but she devised a series of exercises which seemed to slow down the process. She did them every morning.

With the heightened vigor the exercises seemed to produce, she got ideas in the evening. She went through Barney's letters again, listing in a small notebook names and addresses of his correspondents, putting a small pencil mark next to the name each time it was repeated. There were carbons of letters to the billing departments of publishing companies, concerning invoices or delayed payments. There were two letters from Barney's brother, referring to a loan Tessie didn't know Barney had made: one thanking Barney, the other, dated a year later, thanking him again and indicating repayment. Ha, she thought. Philanthropist. I got you now. She wrote her brother-in-law, asking him if Barney had by any chance lent him $20,000 recently. He wrote back, saying no, adding "nor any part thereof." She was looking for a letter to Fishman, unmailed perhaps, attached to stocks or bonds, or a bank check or the deed to a house, saying, I want to arrange my affairs so Tessie benefits in case of my sudden death.

There was a letter from Bookfind at a post office box in La Jolla, California, saying they were unable to locate a copy of e. e. cummings's *Santa Claus*. There was a letter from a man offering to sell his library to Barney. She wrote him and got a courteous reply, saying he was sorry to hear of Barney's death, their negotiations had gone no further than the one letter, in answer to the man's original ad in the

Bookseller, and would she care to consider his offer?

There was nothing to Fishman, no stocks, no bonds, no deeds, no letter from M. H. Ross, nothing about G.d.B. Nothing.

She thought of saying to the browser one day, when she saw him smiling below the eyes like Barney at some book in his hand, "Give me a hint," or "Why did you do this to me?"

Barney would keep the smile, though his eyes would change. He would put the book down. Maybe rub his eyes like that.

"You couldn't have jumped out of the way when the books began to fall? You couldn't have stopped what you were doing just a second sooner and jumped out of the way? Ah, Barney, what was so important?"

"I was looking for a book, a copy of . . ."

Tessie shook her head. She knew. What else? "Did you at least think of me?"

"Think of you? My last words were Tessie, Tessie, Tesseeee. Right before I breathed my last. I was only sixty-four."

She thought of Mr. Hirsch, of old men with poor memories, trying to remember to do widower's tasks, standing in the supermarket trying to decide between Fig Newtons and Lorna Doones. Pitiful. "Maybe it was best you went first," she said.

But then the browser's stiff-backed resolute way of walking, turning to look for something, absorbed, unmindful of her, as if she didn't exist . . .

"And what about me?" she demanded.

The browser turned, startled. She waved her hand at him, never mind.

"And what about me, Barney? Look what you left me with."

Something of value, was what he had said.

The browser's eyes were brown, direct. Not a liar's eyes, maybe.

"You really believed that?" Tessie said.

And then he let her have it. "All these years you had the inside line on what was going on in my head. You never let me answer a question with a plain yes or no. It had to be more. It had to be dramatic. It had to be your way. I meant this or I meant that, as if I were a blue jar of beans and you were going to estimate my number the hardest way. What if I meant only what I meant? What if I never meant anything at all?"

"Is that it, then, you son of a bitch? Did I make you up right from the beginning? Did you trick me? Did I trick me?"

"You tell me," he said. "You know it all."

As if closing a book, she brought herself back to the present, blinking, rubbing her eyes.

Weather resumed, a light, melting sleet with bits of ice now and then tapping the window. The browser returned, a reflection.

Tessie turned back to the counter. He nodded and slid a book across to her. His fingers nearly touched hers. The faded, gummed label in the corner of the book said "$1.25." He dug in his pocket and took out one of those small leather pouches that open on springs.

He has an accent, she thought, and waited for him to speak. He only smiled, confirming the silence that had been between them for weeks. Now it no longer seemed natural to her. She clearly felt the space for speech and saw it, an erasure in the middle of a page.

I will, she thought, but she didn't. Resisting, she felt as though she were yielding.

In unmistakable pantomime now, he turned the edges of his smile down and raised his brow, as if to express the words *When? Will you?* and she pushed price, tax on the register keys. As she was ringing up the purchase, bagging it, tearing off the receipt, she was planning to speak: do you live nearby, nasty afternoon, have a pleasant day, come again soon. Because the intimacy had gone much too far, the silence had gotten into her legs and even between. When he put the money in her open palm, the slight pressure made her flush.

He held up the book in a salute. Tessie nodded, the doorbell jangled. Gone.

She sighed and sat down on the stool behind the counter. It had been a slow day, only six customers (not counting the two who had stopped in to shoplift). Now, though it was only five o'clock, she was tired, she had had enough; it was time to close.

She was standing near the door with the awning rod in her hands (a shepherdess?), trying to decide whether to roll up the awning or risk letting it flap all night in the windy weather, when the browser came out of Hum's, a brown bag in his hand. He waved, and she raised her hand to wave to him, but then turned her back, went in quickly, locked up.

She couldn't move, yet she couldn't settle down. Her heart was shivering, like a cat coming out of the rain, and her mind fluttered from thought to thought, like thoughts were hot pot handles. She told herself to go downstairs, heat up a little of the stew Louise had brought her (with the gratified, worried look of a daughter in ascendance: "Something hot, mama"—and Tessie thinking, Not something, some*one*, maybe me because hotness was in her mind, something about it was in her mind), but she just couldn't budge. The more she kept her lip buttoned, the more this something expanded inside her. A new thought. As if all those years of wagging her tongue had been giving it away. Was this what Barney had been up to? And how strange, after years of complaining about his silence, here she was, wanting it for herself. Liking it. Relishing it. Hungry for it.

Oy, Tessie, she thought. Now you're getting hot for an old stranger? Because he doesn't open his mouth, like you-know-who? Is this a reason? She tried to walk it off, squaring corners of book stacks, pulling half-curled tabs of Scotch tape off corners of old posters, but finally, she went back and sat down on the stool behind the counter again. Somewhere outside, someone passed, and a shadow crossed the counter.

What do you want? she silently asked the browser.

The interrogatory shadow faced her across the counter, and in his firm, demanding silence, said, What do *you* want?

The friction of bodies saved lives of Nazi war victims freezing in the snow during World War II, this was a scientifically proven fact, she said.

You, what do *you* want?

She sighed. Kisses, not too prolonged, because of your deviated septum; during the long ones you can take quick breaths out of the side of your mouth, as if you were playing on the clarinet. Your wide, soft belly that I teased you about, and folded over with my hands; the dimple-scar left over from your surgery; your breasts, as you have gotten older, which made me look away from you on the beach, but are so soft to the touch; the small of your back.

And?

Head-to-toe contact, like six months ago, when we turned in the narrow aisle, surprised, like strangers. Your hands in my hair. Your tongue. Over here. Over here.

More?

No, not really, It was never such a big deal.

Uncompromising silence.

I could never tell you. You referred to it as "doing something." You said, "Do something for me." Then I took you in my mouth. You were so grateful. I couldn't tell you. I always wanted you to . . . let it go, on my body, so I could rub you into my skin like lotion, but I could never think of a way to say it, and you . . . let it go in a tissue, your chin crumpled up in shame.

She stood for minutes, one hand rubbing the smooth lip of the counter, one hand touching her own lips. She lifted her blouse and rubbed the roundness of her stomach. Here. Over here.

What's gotten into you? she said to herself,

trying to shake it off by going away from the counter again. But then, whatever it was stayed, and she put her arms around the cool, damp wood of the bookcase and laid her cheek against the books, wanting suddenly to cry, in a confusion, thinking the release would be, after all, tears, and pressing her lips to the spine of a book, she came.

The little room she slept in was in the corner of the basement, near the bathroom. It had no door. From the bed, all she could see were books, boxes and boxes of them. In maybe one-third of them, maybe one-fourth, someone said to someone "I want," or "I want it," or "I want you." Maybe half. I want.

The importunate shadow—ghost, regret, or her own desire—settled itself on her like a warm body. She closed her eyes. Not bad, she thought, plumping her sagging breasts into a nice cleavage and slipping her finger into it. Not bad at all, and then she fell asleep.

Dear Mrs. Goodman:

Please forgive my long silence. I have been concerned about some things concerning the purchase of your store. These need not concern you. I see that you are making some changes in the store, so far all to the good. But I would not want to go too

153

far, or discard too many things, because many things of great age can also be of value (you included, my dear lady).

M. H. Ross

"Don't throw anything else away," Louise said.

"I wonder what he looks like," Victory said.

Spring comes to the Wilds through cracks in the sidewalk, untidy stubbles of grass which persist until they lift corners of the old pavement for people to trip on. People stumble through the street, sleepy with the mild weather and a focusless hope.

The hope is brought on by an illusion of safe arrival into the season, and a smell made up of exhaust fumes of buses, camphor of spring coats, and the blossoms on a single tree. It makes people want to have new things. Shopkeepers prop open their doors with chairs, books, or blocks of wood. They will sell dust mops, potting soil, new buttons, furniture polish, picture frames, shoes, something to read while waiting in the doctor's office for the checkup no longer postponed because of bad weather.

A window washer made his way up one side of the street and down the other, and when he was finished, the still-cold sun flashed off the clean windows and a river of soapy water he had emptied into the gutter ran down Burnside Avenue and pooled at the bottom. For once, it was not stopped by a body, derelict or dead, and the hope surged.

The borough president was on a walking tour of the area with some media people, and the representatives of the Puerto Rican Acción Locale were showing him the sights. Torn between pride and need, they didn't know whether to show him how the residents of 263 had overhauled their own building, or whether to hide it for fear it would make him withhold city funds if he thought they were doing so well on their own.

A car turned onto Burnside, splashing the sidewalk as it went through the water. The driver parked, stopped off at the McDonald's, and then stood in the recessed doorway of the bookstore, sipping from his container of coffee from a slot he had torn in the plastic lid. He was waiting for the store to open. The sign said "Closed. Will Reopen at 10:00, Wednesday." but it was 10:30 and there was no sign of life.

Inside, Tessie Goodman watched.

If she let him in:

"Mrs. Goodman? Marty Ross," and his hand

shoots out from behind his back to shake hers. She begins to tremble, because this, finally, is M. H. Ross. He asks her to please forgive him for the long delay in getting to meet her. He hopes she is well, he hopes she has considered his offer.

She, thinking it would be a good idea not to show how eager she is, how much she wants to cry, "Where have you been, take it, it's yours," pretends that for a moment she has forgotten what offer he is referring to. He smiles at this ploy.

Oh, she can't believe this M. H. Ross. This is not the right M. H. Ross. This one is too young; M. H. Ross is old. This one looks slick, like a book salesman; M. H. is more, uh, kindly. This one is too smart; her M. H. Ross is a bit of a fool.

But she goes on. He explains to her that he has been in the book business for ten years now ("Getting to be an old man," he says, and smooths his hair back) and of all the accounts he has had, it is hers that has touched his imagination (he says that: "touched my imagination") and when he began to consider settling down and buying a store of his own, it was hers he thought of. And then, when he heard about Barney's untimely accident (here he falters, to show he is troubled at this connection between the rise of his hopes and Barney's death), he thought Tessie might be wanting to sell. Bad memories and so forth.

She doesn't believe a word of it.

"What are you up to, Ross?" she says. "Why did you write me those crazy letters? Why didn't you just knock on my door like you did just now?"

He smiles, squeezing his eyes shut at her, a double-wink. "Sales technique. I wanted to get you curious," he says, thinking frankness will fool her.

She plays it cool. "So, maybe you did and maybe you didn't," she says.

". . . and interested. I hope you are interested," he says, with sudden concern.

"I don't know about that," she says. "Tell me first, did you know Barney? Did you ever approach him about selling out?"

Marty looks at her with a good imitation of honesty in his eyes. "No, no, no, not at all," he says.

"You did, didn't you," Tessie says. "And he turned you down flat."

"Not flat," Marty says. "He said he would think it over."

"Liar," she says. "Barney would never have let the place go. There is something of value here."

"Here?" Marty forces a laugh. "Are you kidding?"

"Yeah. No." She finds herself talking like him. "Yes, there is." She wants to grab him by the collar, shake him, rough him up. "Don't you laugh. There is something here, and you know it. Why don't I know? Tell me."

"I'll tell if you sell," he says.

"Oh, no, you little bastard. Tell me first."

He shakes his head no. "What's your price?" he says.

"Why, you bully," she says, taking him by the collar, shaking him. "You can't push me around. I said I won't sell. Not until I know. And if I never know, I'll never sell. Now get out."

And she picks him up by the shoulder pads of his blue suit and tosses him out the door.

The young salesman was getting impatient. His coffee was cold, soaking right through the container. He saw, coming out of the McDonald's, a trio of young toughs and he wondered if they were looking for trouble, if they were going to come over to him. He felt too well dressed. He wished the old lady would open the damn door so he wouldn't have to face them. He was just deciding to run back to his car when the door opened. He smoothed his hair back and straightened his collar and tie.

"Who?" she said through a crack in the door.

"New American Library," he said, feeling like he was giving a password.

"Go away," she said. "I'll reorder by phone."

He was about to say, "Just let me in for a minute," but he saw the danger had crossed to the other side of the street. And a good thing too, because the old lady had already closed and locked the door.

Barney's Message from Beyond: If you look hard enough (and listen) the store will speak to you.

"Oh God," Louise said. "Now I'm worried."

Well, she had tried everything else. She had Barney's book box, the so-called treasures, appraised. Nine hundred, give or take fifty, the experts said. And that included Gypsy Rose Lee. Hardly something of value.

She went over every bit of correspondence again and again. Russell and Louise (collectively—does that girl ever think for herself?) were still convinced that Barney had bought a money market, or a CD, or some kind of annuity, and the documents were simply lost. Misplaced. Tessie knew they were not convinced that she had searched thoroughly, and she suffered them to go through her apartment

159

again, to be sure. She, on the other hand, was more and more convinced that what she was looking for had something to do with the bookstore, though she couldn't think what it was.

"Let us help you look," Louise said.

"No," Tessie said. She wandered up one aisle, down another, staring at books as if with piercing glances she could discover something, get an idea. She became suspicious that every book might hold the secret somewhere between pages 101 and 102. Customers began to notice a reticence in her when it came to selling them something.

One day she found a two-shelf sentence made by juxtaposed book titles. It began, *Harry Truman Meet the Metric System,* and ended with the phrase *Second Thoughts of an Idle Fellow on the Edge of the Cliff,* and she decided that Barney had left a message for her by placing the books in such a way. She stood in front of the two-shelf sentence, which didn't make sense all the way through, for a good hour. Finally, though, she had to let it go. But she took a yellow pad and pencil the very next morning, and went looking for other sentences among the titles. After a while, she decided to disqualify certain things, like lists such as *Jumbles, Crosswords, Games for the Superintelligent,* and rosters of names, from Biography. And eventually she became bored by certain juxtaposed titles which gave stilted or stiff sentences, so for more grace or originality she skipped a book or two, especially if her eye caught an interesting phrase, such as *A Wild Patience Has Taken Me This Far/To the Lighthouse*. Phrases like those were, of course, not messages — of that she was sure — but they did have a nice ring to them. She began branching out, looking for Barney's message *and* phrases with nice rings.

After a while it seemed a good idea to rearrange the books to preserve the sentences and phrases she spotted, so they would be there permanently for her (or others who cared to notice) to think about. But by and by, despite her absorption in her work, she felt a disappointment at the literal nature of the arrangements, so she decided to adjust the books to conform to a greater logic. She put *Naked Lunch* in the cookbooks because it made her smile. She took General MacArthur out of his proper era and put him as far away from Truman as she could, in Baltic history, because that is what the man from Independence would have wanted. She toyed with other ideas: Titles with "in the," like *Joy in the Morning*, *Intruder . . . Dust*, *Wind . . . Willows*, *Catcher . . . Rye*, which provided a certain rhythm as you read across. Or pairs of things, giving a pleasing symmetry to the line, like *Pride and Prejudice, Crime and Punishment, War and Peace, Fathers and Sons.* Titles descriptive of materials occurred to her, like *Grass Harp, Glass Menagerie, Leatherstocking Tales,* and *Working with Wood,* or things to do with time and place, *English Hours, South Sea Tales, Pitcairn Island, Tropic of Capricorn. Tropic of Cancer* would probably go in Health.

One day she thought, I could arrange the books entirely differently, ignoring the titles altogether, because she was sick of titles by this time, anyway. She could do them according to size place, like grade-school children, if she wanted to, or according to jacket color, which would make a pretty store.

A bookstore itself can be read, she thought, and stopped her book arranging to make a sign to that effect, which she hung over the entrance, a couple of feet in front of the door, so it hit your eye even from the outside. Other signs followed, clear, hand-lettered signs that pointed out the different sections of the store, according to topic. Someday I will have to rearrange the books that way, she thought. But in the meantime at least, the signs would be there for a start.

She began to enjoy walking down the aisle and reading the signs, especially the ones Barney had never had, like Women's Studies, How-To (he had bunched them in Reference), and Sex (he hadn't even labeled it Pornography, treating it like the druggist treated Kotex: lowering the eyes, pointing discreetly). Not in Tessie's Place, she thought, and up went a temporary sign above the door: "Tessie's Place."

When the Random House salesman came, he said he couldn't put his finger on it, but the store had a new look.

"I like it," he said.

He hadn't been covering their account for several months, and Tessie asked him why. She knew it was because she didn't buy enough, but wanted to hear him wiggle out of it.

"You don't buy enough," he said.

"And *you* didn't make an appointment," she said. "You drop in like this on Barnes & Noble?"

He offered to leave but she liked him, told him to stay. He had trouble doing an inventory, because of Tessie's categories.

"I'm still fixing," she said. "I'm still in transition."

He removed books from the shelves as he went along.

"These can be returned, they're dead."

She looked at the pile. Barney had never returned books. The basement was filled with the ones she used to call turkeys and dogs and lemons, and here she was, she thought, doing the same damn thing, mistaking their familiarity for fame, saying to him, "Are you sure about this one?" protecting them like weak children from his inventorial assault.

"Just leave them for now," she said, patting a space near the counter. "Here. Put them here. Maybe later we'll make a bonfire."

The salesman opened his book. Tessie rubbed her hands together. "Let's go," she said. "Did you read this?" pointing to the first glossy page in his sales binder.

He flushed. "I didn't have the time."

"What is it, more flaming desire? You can't sell that stuff to me, sonny. Flaming desire in my crowd? Gives my customers a heart attack. Wait" — now she had done the joke — "put me down for six. Next."

He showed her a book on politics, by former senator Cox.

"That dog," she said. "Three."

There was a series of mysteries, a Swedish detective in four different adventures. She took five of each. She bought a little of everything, impatiently, greedily. The salesman got nervous. Small owners had been known to order heavy to show off, and then call the office and cancel.

"You're sure I'm not loading you up?" he said, but Tessie shook her head.

"I'll sell them," she said.

The browser came in. Tessie saw him. Today he seemed to be M. H. Ross. She was convinced today he was M. H. Ross. She poked the salesman, and spoke loudly, for the browser to hear: "We bought the store in 'forty-two, it was nothing. Nice, I mean, but really nothing. We built it up. Barney refinished those wooden shelves with his own hands, they're still good. And we have the finest stock in the Bronx. You should see my basement, god knows what valuable items I have. You think we do a slow business, because it looks empty all the time. You should only know what we do by mail."

The browser stirred. He was listening, she was sure.

"Old people like to read, what else do they have to do? That's why this location is perfect for a bookstore. More than perfect. You think I'm crazy? You think I should sell out and go to Florida? I'm telling you. This place has a future."

The salesman's coat was on. "You know, eventually all the buying is going to be over the phone," he said. "I'll miss my little stops." He put the order sheet before Tessie.

"All right, save the grease job," she said, but smiling, as she signed.

"Are you sure," he said nervously, "you need all those mysteries?"

"Nobody loads me up, sonny. You come back next time, those mysteries will be gone. I have customers. I'm going to do a window with mysteries when I get a chance."

The salesman left and Tessie was alone with the browser, who had so often seemed not real. Today he was not an ectoplasmic Barney with thinning hair and a droopy mustache of brown and gray, nor the ghost of her sex life, nor an Ichabod of her medical state. Today he was M. H. Ross, but real enough to speak, to state his business. She stayed behind the counter and waited.

She opened the complimentary copy of the mystery the salesman had left her. "Curry was down on his luck," it began. Big deal. That meant he would either kill someone, steal something, or sell something. She slipped to the end. "Curry lit a cigarette. He looked out the window where dusk was overtaking the cool, gray noon. The neon of a Chinese restaurant sign tinted the pavement. Would Maureen ever come back?" Not if she's dead, Tessie thought.

The browser stepped out of the aisle. He had the mark of glasses on the bridge of his nose. He was as ready to talk as Tessie.

"You have some nice books here," he said. He was looking at the pile the salesman had made. His voice was nasal. No accent, she noted.

"Yes," Tessie said. "But nobody buys."

"Oh? I thought I overheard you saying just now that the store does quite well. Excuse me for listening."

"Ahhh," Tessie said. "I wasn't telling the truth. The truth is, the neighborhood is falling."

He nodded. "Failing," he said.

"Falling down, mister, like a crippled old man."

He looked surprised.

"You have to be crazy to try and make a living in a place like this. Do you know how many break-ins there have been in the last year alone? Do you know how many old-timers closed up and got out last year?"

He shook his head.

"Guess."

"I don't know."

"Guess."

"I really don't . . . Oh, well, I'll say four."

"Four? Four? Did you say four?"

"Well, I was just guessing. . . ."

"Say five you would be wrong, say six, you would be wrong, say seven."

The browser waited.

"Go on," Tessie told him, "say seven."

"Seven," he said.

"You're wrong," Tessie said. "It's eight. Eight old-timers in one year."

"So why do you stay? If I may ask?"

If you may ask. Of course ask. I want you to ask. Tessie shrugged (a little dramatic stuff here). Tessie sighed. "Where would an old lady go? To Florida? To live her final days with her children and become a burden? This way at least I always have something to read. And one day the bookstore won't open and everyone will know I am dead."

The browser looked embarrassed. "Ah, yes . . . ," he said. "Well . . ."

He paid for the book from his small purse.

"And the mail-order business you mentioned?" he said. "Is that . . . ?"

But Tessie didn't want to talk anymore.

"Forget it," she said. "Have a nice night."

"And yourself," he said, with his hand on the doorknob, "a pleasant evening."

"Teach you to play games with me, Ross," she said, after he was gone.

PSYCHOLOGY

SOCIOLOGY

WOMEN'S STUDIES

First there were two of them in the Mc-Donald's: Mateo and Bobby. It was still early, and they had the place to themselves, except for the old lady in the corner. Mateo noticed her and was going to say something, but then Richie came in, and stupid Rivera, and they sat around drinking coffee and smoking, not talking much. Bobby was going to the Unemployment. Mateo had promised his mother he would go for a job at the Bronx Hospital and the promise, and a dream in which people were pushing him around, and a dull ache in his stomach all added up to a bad mood.

"What kind of a job?" Rivera wanted to know.

"A doctor, man," Richie said. "They got a opening for a doctor, and Mateo here, he just right."

"Yeah?" Rivera's eyes widened. Richie laughed but Mateo didn't.

"*Jíbaro*," he said. "Someday being so stupid gonna get you in trouble."

But Rivera just laughed, as if Mateo had made a joke.

The old lady made a sound.

"Whatta you laughing at?" Bobby said, although she wasn't.

She tried to act like she didn't see them. She made Mateo remember the grandmother, his mother's mother in Puerto Rico, her hair was pulled tight back the same way, and she sat stiff like her.

Most of the old people stayed out of the way, got out of the way if they saw the place was taken. But this one, she sat stiff against the brown wood wall making believe they were invisible, just asking for it. It bugged Mateo. He thought of the other one, the one who gave him the garbage. This one, the other one, they were all the same, only he wasn't going to take no more garbage from one of them.

"Whatta you looking at?" he said to her, and even though she was staring at the brown wall, the way she blinked he could tell she heard him. The grandmother, she lifted up a nice hand and whammed it across your face so fast you didn't see it move, if you talked back.

"Hey," he called. She put her pocketbook up against her chest, and he noticed the watch on her wrist, and the gold thing, star, on the chain on her neck.

172

"Hey, lady." Now Richie and Bobby were smiling, and Rivera was lighting up a cigarette, like getting ready for the show.

She didn't answer Mateo, but he knew she was listening, because every time he said something she did something with her hands, or wiggled around in the seat, like he was pulling her strings. Or she was pulling his. Every time she moved around he felt like talking back to her.

"Hey, Sadie." Hand to neck. "Yeah, you." Sip.

The sun came out, threw a thin bar on the brown vinyl floor between the old lady and Mateo. The manager, the only one there this time of morning, had disappeared into the back.

Didn't she know something was going to happen to her?

"If I was you, lady, I'd leave," Bobby said. She moved, but didn't get up.

When Mateo stood at her table, she stared at his belt, wouldn't look up into his face.

"Excuse me, lady, could I trouble you for change for a dollar?"

"Only he doesn't have the dollar," Bobby said, and they all cracked up laughing.

She snapped open her purse and looked inside. Her head shook or she shook it, and then Mateo shook the table and very calmly put his fist into her breast, and very calmly pinched her face into a pout with his left hand, and made her look up, and punched her in the face with his right. He ripped her glasses off her, and she stared at him. Bobby and the others had come behind him, as if he might need help. She was making grunting sounds, and panting like she was out of breath, but she didn't scream, and Mateo wanted to hear from her.

"Stubborn fucking old bitch" was his rhythm, four blows each time, he was out of breath and the old lady's eyes were tearing but she still wasn't screaming or begging him to stop and finally it was stupid Rivera who had to say, Come on, quit it, let's get out of here, and Mateo almost didn't take the money, almost forgot the watch and the chain — stubborn old bitch made him so mad — but then he took it.

There was no one on the street.

"At least she didn't come after you," Richie said, and they all laughed, because yes, even though the old lady didn't fight back, she was asking for it.

At night, in his sleep, Mateo felt tightness across his eyes and saw black. There was a hiss and sizzle of devil's breath. Sharp scream sliced him from eyes to belly. Blood, big green head of lettuce, mustard, all gushing from the slit body, lying dead, moving, saying in Mita's voice, *"Tu has sido muy malo, no se me acerque, no se me acerque."* Don't come near me. I'll get you. *"Yo te haré lo mismo."* I'll do it to you. The band tightened.

"Now you're blindfolded," Georgie said.

Mateo gasped and woke. He twisted the tiny wrist lightly. "Get away," he said. *"No se me acerque."*

Georgie ran crying.

Then *she* came, bacon stink all over her. She swung her hand, but Mateo rolled away fast. "Missed," he said.

"Animal," she said and went back to the kitchen.

The wall felt cool on his cheek. He stayed pressed against it until it was warm. He could smell his own breath, it smelled like beer. Georgie came back.

"What's this?"

He was holding the shirt Mateo had bought yesterday, with the money from the old lady. Mateo swung his legs over the side of the bed and Georgie dropped the shirt, leaving a small yellow smudge on the collar.

"Now you're dead," Mateo said, rubbing his eyes.

Georgie waited, halfway to the kitchen, one foot ready to run, as if Mateo had said, Ready, get set ... but Mateo only reached for the shirt. Georgie ran anyway. Mateo scraped at the spot of egg. Fifteen dollars. He had better cut the tags off before she came back and started asking him where he got the money and if he went for the hospital job. He hadn't given her anything for the house in three weeks.

"Hey, Georgie," he called.

Georgie came but stood at the other side of the room.

"C'mere," Mateo smiled. "I ain't gonna hurt you."

Georgie approached slowly.

Mateo laid his palms flat out and smiled again. After a moment, George came close enough to slap them. "Faaahv," he breathed. Mateo caught his hand.

"I want you to do me a favor," he said.

Georgie tried to pull away.

"No, c'mon, I ain't gonna hurt you. Go get me a scissors in the kitchen drawer. Don't let Ma see. That's all. Cool?" He let his brother's arm go and laid his palms out again. Georgie hesitated, then he said "Cool" and slapped Mateo hard.

"Owww," Mateo said, exaggerating, blowing on his palms. "Man, you're a killer."

Georgie grinned and went to get the scissors.

He left the shirt cardboard for the kid to draw pictures on.

She came in again. "Where were you last night?" she said.

He pretended to sleep.

When she went out of the room he went into the shower and stayed there until she went to work, taking Georgie with her, dropping him off at the day care on her way. When he heard the door close he came out, dried himself, and went into the kitchen. The bare floors were cold, he better get himself some slippers. Leather, nice. He made instant coffee and lit a cigarette. No eggs. In the breadbox were an empty Wonder Bread package and a bakery bag with two bagels.

"What do you buy Jew food for?" he had asked her.

He tore the bagel in half and ate it. Then he got dressed slowly, stripping the cellophane from a package of new T-shirts, slipping one on. New things made him feel good. And the apartment was empty, that made him feel good, too. As if this was his place. He wouldn't have a place like this, though. Old toilet, old everything. Old landlord, old people in the building, old people outside, looking for pennies on the ground. The whole neighborhood was old, and the old people they thought they owned it, well the shit stores, yes, and the gates at night, and they pressed tissues against their mouths to keep from breathing his air, their air full of mothballs made him choke. He even felt old, his eyes worn out seeing the same things, and then Mita again, this time in the stomach, speaking inside him on the left side and then in the middle, her words like hot coals and ice picks, and he had to go back to the bathroom and he soiled the tail of his new shirt.

Finally, he went to Mrs. Gloria Muñoz, who spoke to Mita. Through Mrs. Muñoz, Mita said he would never be good again, because of the mean streak that ran down him a mile wide, and Mrs. Muñoz said that Mita said it served him right if his belly ate his belly, for being a low-class Puerto Rican, a *jibaro* from the hills, and for all the bad things he had done which people in the community knew all about. He told Mrs. Muñoz to speak to Mita, say he was possessed at the time, it was *el ataque*. Mita said, through Mrs. Muñoz, don't give me that shit. But then Mita said she would see what she would see, and if he really wanted to be dispossessed of the evil spirit, he should take a good hot bath to cleanse himself, with a candle at each end of the tub, and keep away from the other animals without surnames, and she would

178

be watching to see if he did it.

He took the bath, but didn't stay away from Richie and the others, and two days later Mita spoke again, and this time his mother had to take him to the emergency room.

The doctor on duty said, "What did he do, swallow his knife?"

He had to stay overnight, which was all right with him. He didn't want more trouble. He whispered to Mita all through the night. He was ready to listen, he told her. Ready to do what she said.

The borough president was long gone, a week or more, and back in the county offices, when Victory got mugged in the McDonald's, and it was not something important enough for him to have heard about, so Tessie called to let him know.

After the beating, Victory had called for help, but when the manager (who might have disappeared for good) did not come, she managed to make her way out of there and stumble to the door of the bookstore, where she collapsed and was discovered by, of all people, Tessie's daughter Louise.

Louise, as she tells it (again and again, Tessie thinks but doesn't say), was coming to take her mother shopping. As she approached the doorway (slowly I turn, step by step, Tessie thinks) she saw the shoes of a woman. She shivered (Tessie notices she does the shiver each time she tells it). She thought it was one of those bag women (here she stops and casts her eyes apologetically to Victory, who is lying in the hospital bed doped up like a zombie and couldn't care less). She recoiled at the thought of having to touch the old woman to rouse her (making something cleverly candid out of the repugnance which might otherwise make her look heartless). Then oh, oh (she rubs her eyes), there was an apple at the woman's side, in her fist, Louise saw it, it was not an apple it was her fist, red as an apple. Covered with blood. I thought it was my mother, she says, in a whisper. (Victory is almost a foot taller, with steel-and-white hair, but all right, Tessie thinks.) She describes how she fell to her knees, calling Tessie's name (which had moved Tessie when she first heard it but doesn't anymore, since it is a tale now, and sucked dry).

"I thought I would die," Louise says.

Tessie pats her hand comfortingly, thinking, Since I was the one you thought was beaten, shouldn't it have been me you thought would die?

Louise had banged on the door, and Tessie, who had been coming up the basement stairs, heard her and opened the door. Victory's upper lip was torn, a tooth lifting and falling back against her torn flesh each time she breathed. One eye was full of blood, and there was blood all over the front of her.

The hospital room is warm and Tessie is going to be sick.

Louise had acted quickly, calling 911, calling an ambulance, while Tessie sat on the ground holding Victory in her arms, berating her, calling her a disaster waiting to happen, and finally begging her to wake up, dammit, Victory please, holding her face against her face, kissing her.

"Let me sit," she says to Pearl, who is occupying the only chair in the hospital room.

Victory regained consciousness in the emergency room, but has not spoken. It has been two days. The function is there, the doctor says. She just doesn't want to. Tessie knows this is true, because actually Victory has said one thing, or Tessie thinks she heard her say it. But it might have been a sigh. "Ashamed." Or it might have just been a sigh.

"I thought it was my mother lying there," Louise says, again.

Tessie gets mad then, and wants to say it wouldn't be, couldn't be, I wouldn't let it, and wants to tell her about how the three punks had attacked her on the bus, and how she had beaten them off, scared them away, outsmarted them. But it is suddenly clear to her that if they had wanted to, if they had really been serious about it, they could have done this to her. The baby-faced boy, all the baby-faced boys, could have, and could, and she is ashamed of having been stupid enough to think different.

"The problem with this kind of trauma," the doctor says, sucking on *trauma* like it is hard candy, "is that it reverberates. When the physical injuries are all healed, the victim expects to feel fine, but the psychic damage is just beginning to set in. There is sleeplessness, anxiety, depression. The victim often blames herself." Victory continues to stare at the green hospital wall.

"Like rape," Louise says.

"She'll be all right," Helen says, pulling her coat around herself. "We'll keep her busy."

"Exactly like rape," the doctor says.

"We have to get her mind off it," Helen says. "So she doesn't dwell."

The doctor is young — everyone is young these days, muggers, doctors, policemen — and he clearly cares; his cheeks are rosy with concern. He contradicts Helen gently, like she is his grandmother.

182

"Strangely enough," he says, "it might do her some good, not to dwell exactly, but to think about it, think it through, you see. So she can get in touch with her rage."

Helen squints, to see his point; Tessie knows she is shocked. "Oh, rage," Helen says. "I don't really think Victory, you know, has that sort of thing." As if Victory is a shopkeeper who does not stock a certain item.

Tessie looks up and meets her daughter's eye, in brief and unusual accord.

"Of course she does, everyone is supposed to," Pearl says, impatiently.

"Well, I don't know," Helen says, uncertainly.

"Her son is coming from Arizona," Pearl says.

"*May* be coming," Tessie-Who-Has-No-Faith-in-Children says. "If he can get away, he says."

The doctor looks uncomfortable, and Tessie thinks he has a mother he has put off a time or two. "Well, let's just get her body well," he says, looking at his watch. "Then we'll worry about the rest."

Helen nods, relieved that the discussion is over. Pearl follows the young doctor out, to tell him, Tessie is sure, about her nephew who is a big man in neurosurgery at Mount Sinai.

Helen is buttoning her coat, and Louise

is putting on hers.

Louise waits until Helen goes in search of Pearl, and then says to Tessie, "Mom, please come home with me. Stay with us for a while."

Tessie almost says yes. If Louise had asked at the moment that their eyes agreed over rage, she would have. But now she is irritated at Victory's son, and thinks it is Louise's way of saying, "Look what a goody-two-shoes child *I* am," and doesn't want to let her get away with it. She thinks if Louise said "Stay with *me*" instead of "Stay with *us*" she might have said yes anyway. She says no.

"Please," Louise says, but says too quickly, and Tessie notices she is hurriedly buttoning her coat.

"Soon," she says. "Another time." Then she decides to let her off the hook. "I want to stay around to make sure she's all right," she says, gesturing at the bed. "Then maybe, all right?" She looks up at Louise, who is standing behind the chair.

Louise hesitates, then sighs and says all right. "Just promise," she says, "you will take a taxi home, don't take the bus. They aren't safe at night."

"They aren't safe any time," Tessie says. "I have the car."

Louise is surprised to hear Tessie is driving

again, and Tessie pretends to be surprised that she is surprised, though she had deliberately not told anyone, even herself, preferring to sneak up on it, so she wouldn't scare herself.

"Well, be careful walking after you park," Louise said. "Where are you going to park?"

Tessie is irritated by Louise's concern. She reminds herself she would also be irritated if Louise wasn't concerned.

"Gonzalez is saving me a spot in front of the house," she says. "He took up two spaces and when I come home I'll honk and he'll come out and move up for me," she says. This is not true, but it occurs to Tessie that it is a good idea, and she promises herself that if she survives the walk from wherever she parks tonight, she will arrange something like that in the future.

After Louise is gone, and Helen and Pearl leave, Tessie says to Victory, "This was the worst one yet. When are you going to stop? If you're looking for attention, you got it. But I'm telling you right now, it isn't going to bring George back, and it isn't going to bring Mindy to life, and between you and me, Victory, Mark isn't going to come running so fast, either. You want me to roll you down?"

When Victory doesn't answer, Tessie rolls her down, and lowers the fluorescent light above her bed.

Victory's bed is near the door. A woman with no jaw lies sleeping opposite. A woman with long black stitches that go from her ear-lobe past the V of her nightgown coughs care-fully into a large, brown-spotted handkerchief. A fourth woman, whom Tessie has come to think of as Victory's twin, lies staring.

This is a hospital, Tessie thinks. She remem-bers once when Barney had dragged her to Miami, to visit another one of his sick cousins who had just had a stroke. The hospital rooms were all painted in different pastels, like after-dinner mints, with stenciled flamingos on the walls, and she had never once smelled medicine smells. Suntan oil, she had told Barney, they pipe it in through the vents. Well, they charged enough. The cousin's wife had let her know that. The barium drinks came in malted flavors, the cousin's wife had told her, enthusi-astically, as if she was in charge of publicity and this was a fancy hotel. There were palm trees in the visitors' lounge.

A medicine cart clicks somewhere down the hall. The woman with the stitches coughs again. From somewhere comes a high, piping, two-note cry, like the cry of a child: Mom-my, Mom-my. It has no urgency, but it goes on like an unanswered phone, so long that Tessie be-gins to count the cries. She gets up and stands in the doorway, and sees a nurse stop at the door of a room down the hall, put her finger to her lips, and then move on, shaking her head. The cries continue. Tessie walks slowly toward the room and stands outside, listening. Then she looks in. In the middle of the bed is a tiny, very old woman, older than Tessie can imagine ever being. Her gray hair is fanned out over the pillow. Her hands, knuckles enlarged, are curled quietly on her chest, and her lips open and close periodically to free the cries. Tessie goes back to Victory's room.

"This is a hospital, all right," she says to Victory, "not like that Eden Roc for the Sick in Miami Beach. You want to lie around in a place like this?"

Victory groans, and Tessie nods.

"I know," she says, "but don't drag it out by being in shock. We aren't getting any younger, Vicki. Did you see Helen tonight? She looks terrible, she looked old. You don't look so young either, if you want to know. You want to go to Arizona and live with Mark and get ignored on a daily basis? So go. You want to go to Florida? Pick yourself up and go. You want to stay here? Put your rings in the vault and start watching yourself. But you better make up your mind soon, Vicki. You better stop futzing around, you hear me? I'm not talking to myself,

187

Vicki, do you hear?"

Victory groans again and then says wearily, "I hear you, I hear you, now will *you* go?" which is about as angry as Tessie has ever heard her sound.

"Good," Tessie says, picking up her coat and pocketbook, "you're getting in touch with your rage."

Before Tessie got into the car, she checked on the floor and in the backseat to make sure the thick shadows contained no young muggers, yet all the way home she felt them there. When she parked the car, halfway up the block from her house, she made sure there were no young muggers or even old women who might be young muggers in disguise as far down the hill as she could see, calculating her speed to her door in case they should be approaching, just beyond the bend of the street. She ran all the way, and there was no one behind her, yet when she reached her door she turned quickly, to catch them at her back.

The apartment, which she had moved back to the day Victory had been attacked, still smelled and looked and felt vacant, the way it used to when she and Barney returned from a week's vacation somewhere. Someone had come in while she was gone and scooped out the insides of chairs, they were like shells, if she had lifted one it would have been light as a shell, and when she spoke (Come out, I know you're in there, entering each room) they took her voice and sent it back hollow. She put on all the lights. Her bed was covered with papers, the old accordion file lying empty on her pillow, and she thought "ransacked" and felt a hot flash before she remembered that she had never put them away.

"Tea," she said, "coffee," and went into the kitchen, where the air seemed more normal. While she waited for the water to boil, she counted the tulips that rimmed the cup. She had bought these cups twenty years ago, and the flowers had never been so clear. Someone had come in and repainted the flowers while she was gone. Someone had left a cup and saucer in the drainboard. She examined her fingernails, chipped, yellowed, and unpainted. She watched her hand holding the spoon, dipping it into the coffee jar, coming up with too much, dipping again and leveling it by shaking the spoon — was she shaking the spoon or was the spoon shaking her? After the coffee she walked into the bedroom, intending sleep. She still felt followed, but by a smaller presence, a cat padding after her. She looked down. When she looked up she caught herself in the mirror.

"Oh, my god, look at you," she said, and gave herself a temporary face-lift by pushing the skin up at the sides of her face. "What you need is a touch-up," she said. And so, instead of going to sleep, she went into the bathroom, set up her equipment, and retouched her hair. While she waited for the bleach to take, she manicured her nails, and while she waited for the polish to harden, she went into the living room and sat down and got up from every chair, the love seat, finally occupying the sofa with her whole body, staying there and blowing on her nails until they were dry. When she got up she felt at home again, and the shadow cat was gone.

Yet in her sleep she heard, or dreamed she heard, the old woman crying the two-note cry, and when Louise called in the morning, her voice cracked, and she said, "I didn't sleep well."

Spring comes to the Wilds in a rash of robberies, push-ins, disagreements in alleys behind after-hours clubs late at night; the beautiful cantilevered park with the circular sitting area enclosed in blossoming shrubbery at top, which gracefully winds down in old-fashioned cobblestone steps level after level to the circular playground below, is bustling with drug transactions. People are stricken with a focusless hope which makes them want to change the numbers they play, from their birth date to something new, and put twice as much money down as usual. In the back of Hum's Chinese, Joe Figueroa was busy.

Gloria Muñoz, the spiritist, was busy, too, because now was the time people wanted to clear up their troubles. She conducted séances to get in touch with protector spirits, conducted dispossessions to get rid of destructive spirits, prescribed and oversaw a *limpieza*, a sort of spiritual dry-cleaning process, to remove the stain of corrupted spirits. Many of these spiritual matters had to do with housing, job discrimination, alcohol abuse, and family trouble.

A man had to go to court, because he was found in possession of his friend's gun, which the friend had asked him to hold because he had just found out his girlfriend was cheating on him and he didn't trust himself with it. Mrs. Muñoz dispossessed the man of the spirit that was urging him to take the gun and hold it to his friend's head for getting him in trouble; she also explained about plea bargaining. The protector spirit was invoked to help a young widow fill out the papers against her landlord, who had been overcharging her on her rent for two years. Mothers came with their sons, to

191

keep them out of trouble.

Mrs. Muñoz wore white during these gatherings, because it was ceremonial and because she knew she looked dynamite in white. Around her neck was a large white sand dollar, on a piece of white satin cord. She wore this even when she was in her street clothes, and people knew her by it, and thought of it as magic, because she was in the habit of rubbing its light, papery face against hers when she was thinking or going into a trance. She was tall, and her shoulders broad as a man's. She wore high heels to make herself taller, and shoulder pads in her dresses to make herself broader. Her facial features were regular: large brown eyes, tiny, slightly broadened nose, prettily full lips; but there was something in her expression, an exclamation or a kiss always poised and ready to burst forth (though she never blew kisses and her exclamations were often angry), an irony manifested in the hollows of her cheeks, energy in her eyes. Her hair was thick curls, short and dark, streaked with gray.

This night, before the séance began, several people were talking about prejudice against the Hispanic community and prejudice in general. The conversation stemmed from the experience of Mr. Velez, who had been passed over for manager of a store twice because, although his boss admitted he could do the job, he also admitted he didn't think customers would like the way he talked. You can report him, someone said. Someone else laughed: And get fired for your troubles?

Mrs. Muñoz let the talk go on, postponing the ritual. The talk often was the best part, a way of coming together and making some sense out of a strange and often cold environment. Sometimes, on the other hand, it was the mumbo jumbo that had the most value, connecting people to the home culture in old ways, and taking some of the pressure off, since spirits, even bad ones, were easier to deal with than city agencies.

There was a light tap on the apartment door, and someone else arrived. It was Iris Colon with her son, Mateo. This one was trouble. This one Mrs. Muñoz had no use for, and the more he said he would do what she said, the more she didn't trust him. She wondered, smiling at the thought, if *she* was prejudiced in this case, if it had anything to do with the fact that the boy looked a lot like her second husband: too pretty. But the mother, she tried so hard, Mrs. Muñoz didn't like to send her away.

This time the boy had lost his job of three days, for cursing his boss.

"He called me stupid," he said.

She could see he was sorry, and seeing that made her know he was a hopeless case. If he were not sorry, she could have made him sorry, and he would have begun to act better. But this one thought better of being sorry, and his anger was the king of him, and she thought it would be the death of him. Still, she tried. He was a sickly boy, and she worked on that, offering health in exchange for good behavior, threatening pain as a result of bad. She suggested candles to light for the mother, and to him she said she would speak to someone she knew about getting him another job and meanwhile to watch who he stayed around with.

It was late when the evening ended, and her last visitor had gone. She went inside to the bedroom to check on her two sleeping boys, cursing as she felt how cold the room was, touching the radiator and cursing again. It wasn't enough that spring would soon make the room warmer; spring would also get the landlord off the hook, and he had been getting away with it all winter. There was no sense in bothering the super, he could do nothing; the boiler broke and he called the landlord, he tried; the landlord wouldn't send anyone to fix it from one end of the year to the next. The landlord was notorious, but up to now, untouched by the law; this was because the lawyer for the Acción Locale, who was supposed to be taking care of it had the brains of a mango, she thought. She had a sudden inspiration.

The next morning, she called the landlord's office, and spoke in a friendly way with the landlord's secretary, pretending to be from a heating and air-conditioning repair company interested in submitting a bid for the landlord's business. In this way she learned the name of the company who presently did his repairs, and the secretary's first name as well. Then she called the repair company, said she was the landlord's secretary, and gave them a work order, ASAP, rush, top priority. By late afternoon, they had heat.

That evening she put Mateo Colon's name on the Acción Locale job bulletin board. She could not write "experienced"; "intelligent but sneaky" entered her mind. She settled for "intelligent and willing to work" and then worried that she had gone too far. There was a meeting of the committee, and they urged her to stay. She said no, she had other commitments. The truth was, lately she couldn't stand their snail, turtle, mouselike approach to every problem: slow, slow, talk, talk, talk, where was all the action? If she stayed she would end up screaming at someone, so she went.

The borough president wouldn't come to the phone. Tessie spoke to a sympathetic aide named Sharon who turned not so sympathetic after Tessie's ninth call. Then, after Sharon wouldn't come to the phone, and Tessie had exhausted Jeffrey and a third person who refused to give his name, she finally decided to write a letter. The letter was reckless in its scope, detailing not only Victory's mugging and the attempted break-in of the bookstore, but also sanitation department neglect (all right, Barney?), postal delivery irregularity, potholes, stray dogs, cats, people, and her suspicion that all of these things, including the never-completed urban renewal project, were a ploy to line certain politicians' pockets. Her indictment included Sharon, Jeffrey, and the third person who refused to give his name. She read the letter over twice, changed "dishonest politicians" to "crooks," and sent it. While she waited for an answer, she thought of other items she should have included, so she sent a second letter. After a week, she received a form reply, thanking her for her interest (which was like thanking a rabid dog for frothing at the mouth, she said), not even mentioning any of her points, and suggesting she contact the

Local Action Committee, which was the liaison between the community and the borough president's office.

She banged on Gonzalez's door.

"What the hell are you people doing about the muggings?" she demanded. Gonzalez's feet were bare, his hair was rumpled, and he looked somewhat sleepy, all of which, Tessie felt, was his way of telling her her demands had come at an inappropriate time. Therefore, she escalated them. "I want some action *now*," she said, and then stood there while Gonzalez rubbed his face. The rubbing went on too long, and Tessie found herself staring at Gonzalez's feet. "Well?" she said, finally. Gonzalez responded softly and politely, saying the matter was coming up the next evening at the Acción Locale meeting, and she was welcome to attend, he would take her there. He waited a moment, and then, to her surprise, quietly and firmly closed the door, leaving her to say "I'll see" to the chipped green wood panel. Afterward, going back upstairs to her apartment, she remembered that he was having troubles of his own, his wife had had a breakdown after the daughter died. She was sorry she had yelled at him like that. So the next evening, when he knocked at her door, she was ready and apologetic, which made her very nervous.

Walking alongside Gonzalez made her nervous, too, because they were a couple, and she hadn't walked alongside a man in a long time.

"How is your wife?" she said, to say something.

He shook his head. "No good. She screams inside her sleep, every night, every damn night. She stays by her sister, she don't let the nieces alone, her sister can't take it. She calls me up and tells me to take her home, but when I go she don't want to come home. She wants to stay there and keep an eye on the nieces. *No puedo más,* I can't take anymore. *Me tiene hasta aquí,*" he said, striking his nose. She understood this to mean he was fed up.

She surprised herself by patting his shoulder. "Children," she said, because it was the daughter who had brought all this on.

"I have a boy back home," he said. "Puerto Rico. With my brother. I am thinking to send her there. He is a good boy. But he can't take care of her. He is only ten years. How can he take care of her? My brother is poor, too, how do I put this on him?"

She saw suddenly that Gonzalez was a much younger man than she had thought he was, and that he had been made old by troubles, more troubles than she had. Her heart filled with warm sympathy. She wanted to help.

"Did you take her to a doctor?"

"Ahh," he said in disgust. "They give her pills, but they don't do nothing. She stops screaming when she takes the pills, but then she doesn't clean up, doesn't do nothing but lay around the house."

Tessie shook her head. "Tranquilizers," she said. "I don't like them either. They zonk her out."

"*Qué?* What?"

"Zonk," Tessie said. "They knock her out."

They walked on in silence for a while, Tessie wondering whether she ought to recommend a good doctor. Gonzalez stopped her with the length of his arm from stepping on a broken bottle. He swept the glass to the curb with the side of his shoe, and they walked on.

By the time they reached the storefront she no longer felt nervous, and understood, though vaguely, that she was grateful to Gonzalez. She wanted to say something to him about Barney, how much Barney had liked him, but she couldn't think of how to say it, so she said, "Well, if there is anything I can do . . ."

There were ten people in the storefront. A *minyan*, Tessie thought. The lawyer, who was the president of the committee, called the meeting to order. He was a tall, collegiate young man with horn-rimmed glasses, and reminded

199

her, as he had when he had come to pay the *shiva* call, of her son-in-law. He extended the similarity by welcoming her with an exaggerated courtliness, saying her late husband had been one of his favorite people, and that in his practice he met many fine Jewish people, both as clients and as colleagues. Tessie wondered whether he was going to tell her next that lox and bagels was his favorite dish and wish her mahzel tough. Then, Russell-like, his eyes shining with his own importance, he said, Now that the formalities were completed . . .

And now, she thought, that the bullshit was over . . .

But the bullshit was just beginning.

Papers and forms. All these people did was to fill out papers and forms and talk about proper procedures for appeals and appeals of appeals. This one was writing to the HRA about licensing the day-care center which had failed to meet standards last month; that one was writing a complaint about city agency neglect of landlord neglect. She had to wait through ongoing cases, second appeals, and it wasn't until ten o'clock that she got her chance to speak. And when she did, she didn't know what to say anymore. She felt disappointed, because they were so dry, and businesslike, and maybe tired. Where is the hot Spanish blood, she caught herself thinking, and then laughed, because it was in the same place as the lox and bagels and the hora and the cha-cha. She felt silly, yet relieved; sorry and not sorry. She filled out a form asking for additional police patrols and signed a petition requesting a Senior Citizen Task Force representative to come and speak to Senior Citizens about how to protect themselves from muggings. But she didn't get a chance to yell, and holding it in made her as tired as if she had been holding it on her back, and it was heavy.

When she got home it was late, but she called Louise anyway, and accepted her invitation to come and stay with her for the Passover holidays.

In the suburbs, the baby-faced muggers with the nasty smiles were no longer everywhere Tessie looked, and at first that was enough. The streets were clean, she said, enthusiastically, as if that was what it took to be happy. She sat in the large, bright kitchen and watched Louise concoct complicated health-food meals with long lists of ingredients.

"I never cooked," Tessie said.

"I know," Louise said, with a little smile, so Tessie got up and went down to the basement room Louise had fixed up for her with such attention to detail as a picture of Barney, sour balls in a mason jar on the end table, and designer-boxed tissues. Eventually, Louise came down, still in the apron that said "Gourmet Kook" across the front, smelling of steamed garlic and phony good humor.

"Where did you disappear to?" she said, or "Are you all right?" or sometimes "Can I get you anything?" as if Tessie were an invalid.

Tessie always replied appropriately, "Just resting," "Yes, I'm fine, dear," or "Nothing that I can think of."

Once Tessie did not leave the kitchen, but stayed there, watching, and finally said, "I don't know how anyone who is supposed to be a health-food fanatic and makes innocent babies eat plain yogurt, and makes a federal case out of a lollipop can use so much butter," but Louise did not rise to the bait.

She had been there a week, and she knew she was being difficult. But Louise drove her crazy. Louise drove her everywhere, chattering, chattering as if she were a real estate agent out to sell her mother the neighborhood, all about "our" mall, "our" temple, "our" dry cleaners, for godsakes, as if she had built it all for Tessie's approval. Tessie thought she was leading up to asking her to stay, live with them. Louise had driven her past the Senior Center

202

six times in one week, to show her how close it was to their house, and tell her about the trips they ran to Atlantic City and to Englishtown, New Jersey, for the antiques.

Tessie watched daytime television with Louise, which Louise claimed, her eyes glued to the screen, she never watched. So Tessie wondered why she was watching it now — was it for Tessie's sake or her own? — and decided it was for both of them, so they wouldn't have to talk. Sebby joined them after school, just in time for "Divorce Court," but when, mimicking her grandmother one day, she said the defendant was a horse's ass, Louise decided it was best that she use that particular time slot to do her homework in. Tessie became an expert on the daytime version of "The Pyramid," so when the whole family watched the evening version, she knew all the answers before the contestants did, and was treated, by Russell, to patronizing little claps of his hands. She wondered if she was going feeble-minded, to stand for this.

"Daddy and I never watched much TV," she said.

"Neither do we," Louise said quickly, "just sometimes."

One night, when Russell came home early from the office, he rubbed his hands together and proposed they all sit down in the living room for a little talk.

She wondered if now was the moment they were going to ask her to stay.

"Tomato juice for you, Gram?" he said heartily, and Tessie nodded and Louise went to get it.

It was time, Russell said, to talk turkey.

"Save the turkey for supper," Tessie said.

Both sets of eyes registered her irony, but, Tessie noticed, not to each other. Russell looked at the ceiling and Louise looked down. Tessie suddenly knew that the marriage was in trouble.

"Go on," she said.

"What Russell wanted to say," Louise began, and this time his glance went right to her and cut her off.

What Russell had wanted to say, he said, was that it was time for Tessie to stop fooling around and start thinking about what she was going to do with the store.

"Sell it," she said.

"When?" Russell said.

"When I get a buyer," she said.

"This mysterious buyer who wrote you the letters?" he said.

She had almost forgotten about M. H. Ross, and the thought of him came as something of a shock. "Him, or someone else," she said. Him and only him, she thought.

"Well," Russell sighed. "That makes sense." Yet it was clear he was still not satisfied. "What is your timetable?" he said.

"My *timetable?* Look, Russell . . ."

"Look, Tessie," he said.

"Look, Mother," Louise said. "We feel that —"

"Look, children, my timetable is my own business," she said firmly. Did she have a timetable? She thought she did, oh yes, she did, even if it was without hours or days assigned to it. "And that is that."

And because Louise and Tessie never argued, Louise put her hand on Russell's arm, and since Louise and Russell never argued either, Russell took one more good look at the ceiling and dropped the issue, and they went back to the television in the den.

Tessie and Louise never argued. It had been well over a week filled with no arguments.

They had just returned from the supermarket, where they had been shopping for the next day's Passover dinner. There were no arguments between them in the supermarket, either. Tessie had pushed the cart down each aisle, Louise followed. Tessie moved fast, tapping an occasional cracker box, scanning the shelves as she passed, a speed-reader. Louise went more slowly, picking up groceries until her arms were full, then hurrying to catch up and dump them in the cart. Once, Tessie caught a box of macaroni in the wheels of the cart and twisted it and jerked it to dislodge the box, but Louise finally bent down to remove it. She locked wheels with an old man, and pushed him so hard he fell against the meat counter. Louise blushed. Tessie contested Louise's choice of tomatoes, and pressed her thumb disparagingly through the skin of her avocado.

"Too mushy," she said.

Louise smiled at the produce man and said, "My mother's with us for a while."

She chattered all the way home and was still chattering as she unpacked the groceries and began her preparations.

"Why don't you make the soup first," Tessie said, as Louise set about making the cranberry sauce. She was rewarded with Louise's first silence of the day. Sebby was racing about, chasing the cat. She was a very thin child, and sober; she reminded Tessie of Louise when she was small: she didn't smile easily, paled to the lips rather than flushing with emotion. But Sebby was more straight-forward, not as timid as Louise was. Still is. Not afraid to show how she felt.

"The child never stops," Tessie said, thinking of Louise's nervous chattering, but pointing to Sebby, who had dashed out of the kitchen.

"Don't forget your jacket," Lousie called to her. "It's chilly."

"I used to underdress you, I think," Tessie said. The word *underdress* made her think of the morning, when Russell had shocked her by walking in front of her in his Jockey shorts. She had wanted to tell him, "I am not a brick wall, I am not a nothing for you to be parading in front of in your underwear." But she had said, "You look like the New Year's baby," and she could have sworn his penis perked behind the diaperish white cotton.

Now she wanted to go home, urgently.

"She's fine," Louise said, defensively.

Suddenly Tessie wanted to shake her, to shout at her, "Stand up to me." Sebby burst in, breathlessly, a cat struggling in her arms.

"I've got her," she said, and swooping down, poked the cat into Tessie's face, rubbing the cat's nose roughly on Tessie's cheek, saying in a high, excited voice, "Here, kiss the little grammy, cat, kiss the little grammy." There was a faintly sour, metallic smell about her, nervous sweat, Tessie thought. The child's initial delight in having Tessie there had declined over the week, and she could not hide it. She sees how frightened her mother is of me, and now she hates me.

"Sebby," Louise screamed, "be careful of Grammy," and made a lunge for her, but Sebby dropped the cat and ran out of the kitchen.

"I'm sorry, Mom," Louise said in a shaky voice. "Is your face all right? Did she hurt you?"

"I'm fine," Tessie said, though her cheek stung, as though the cat had scratched her. She heard her own voice, it sounded angry, responding as always to the worried pleasure, or pleasurable worry, in Louise's voice.

"All that excitement," Louise continued. "Big dinners and little children really don't mix, too much stimulation, overstimulation. It's too much for her."

And Tessie thought, Stop fussing, but for some reason she could not stop tears from coming to her eyes. I'm too much for you, she thought.

That night she did not sleep, yet woke at four, with the words *I was too much for him* in her mind. She was wet between her legs and for a frightened moment she thought she had become incontinent, but then she knew. I scared the pants off both of them, she thought.

The paschal lamb — a turkey — was in the oven. The Passover table was set, and in the kitchen, Sebby was arranging the symbolic foods on a large tray, while Louise entertained Russell's cousins, who had arrived from New Jersey almost two hours early.

Tessie had resolved to be gentle and agreeable and to offer no suggestions to her daughter or anyone else, but she was realistic enough to admit her own limitations, and estimated she could manage that for one night at the outside.

"I'm leaving tomorrow," she told Louise. "I have to get back to the store." She was ready to argue, but there were no arguments. "Show Grandma what you are doing," she said to Sebby, turning away to hide her surprise.

Sebby proudly explained the Passover plate to Tessie: shredded romaine lettuce was the bitter herbs, to remind us of the suffering in Egypt; chopped apples and nuts mixed with honey, the mortar with which we worked; a turkey's neck, meant to be a shank bone, was the sacrificial lamb; parsley and salt water the meager food we ate, also our tears; an egg, symbol of the meal; horseradish, more bitterness. An extra wineglass was filled for Elijah the prophet and placed in the center of the table. Later, someone would open the door for him to enter, as he would one day, to herald the Messiah.

Tessie, who had practiced this ritual for many years, felt a slight swelling of emotion. She attributed it to the sweet, self-conscious incantation of her granddaughter.

"Give Grandma a hug," she said.

She took one off the stack of Haggadahs — the instruction booklets for the ceremony — and thumbed through it. She remembered the ones her mother had, tucked away in the bottom of the huge, ornate sideboard and taken out once a year, wine-stained and dried out from the heat of the house. They had borne the imprint of the Manischewitz Kosher Wine Company, which had distributed the copies free of charge. There had been a few from the Maxwell House Coffee Company as well. Louise bought hers at a dollar a book.

Tessie read: "Some people begin the meal with a hard-boiled egg dipped in salt water. Someone once asked Rabbi Meir Shapiro, famous Rabbi of Lublin, why Jews eat eggs on Passover. 'Because eggs symbolize the Jew,' Rabbi Shapiro answered. 'The more an egg is burned and boiled, the harder it gets.' "

The saying made her think of herself. A hard-boiled dame, Humphrey Bogart would have said. She hadn't been to a movie in over a year. She had watched fifteen old ones on

Louise's cable TV. Hard-boiled dames and strong silent types, she thought.

"Are you going to live with us?" Sebby asked.

Tessie gathered the child in her arms, feeling the resistant back of her, like integrity made bone. She wanted to say, playfully, Do you want me to, but was afraid of what she would hear.

"No, absolutely not, tootsie," she said, and felt her own relief as the child sighed. "Absolutely not."

At the Seder were Russell and Louise, Tessie, Sebby and the baby, the cousins Mike and Bonnie, and a widowed neighbor, old enough to be Louise's mother, but much younger than Tessie. Louise called her her "friend." Tessie was jealous, surprised to be jealous. Louise had always had "friends" like this: schoolteachers, piano teachers, dancing teachers, neighbors who used to, were always willing to tell Tessie what a wonderful little girl she had, in case she hadn't noticed, or inform her what her little girl thought or felt. The widow has her eye on me, Tessie thought. Once, she saw the widow smile and wink encouragingly at Louise.

Sitting here, at their Passover table, as Sebby raised the ceremonial questions, Tessie raised a question herself. Why had she never been here before? It seemed clear, from the conversation, that the cousin had been here before on Passover, and the neighbor referred to last year's turkey.

The neighbor complimented Sebby on her arrangement of the Seder plate.

"She has her grandpa's taste for ritual," Tessie said. Now what did I mean by that? she thought. All Barney had ever asked was that she keep two sets of dishes, but she had enlarged it into a major obsession. Had even made him (mythically) so religious that he was their excuse not to come to Louise's on the holidays. "Daddy doesn't like to travel," she used to say, when of course the truth was, she hadn't liked to . . . what? Her face tightened with the effort of getting through the small opening of *what* to an answer. Not now, she thought, putting her hands up to smooth her cheeks. Yet something, her feeling of being a stranger here, her regret, made itself known at the table, and there was a sudden silence.

Tessie resisted the desire to fill it. It was hard. She concentrated on the mounds on her plate, red cranberry sauce, orange carrots, white potatoes, brown turkey. She noticed Bonnie, how she pulled the food off her fork with her teeth, holding her lips apart so they didn't touch the food. How will she manage the pudding, Tessie thought.

Finally, Sebby said, striking just the right note, "Was my mother a good girl?" and Tessie was grateful: she was the insider at her daughter's table after all, the only one able to answer such a question.

"Are *you* a good girl?" Tessie asked, with unaccustomed coyness.

Sebby considered, then answered seriously, "Yes."

"So was your mother. A very good girl. And smart. Your mother was always using her head."

Louise looked up, smiled, there were tears in her eyes. But her voice was surprisingly tart.

"She used to test me," she said. "To see if I used my head." She spoke to the center of the table, though Tessie sensed she was saying this to the neighbor, the rival mother. Tattling.

"I did? How did I do that?" Tessie said, calling her bluff.

Louise kept talking to the center of the table. Tessie kept her eye on Bonnie, who was managing the cranberry sauce remarkably, look Ma, no lips.

"Once she sent me to the incinerator with my blouse half off—'Hurry up,' she said, 'the bag is dripping'—and when I got outside the door she locked it. And watched me from the peephole."

Tessie touched her own hand. It was cold. "I

just wanted to see what you would do first," she said. "Bang on the door to get in, or button up." She turned to Sebby. Sebby said "Button" and Tessie nodded her head approvingly. "Right," she said. "That's just what your mommy did. Smart. I knew she would."

Everyone laughed. "What else did she do?" Bonnie said.

Tessie wanted to say, Cut it.

"The burglar test," Louise said. She turned to Tessie. "Remember?"

Tessie said no, although she did.

"Sometimes, when she came home from the store, instead of using her key, she would impersonate a burglar."

Bonnie shrieked. "No."

"Louise, not now," Tessie said. "We still have more ceremony to do."

But Louise made believe she didn't hear.

"First she would pound on the door and rattle the knob. If I let her in, she took my key away for a month. If I asked who was there, she didn't answer me. If I opened after that, it meant no key for a week. When I asked for identification, she mumbled something." Louise made a funny sound to illustrate. Everyone laughed but Tessie and Louise. "In that case letting her in was not a punishable offense, since I had been deliberately misled."

"Led down the garden path," Tessie said, drawn in. "I remember. What would you do after the door was open and you were faced with a burglar, ready to maul you?" she recited. She had used the word *maul*. She turned to the neighbor and explained, "It sounds a little crazy, but I was just teaching her to be careful."

Louise grinned. "If you are a burglar I am running outside," she said.

"Out? Why not in? Wouldn't you try to lock yourself in?"

Bonnie shrieked again. "Oh, you are too much, Tillie."

"No way," Louise said, "no way. Because it is safer out in the street where I can run for my life than locked in with you."

Their eyes locked then, and Louise's filled again. "With a burglar," she said. She turned to Bonnie. "Tessie," she said. "Not Tillie. My mother's name is Tessie."

It was time for dessert. In addition to Louise's pudding (she called it "flahn") was the neighbor's sponge cake, which had a good reputation from previous Passovers. The neighbor was modest, and diverted attention to Bonnie's offerings, brought all the way from New Jersey. There were two, both feats of magic performed without flour, everyone was assured by Mike. The secret, he confided, was marshmallow fluff. Tessie accepted a lump of everything on her plate, and listened while the conversation moved from recipes, to traffic, holidays, children. Tessie was very tired. She took her coffee into the living room, which adjoined the dining room but was cooler, and almost dark. After a moment, the neighbor joined her on the couch. Her name was Irene.

"Wasn't that delicious?" Irene said. "Your daughter is a wonderful cook."

"Do you have a daughter?" Tessie said.

"Yes," Irene said.

Tessie raised her eyebrows but didn't say anything.

"We don't get along," Irene said.

"How nice," Tessie said. They both smiled.

Irene left at eleven. The children had gone to sleep at ten. By eleven-thirty Russell and Mike were dozing on the couch, and Tessie and Louise were struggling not to fall asleep as well. Still, Bonnie made no move to leave.

Tessie was feeling more like herself. "I would throw them out," she said to Louise, in the kitchen.

"Mom, please, let me handle it," Louise said.

Louise's makeup was worn off, and Tessie stifled the impulse to tell her so. She smoothed her daughter's hair off her face, an infrequent gesture, though the comment that usually replaced it — too messy, too drab, needed a wash

216

— was on the tip of her tongue. She hates me, Tessie thought, as she had of her granddaughter earlier. The thought was not altogether bad. All the time she was disapproving of Louise, Louise was disapproving of her. It had a symmetry Tessie liked. They were even. That's my girl, Tessie even thought.

They returned to the living room together, Tessie's arm around Louise's waist. She tried to be tactful: "How long does it take you children to get home from here?" she asked Bonnie, solicitously.

Louise gave her a warning look.

"Not too long," Bonnie said.

"But I imagine the traffic is going to be heavy," Tessie said.

Louise sighed, and then said quickly, "Why don't you two stay over?" She rushed on, about how it would be no trouble at all, to open a Hide-A-Bed. Tessie was aghast, but all at once realized with pleasure and surprise, that Louise was being clever. Devious and clever, my god, Tessie thought. And it worked.

"No, no, honey," Bonnie said to Louise, shaking Mike to wake him. "We would really love to, but we can't."

"Are you sure?" Louise said, innocently.

"No, really," Bonnie said. "We have to go to the cemetery tomorrow."

"Oh, I'm sorry," Louise said.

"No, no one died," she said. "I mean not recently." She glanced at Tessie. "We're just going to show Mama and Papa the new Mercedes," she explained.

Louise gasped, and Tessie coughed and covered her mouth and excused herself and Louise ran after, saying "Oh, Mom, let me help you," and they were gone so long Russell had to see his cousins out.

And so it was that mother and daughter finally fell into each other's arms, laughing until they cried, and crying until Russell had to come and see what was going on.

When she left Russell and Louise, Tessie promised them she would do something about the store.

Well, she had, she thought, though not exactly what she had promised to do. She had intended to put an ad in the newspaper once and for all, for a buyer for the store. She had even sat down at the typewriter one morning and typed it out in capital letters on white typing paper: BOOKSTORE FOR SALE. (Can you sell a bookstore and keep the books? I'm not finished going through them yet.) EXCELLENT UP AND COMING (all right, down and going) WEST BRONX NEIGHBORHOOD. FAIR PRICE. But

218

then she couldn't find a #10 envelope. And she was out of stamps. It was days before she found a #10 envelope, in the bottom drawer of Barney's desk. And the stamp, which was in the change purse of an old wallet, had no stickum on the back, and by the time she found the old, half-used bottle of Le Page's glue in the hardware drawer in the kitchen, and cracked it open, the stamp was gone again, and the white typing paper was all dog-eared and smudged with something that looked like grape jelly. She had fully intended to retype the letter. But in the meantime (she thought), just as a preliminary measure (she told herself), to test the waters (so to speak), why not just put the dog-eared copy of the ad on the Local Action bulletin board? To see if someone local (that lingering fever, M. H. Ross?) would be interested in buying. Yes, that was a better idea. She was glad she had come up with it. But it was days before she managed to remember to stop off at the committee headquarters, and when she did (oh, too bad) the storefront was closed. The next time, she couldn't reach the bulletin board, she was too short. After she left, she realized she might have stood on a chair, or asked the woman at the desk to put it up for her. She said to herself she would try that when she went back. And she did, some time later.

By standing on tiptoe, she found she was tall enough after all, to reach the bulletin board. But, uh-oh, no tacks. She was turning to go, when the girl at the desk said, "Why don't you take one of the old ones down, those over on that side, and use the tack from it?" Why don't you mind your own business, Tessie thought. But because she was really trying, she did.

The notice she took down said part-time/full-time help, intelligent and willing to work, and suddenly it became clear to Tessie that what she needed was someone intelligent and willing to work to help her fix up the place, and *then* she would be in a position to ask a good price. So she threw away her own notice, ripped it into little pieces, and went home to call the job seeker.

Matthew. He was light brown, about twenty years old, but with a frail, sickly physique which made him look either like a boy of twelve or an old man.

When she had asked him why he wanted the job, he had shrugged. And when she said she would hire him, he didn't smile, or thank her. He reminded her of the one who had stolen her garbage, or one of the three from the bus: the one who looked straight in her eyes. This one did, too. Yet he did not frighten her, though she was sure he meant to. Do I know you? she had said, and he hesitated, and said no. Since she was in no mood to be friendly, his sullenness freed her.

The first day after she hired him, she didn't know what to tell him to do.

"Wait here," she had said, and walked to the other end of the store, to think. She and Barney had never had anyone work for them, although Tessie had always tried to talk him into it. She liked the idea of being a boss. She would be good, but she just didn't know how to get started. When she came back, he was sweeping the floor.

She never had to tell him to sweep. She never had to tell him to do anything. He was an excellent worker. As a matter of fact, the only time he did not do something was when she told him to. She noticed this, and now pretended not to notice.

"You should keep those windows clean," he said one day, and then climbed in and did them. He carted the trash from the basement for the pickup. He used a little implement with a sharp razor inserted in it, and slit the sides of each carton, flattened it, folded it, so that what used to take up all the alley space behind the store now only occupied one large box. It used to take Tessie two trips, sometimes three, arms full, to carry up the trash. Matthew did it in one, though he couldn't lift the box and had to drag it up one step at a time. He worked quickly and efficiently at everything, as long as she didn't give him orders. If she did, he sulked at her, as if everything in the store, in his life, in the world was her fault. He glared as if to say, I could do something or, I could say something if I wanted to, and sometimes even cleaned his fingernails with the razor, in an imitation of some tough guy, to frighten her, she was sure. She was not frightened.

She knew he lied, yet felt he was honest. He came in late every day. Always with an excuse.

"I got to drop my brother at the day care."

"I thought your mother did that."

"Oh, yeah, she does, only today she went to the clinic."

Or,

"I got to take my mother to the clinic, she don't feel good."

"Your nose is growing, Matthew," Tessie said. But he didn't get it.

He dressed to kill, in shiny clothing. One day she told him, "Matthew, you look like a Nestlé's Milk Chocolate bar, all wrapped up in silver and blue. But semisweet, just semi."

He did not understand her jokes.

He didn't always do as she wished. When it was warm, as it had begun to be, he took his shirt off while he worked. She told him to keep it on, that it did not look nice for customers to see him like that. He gave her a dirty look but put it on; the next time she saw him it was off again. She also told him not to smoke down in the basement, it was a fire trap and could go up like *that*. When she came downstairs, sniffing the smoke-laden air, he said to her, "I don't want to hear nothing about smoking. I just lit one which I did because I forgot what you said, and then I put it right out. So don't accuse me."

Tessie raised her hands in mock defense. "Who said a word?" she said. "Don't get so insulted."

"I'm not insulted," he said.

"He's not insulted," she said. "He's above such things. He is defensive, and he is offensive, but he won't admit either. You know what you are? You are a defensive-offensive sandwich." He didn't get it, but was beginning to know her. "I think you made another joke," he said, and she was the one who laughed.

Russell and Louise don't understand why she hired him, why she kept him, how she could trust him. "How can you stand that nasty eye he gives you all the time?" Louise said.

"He doesn't mean it, it's all for show," Tessie said.

The first time Victory saw him, she took

Tessie aside, and trembling, said, "That's him, Tessie, he's one of them."

And although it would have been easy for Tessie to say, "They are *all* one of them," because Victory had been going around accusing everyone, including priests and ten-year-old children, she knew it was possible that he was. Yet she defended him. She wondered about it sometimes. It was not that she liked him so much, it was that she knew him so well. It made her feel safe. She knew him, it seemed, better than she had ever known anyone. She knew the bad of him, and would somehow co-opt it, and she knew the good of him, and would bring it out.

"Matthew," she said, after the third week, "here," and gave him a key to the store. From the look he gave her, he sided with Russell and Louise. But he took it.

The Widows are meeting at Tessie's apartment, to celebrate her return home and Victory's recovery. Maybe *celebration* is not the word, Tessie thinks. Since Victory's mugging, which she refers to as her "accident," Pearl's dog has been hit by a car and Helen has been under the weather. They talk about health.

"I had to go off my diet to bring myself back to normal," Helen says.

"Diet?" Pearl says. "What kind of diet? Look at her, she's on a diet. All ninety pounds of her. You'll drop dead yet from your diets."

Helen says nothing, but lets her eyes rest on Pearl's full bosom, which tonight is encased in a tight, bright green turtleneck. "What happened to *your* diet?" she says, and moves the honey-roasted peanuts away from her. Pearl moves them back and continues eating them. Helen moves them away again.

The two of them remind Tessie of herself and Barney. She sent him to the store one day, to buy soap. He came home with something that smelled of cloves. How she hated cloves. She didn't say so. She just threw the soap away. Came back into the bathroom that afternoon, there it was, back in the soap dish. She threw it away again. Next morning, it was back. Barney never said a word, she never.

Pearl slaps Helen's hand lightly and moves the peanuts back.

Tessie thinks now, I could have put the soap in the incinerator, where he couldn't get at it. She smiles. But that wasn't the point, was it? What was? To be in the game together, their game.

Pearl says, "Mel never *let* me diet," but puts her own hand over the peanut dish. "He always liked me just the way I was." Was that Pearl and

225

Mel's game? She turns to Helen. "Why, do I look fat?" It is, of course, a challenge.

"Of course you don't," Victory says quickly.

"Don't mind me," Helen says, rubbing her face. "I'm all nerved up."

But it is Victory who looks bad. Her face is still slightly discolored and her jaw is still wired on one side, making her usual tight smile even tighter, and more clearly the grimace it always was. Her eyes are sunken in deep troughs and her rouge is streaked. The pencil line which usually extends to her eyebrows so smoothly tonight strays almost into her hairline. Her voice has come down an octave, but it is weak and flat.

"Tired," she says. She has just returned to work.

They talk of vacations.

"Is-real," Pearl says.

"I've been," Helen says. Wherever you mention, Helen's been.

"Or Florida."

"Too crowded," Helen says. "With old people."

"What do you think *you* are?" Pearl says. "What about Vegas?"

"Not for Victory . . ." Helen says.

". . . or even the Coast," Pearl says. Pearl rolls the names of places (most of which she has never been to, Tessie knows) off her tongue like the nicknames of famous movie stars she knows personally.

"Depends where on the Coast," Helen says.

Pearl turns to her, exasperated. "Helen, stop already," she says.

"I'm not interested in traveling," Victory says.

"How can you say that?" Helen says.

"I can say it," Victory says wearily. "If I want the sun, I can take my beach chair outside in front of the building. Or if I want to go to the trouble, I can go up to Orchard Beach."

Helen laughs. "Irwin used to call it Horse-dash-beach, to rhyme with 'it.'"

Pearl shakes her head.

"'Sand is sand," Victory says. "And if I want entertainment, I can turn on my twenty-one-inch color TV, which has excellent reception."

Tessie, who has always resisted going away, feels in some way, in recent days, like a world traveler. Unafraid, almost. "I might like to go somewhere," she says.

Victory looks surprised. Maybe betrayed.

Pearl shifts, releasing a strong smell of perfume and tobacco, like the inside of an old pocketbook. Suddenly, Tessie can smell Helen's perfume, and Victory's as well. A small headache begins over her left eye. She opens the window.

"You'll never meet anyone hanging around the house," Pearl says to Victory. Thus, as always, the talk turns to men.

"Who wants to?" Victory says.

"Not me," Helen says. "He would have to have six million dollars, chauffeured cars, a big house with servants to make me bananas and sour cream and clean up the dishes after, to get me interested. . . ."

Victory nods, agreeing.

"When was the last time you ate bananas and cream?" Pearl says.

". . . and his pants would have to zip up the back," Helen continues, ignoring Pearl's question.

Helen is against sex. She is suspicious if you claim to like it. She says, "Sex shmex," and claims one day she told Irwin, "The kitchen is closed," and from then on he never bothered her with it again.

Tessie supposes her childlessness is a sort of proof that she means what she says, but for someone who doesn't like it, she seems to talk an awful lot about it. Yet there is something virginal, or girlish, about her. Straightbacked, Tessie decides, from not ever having carried a baby low on the hip, or bent over a playpen or toilet, crib, bed, floor, kiddie pool, bucket swing, damn Louise, I wasn't that bad.

Pearl's face is red, as if she is accused of something. She puts her hands up to her breasts, protectively. "I don't miss sex, either," she says, "but companionship . . ."

"Who said *miss* it," Helen says, spraying her drink. "I never liked it in the first place." She tosses her head, daring anyone to top that.

There is no changing the subject with Helen, either. "Half the women who say they like it are lying," she says, glaring at Pearl, and then at Tessie. She gets up to mix herself another drink as Tessie murmurs, "Who, me?" She bumps into the coffee table. Victory raises her eyebrows when Helen's back is turned. Pearl averts her eyes, scrutinizing the brown velvet of Tessie's couch.

"Bring me a wine," she calls to Helen.

We are like couples, Tessie thinks. Victory and me, Pearl and Helen, loyal, sharing little secrets, sniping now and then, helping one another. Sniping. There is something wrong between Pearl and Helen tonight.

"Since when do you eat ham, Tessie?" Helen asks, coming back to the couch. A string of pink meat hangs from the corner of her mouth. Tessie thinks of watching fish being fed to the seals in the Bronx Zoo, how they snapped them up. She will say she doesn't want any when I offer it, yet she dangled a piece over her mouth and snapped it up back there in the kitchen. She says she doesn't like sex. She is so hungry, Tessie thinks.

Helen sways, but sets the tray down safely, and Pearl leans over and steadies her as she sinks back down.

"She always ate ham," Victory says.

"But not in the house," Pearl insists. "Tessie always kept kosher. Didn't you?"

She had, until the night Barney died.

And then, after everyone had left her alone, she had gone into the kitchen, thinking she would make tea. She had stood in the middle of the room turning slowly in a circle, as if in a children's game, not coming to a stop until she was dizzy. There were crumbs on the toaster she noticed, and wiping them off she noticed crumbs underneath. Crumbs lead you to more crumbs. She removed the toaster and scoured the counter until the yellow lines in the patterned Formica stood out clearly. The toaster shed crumbs all over the kitchen floor when she moved it, so she swept the floor. She rearranged all the cakes and food offerings people had brought, lining them up along the counter like rows of silver foil buttons. The refrigerator door and the outsides of the cupboards had to be washed, because they now looked dingy in contrast to the newly washed table. And then, thinking she was done, saying she was done, she opened all the cupboards and began removing the dishes and mixing them up, *milchig* with *fleischig,* saying out loud with the rhythm of putting them back in the cupboard, "No more kosher," over and over again. It had been 3:00 A.M. before she finished and went to bed. She had climbed in on her side and lay awake, listening to a distant siren and then to the kitchen clock. For an instant before sleep she wondered what Barney would say when he found out, and then remembered that Barney was dead.

"I wondered why you did that," Pearl says.

Tessie shrugs. "I had to have things my way," she says.

"He would have killed you," Victory says, her voice stronger, proud and proprietary of her best friend's life, secrets.

"I don't believe it," Helen says, supplying the gambit.

" 'Kill' meaning . . . ," prompts Pearl.

" 'Kill' meaning *kill*," Victory insists.

"Oh, come now, Victory," Tessie says. "Let's not get carried away."

" 'Kill' meaning what, then?" Pearl challenges.

"Here we go, rehashing husbands for a change," Tessie says. Yet it interests her. Does she know? Was Barney a killer? Or, what kind of killer was he?

Not violent, like Victory's George. Barney, never. Only that once, in the store window. Oh, twice. Put his fist through something, remember? In the spring. One night, he came home with bloody knuckles. And didn't want to say. Didn't want to, or was playing the coax-me game? She had seen him coming, blood on his hands, slapping the *Post* down on the hall table, reaching for Haig & Haig Pinch in the cupboard above the sink, that was unusual in itself. He had been to a book fair in Manhattan. *What happened to you?* she had asked and he had said, *Nothing. Well, nothing is dripping all over my rug,* she had said sarcastically. Was I always sarcastic? Was that the kind of killer I was? She had pulled the story out of him. On the subway, coming home, a man wouldn't give up his seat to a pregnant woman. Barney had asked him to. The man refused. Barney persisted. The man lost his temper and hit Barney. Barney had hit him back.

It was a matter of integrity, he had told her. And she had laughed. Had she? How could she have? Had it been that shock — she had it again right now: *Who is this stranger?* — that had made her laugh? How could she have ignored the greatness of it, the chivalry, to do

232

such a foolish thing for the sake of a woman. Regret, like a wave of morning sickness, or menopausal heat, swept her. She fanned herself.

"Enough with Barney," she says. "Enough with husbands."

But then she remembered, how could she have forgotten what happened next? After she had laughed at him, he had stopped talking to her. Stopped altogether. Stopped dead. For four months, *four months* he had not spoken a word. How do you forget a thing like that? At first she didn't even realize it, just thought he was Barney being more Barney than usual. Then the silence got bigger, grew like a baby, small and obstinate at first, then demanding attention. It stopped her from eating, sleeping. She pleaded with him at first, oh, Barney, come on. He clenched his jaw, turned away. Then, just as she was getting accustomed to it, forgot about it for a few minutes now and then, Barney had asked her where the cleaning ticket for his good suit was, shocking her so with the sound of his voice that she cried for two days straight.

" 'Kill' meaning clam up," she says.

She had never loved him more. He was so romantic, with that small frown, the jaws clenched so tightly the skin of his face pulled taut and his eyes almost slanted. It was the same look he had had when she made him (had she really made him?) smoke a pipe. His teeth had bitten the stem that way, his eyes had narrowed against the smoke.

"You two were some pair," Pearl says.

"We were, weren't we?" Tessie says.

"George used to call them Stonewall and Jackson," Victory says.

"He too can be replaced," Helen says, unsteadily.

Tessie doesn't know if she would want to replace him anymore, not even with another just like him. It had been such an accidental dance, the logic and rhythm having to do with not tripping over each other: Tessie forward, Barney back, Barney at her, Tessie in retreat (but always with that little come-hither glance over her shoulder to make sure he followed). Equal after all, and what both of them wanted. And now, until the damn money is found, the dance goes on.

"I like living alone," Helen says. "I like my privacy. Do what I want, eat when I want, watch what I want on TV."

She says it defiantly, as if someone won't believe her.

That is the party line, Tessie thinks, yet, at the same time, it is true. So why all the showing off, the bravery about not being lonely, if the truth is you aren't lonely at all, and bravery has nothing to do with it? Part of being the pampered sex. How else can a woman get some consideration? How would a woman sound if she said, right out in the open, I don't miss my husband? But if she says it so you won't believe her . . .

"I can't eat alone," Pearl says.

"That's ridiculous," Tessie says. "An egg is still an egg, a piece of fish is still a piece of fish. What difference does it make if someone chews the same time you do?"

"I don't know," Pearl says. "I don't seem to take the trouble to fix anything if it's just for me. I can't cook myself. I can't eat myself. Look." She holds out the waistband of her skirt.

"Since you're still a fourteen I can't see how it's done you any harm," Helen says. Her face is flushed.

Pearl says, "Well, all I know is I can't."

"Why?" Helen persists. "The portions don't come out right? There is no one to pick his teeth, belch from your cabbage?"

Pearl slams her hand down on the table. If there is one thing Pearl is against, it is vulgarity.

"Helen, stop that. Freddy does not do that. You're being nasty."

Victory and Tessie exchange looks. "Freddy?"

235

"She's having a romance with the man who delivers the dry cleaning," Helen says. Her eyes are red.

"He is *not* the man who delivers the dry cleaning. He owns three dry-cleaning stores," Pearl says. She delivers this explanation with her back to Helen, but then she turns to her again. "And what business is it of yours?" she says.

Helen is rubbing the arm of the chair she is in, back and forth, back and forth.

"I just hate to see you make a mistake," she says. It sounds lame.

How about, Tessie thinks, *Don't leave me. Or, How can you abandon me, what about our friendship, don't I mean anything to you? It is sex that makes this Freddy a more valued friend than I am? You know you don't love him. Why can't a friendship be like a marriage?* And, most of all, *If you need him to take care of you, I will begin to lose hope I can do it by myself. I will begin to think I need someone to take care of me.*

Pearl makes her announcement. Officially. There is no down-talk then, only up-talk; wonderful, beige silk, Is-real in July, prenuptial agreements, small cocktail ring, redecorating the house. There is no talk of love. Helen rallies, amid praise and hand squeezes, and takes one step down, where she will settle for

236

the Bronze Medal, Tessie thinks, because Freddy's captured the Silver. And Irwin, because he is dead as much as because he is a saint, keeps the Gold.

"He's a fine man, Irwin would approve," Helen says, to make up. Pearl hugs her and kisses the air beyond her cheek.

At night, after they are gone, Tessie is sleepless again. Yet she is not restless this night, and settles comfortably into a momentary pocket of clarity, where the questions she wants to ask are sharply and easily formed, and the ability to push forward toward an answer is as uncommon and delicious as a perfect glass of iced tea.

What is this need? To be taken care of.

What can you *not* do, in reality, on your own? Pay bills? Figure things out? Find things? Screw? Change fuses? Light a pilot light? Cook? Eat? Listen to the news? Laugh at something? Have a thought? Drive long distances at night?

Drive. Fine, let's take drive, then. Long distances? Same as short, only more so. You can make them short, by stopping. But what if you have to go on? You don't have to. Fine. Long distances, then, broken up. But at night. Ooooo, night. Stop at twilight. What if you have to be somewhere on time, and can't afford to stop? To get to your daughter's for dinner.

Don't. Be firm and tell her you can't be there any sooner than you can, nor later.

Okay, pay bills. You can't figure things out in the checkbook, you say. Ask someone. The number on the bottom in the column that says "Due" on the statement is the number you pay. You will find it corresponds to the number you saw on the receipt when you took the dress home with you from Alexander's. You had no trouble reading it then. Don't be snide. Well, then, don't patronize yourself. You're not stupid, you know. What if you can't find something? Where are your glasses? On the end of your nose. What if you can't find them? Look for them, and if they aren't there, assume they are lost. Replace them or live without them. Does this go for husbands? Yes. Screw? Well, come back to that. Listen to the news? Can Libya or Lebanon be so confusing to a woman who kept peace between a stubborn husband and a stubborn father? With issues layered upon issues, of power, might, pride, economics? What do you tip a waiter when you find yourself alone in a restaurant? If you are a man there is a rule you were born knowing. If you are a woman you give a little bit more than he deserves or double the tax. Screw? Well, sex then. Get to know Mary Fist. Let your fingers do the walking. Make it a self-service establishment.

What if you grow old? And ugly? Old you will. Ugly you have always been, except in the eyes of those who know you, where you have been ugly and beautiful and everything in between, and in your own, where you have been everything short of beautiful, up to but not including gorgeous.

Who will take care of you if you get sick? Who ever did take care of you but you? If you are too sick to cook soup you will open a can, and if you can't open a can that will mean it is time to see a doctor, who will give you a pill or put you in the hospital. Where doctors and nurses will take care of you, and you will either live or not grow old after all. Who will visit you? Your friends. You made more friends than he did. They will come in the afternoon with magazines and send get-well cards and tie up the hospital switchboard with their calls.

She could ask every question clearly and answer it with a lifting heart, all except one: Who is there for you to take care of?

Matthew.

Twice a week she let him open the store, so she could sleep late. She didn't sleep late, but took her time cleaning up the apartment, watched "The Pyramid" once in a while, walked the six blocks to the store slowly, stopped to pick up a bag of assorted Dunkin' Donuts. She shared the donuts with Matthew in pantomime, because if she offered him one he said "Nah" and waved his hand at her, as if she had proposed something ridiculous, but if she just held the bag up and open to him, he turned his head the other way, so as not to see himself taking one, and helped himself.

He had a delicate stomach. He drank milk straight from the container, a quart a day. Not what you would expect from such a *macho muchacho*.

One morning, she came into the store late, and he was not upstairs as she had told him to be. She went down to the basement, intending to talk to him about it, but when she got there she found him down on his knees, either praying or doubled up with stomach cramps. She asked him, and he told her there was nothing wrong, and moaned.

"Right," she said, "sure," and stood there letting the silence work.

"My stomach," he said finally, "hurts."

"Ahh, oh really?" she said, but then dropped the sarcasm, because he was really in pain. She put her arm firmly about his narrow shoulders and lifted him. He pulled away, but followed when she walked into the bathroom.

"Welcome to the wonderful world of My-lanta," she said, and handed him the green bottle and a spoon.

He backed away. "Nah," he said.

"Come on, what are you afraid of," she said, using the irresistible goad, then moving her lips along with the predictable answer:

"I'm not afraid."

"Look," she said, "it isn't going to hurt you. It'll just coat the lining of your stomach, soothe it." She held it out to him again.

"What's it call?" he said.

She was standing there, holding the bottle in full view of him, and he was looking straight at it, and after about half a minute, it came to her that Matthew did not know how to read very well, if at all.

"My-lan-ta," she said, pointing. Then she did what she did with the donuts, just held it out to him without saying any more. Sure enough, he took it. She left him alone, and after a few minutes he came upstairs. He didn't say anything, but since he was back at work, she assumed he was better. At the end of the day, while she was putting on her coat, he said, "That stuff worked good," and almost smiled.

"Help yourself anytime," she said.

After that, whenever he didn't feel well, he went for the Mylanta. How did she know this?

241

He never said, and she didn't find him doubled up again, but she knew. She could tell a trip downstairs to get stock from a trip downstairs to smoke a cigarette (even before she could smell the smoke) from a trip downstairs to take Mylanta.

A few days later, Matthew was sweeping for the third time, and Tessie realized he had nothing to do. She gave him an invoice, and told him to check in a small shipment of books.

"Nah, I got other things to do," he said, backing away.

"They'll wait," she said. She pulled a stack of books from the box and showed him how to see, on the spine, where the books went: "FIC" meant fiction, "MYS" was mystery, "NF" was nonfiction.

"Can't you do this?" he said.

"You don't know how to read," she said.

"Yes, I do," he said. "I just don't like to."

"Matthew," she said.

"I'm not kidding," he said, and opening one of the books, read haltingly.

"Good," she said, and left him with the invoice. "Take all the time you need."

It took him all day, but he checked the shipment in. She was so proud of him that she was sure he was proud of himself. And she felt so kind, and even fond of him, she imagined he must be feeling the same way toward her.

"You did it fine," she said, and though he didn't acknowledge the compliment, when she closed up that night, he waited while she double-locked the door and then he tried it, saying solemnly, "You got to be careful."

"Don't worry," she said.

"Who's worried?" he said.

The next morning she allowed her eyes to rest on him benevolently. "I am very pleased with the way you are working out," she told him. He nodded like a king accepting his due.

In the afternoon, she was sitting at the back of the store, behind the big old mahogany desk she had moved up from the basement, when the front door was pushed open violently. The shove and clatter of it was like a forced entry (six big ones, it sounded like, she thought) and though she didn't move, her fingers closed over the cheese knife on the desk. When silence followed the burst of sound, she waited.

Then, "Matthew," she called, "the damn door blew open." She called him twice, and when he didn't respond, she swiveled the chair and thumped on the floor with her heel. He was downstairs. He could pretend not to hear her voice, but he'd have to hear the pounding.

He came upstairs.

243

"The door blew open," she said.

"We gotta lock it," he said.

"If we lock the door, how do customers get in?" she said.

"Like the other stores, they ring the buzzer, you press the buzzer, you let them in, you let them out."

She shook her head. "Not a bookstore," she said. "People like to wander in and wander out. Anyway, there's nothing here to steal."

He looked at her sharply. "You got a cash register, don't you?"

"Don't worry, I can protect myself."

"Oh, yeah?" he said, pointing to the cheese knife she still held in her hand. "With that little sticker?"

"I also have you to protect me," she said.

He didn't answer, but went to close the door. He brought back an envelope. "This was on the floor," he said.

Dear Mrs. Goodman:

I paid you a visit last week, but saw the shop closed up and got worried that something happened to you, such as an unfortunate accident. May I say that the violence that is too common in this neighborhood should be a good reason

for you to want to get out.
                    Sincerely,
                    N. J. Ross

N. J. Ross? What the hell was going on? Couldn't he even remember his own phony initials? What the hell was going on?

"Did you see anyone?" she asked Matthew. He said no.

"Lock the door," she said. "For now."

Instead of a buzzer, she installed a big, old-fashioned bell, the kind stores used to have, which jingled and clanged and made a racket every time someone touched the door.

Next time, she thought.

Matthew told her about a friend who gave him good advice. This friend, Mita, was the one who told him to get a job and quit fooling around.

"Good advice," Tessie said.

Mita told him if he was good and kept his job and did it good, she would take care of him.

"I'll make exactly the same offer," Tessie said.

He seemed so devoted to Mita, Tessie wondered if his mother was jealous.

She treated him to Chinese food from Joe Fig's for lunch. He brought it through the adjoining door, which he knew about now and used whenever he wanted to go upstairs and play the numbers. She had black bean sauce without the shrimp, and he had plain fried rice. He bent over the container and ate slowly, as if he were afraid. He reminded her again of an old man. She thought they were friendly enough, so she said to him, "What's the matter?" but his face darkened and he said nothing.

His friends visited him. Three of them. The word *gang* came off them like a smell. Tessie didn't like them, but she didn't say anything to Matthew. They followed him around the store, talking in Spanish, and he took them downstairs, and in the way he didn't turn around when she called his name but just led them down the basement steps, she knew he was being defiant. When he came up without them, she knew he had let them out through the adjoining door into Hum's, and this disturbed her. She said later, "I don't like your friends."

He didn't answer. Then she said, "How does Mita like those friends of yours?"

"Don't worry about Mita," he said.

The bell jangled. It had been doing that more and more lately, and business had been getting better. Barney had predicted it: students, young intellectuals looking for cheap rents and a place to make their own, social workers, it was all just a matter of time, he had said, before you turn around, everyone would want to come, like what was happening to Washington Heights, across the bridge.

"Customer," she called out. But it was not, this time. It was Matthew's friends, again. They looked beyond her, as if she wasn't there. She let them walk past, but followed behind as they went down the aisle to where Matthew was standing, a book in his hand.

"Hey," one of them said, and put his palms out.

Matthew slapped him.

The other one nodded, and the third one grinned. The third one, the big one, took the book out of Matthew's hand and balanced it on his head; it didn't stay and when it fell on the floor, he kicked it. That did it for Tessie. She couldn't ignore what they were up to anymore, and she couldn't pretend Matthew was not one of them. She clapped her hands together, and the sound startled them into looking at her. With a sudden movement she locked her hand inside the belt of the one who said "Hey" and dragged him quickly, like he was a box of garbage, to the front door, which she opened. "Out," she said, and pushed him back through the open door. "Out, out," she said to the others, pushing.

She felt she knew what she was doing, even

though there was a risk, and she also knew damn well that the three of them (all right, four, counting Matthew) could cut her up into little pieces if they got the chance. She knew, she didn't fool herself that even one of them could do the job. All she had on her side was the element of surprise, and her anger. She knew today that she was not Superwitch; she was not the little tailor; and she was not even the little tailor's wife. This was not some fairy tale.

But "Out" she said anyway, and pushed them into the street.

"You," she said to Matthew, pointing her finger at him. "I know who you are." Then she pushed him out, too, and locked the door behind them.

But I am not Victory, either, she said to herself. That I am not.

All night, she was wide awake, imagining repercussions, yet she did not regret what she had done. In the morning she woke, feeling light, rested. When she arrived at the store, ten minutes early, Matthew was waiting. The store key dangled from his finger.

"What do you want?" she said.

"I was going to tell them don't come any-more," he said.

"Sure you were," she said, but then let him

come in. "Sweep up back here," she said. "It's filthy."

He gave her a dirty look. "First I got to do the garbage," he said. She smiled: everything was back to normal. Before he went downstairs he said, "Hey, they ain't going to bother you."

Loyalty, Tessie thought. It was the best revenge.

There were three customers in the store: an old woman with a Macy's shopping bag (shoplifting was a problem, Tessie looked around for Matthew to give him the eyebrow, *Look out for this one*), a young woman with a baby hanging down in front of her in a sling, heavy gold earrings hanging from her ears (which told Tessie she was part of the new redevelopment group and probably had worried parents in the suburbs), and a woman tugging a little boy by the arm. The woman knew Matthew. Tessie wondered if she was his mother. If she is I will have to give her a discount, Tessie thought. Matthew was in Science Fiction, working on the shelves. He saw the woman and appeared to hide. The woman looked for him, looked piercingly at him. He disappeared again. He moved slowly down the aisle, ducking, his head gliding like a wooden cutout in a shooting gallery, and every time the woman fired off a look he dove down as if he had been hit.

Tessie rang up the young woman's purchase, a copy of Dr. Spock. She noted the look of good, suburban nutrition in the girl's healthy face, the worn, torn pants and work shirt. She watched the old woman leave, wondering what, in the Macy's bag, was leaving with her. The woman with the little boy came toward her.

"May I help?" Tessie said.

The woman smiled, but instead of answering Tessie, she looked over to Matthew and called him.

"Hey," she said.

"Matthew's mother?" Tessie said.

"Forbid," the woman said.

"No," Matthew mumbled, eyeing the woman.

"Mrs. Gloria Muñoz," the woman said, reaching a hand across Matthew to shake Tessie's, seemingly by accident threatening to slap him as her hand fluttered by.

"How is he behaving?" she said, pointing at him with her thumb.

He looked at her with clear hatred now, his eyes narrowing. But he did not back away from the hand.

Tessie said "Fine" and wondered what was going on.

"You sure?" Mrs. Muñoz said, looking skeptical.

Tessie didn't like being challenged. "I said so," she said. "Who are you?"

"I am a member of the Acción Locale. We are keeping an eye on Mateo."

"Never heard of you," Tessie said. "Are you the one he calls Mita?"

Mrs. Muñoz looked amused. "No," she said. "But I speak for Mita, to Mateo and others. I . . . translate, you might say." This seemed to amuse her.

"Well," Tessie said, "she certainly sounds like a wonderful woman, and Matthew certainly has a lot of respect for her."

Mrs. Muñoz turned to Matthew. "Go away," she said. He went. To Tessie she said, "Mita is a spirit."

"She certainly is," Tessie said agreeably, wondering how long this was going to continue.

"No, you don't understand," Mrs. Muñoz said. "Many of us who still have strong ties with home believe in spirits who will take care of them and also who see everything they do. That one" — she shook her head toward Matthew — "is a bad one, but a big believer, like his mother. He steals, he lies, he hurts." Tessie opened her mouth to protest and Mrs. Muñoz held up her hand. "His mother brings him to me because he is getting stomach pains and she thinks there is some connection between the

251

things he is up to and the devil in his stomach. . . ." Mrs. Muñoz shrugged. "He has an ulcer, the little animal, serves him right," she said. "But no use telling him that. He won't believe it."

"What does he believe?"

"The spirit sticks him with sharp points, teeth, what-have-you."

"What do you have to do with it?" Tessie said.

"I communicate with Mita," she said. "You might say I'm her New York rep."

"You don't believe it yourself, then?"

Mrs. Muñoz laughed. "Are you kidding? I have a sociology degree from Hunter College. No, I don't believe it anymore. At least not the way I used to. But with some people, it works. It relieves, mobilizes unseen help, gives strength. And it's a living. I'm a widow. I got two kids." She tugged the hand of the little boy. "Not this one, this one I caught trying to lift a toothbrush over by the drugstore. Him I'm taking home. My two are in school where they belong. But this one" — again she jerked her head toward where Matthew had been standing — "don't let him fool you. He's a smart one. And pretty."

"So am I," Tessie said. "Smart."

"Look," Gloria Muñoz said, "it may be none

of my business, but the ethnic population of the community gets blamed for a lot of things, and we are willing to be responsible for our own. But if you take it upon yourself to do your own stupid brand of social work . . ."

"The ethnic population?" Tessie said. "Don't you call yourself Puerto Rican anymore?"

Gloria Muñoz flushed, then grinned. "All right," she said. "Don't listen to what I am saying. But just remember to be careful. You are running a risk, trusting an animal like that."

And the night after that, someone came along and threw something through Tessie's front window, which did not touch off the alarm (which turned out to be broken) and went into the store and messed around, and tossed things all over the place.

"Do you see?" Tessie said to the policeman, and he obediently nodded his head, he saw.

"Anything missing?" he asked, pencil poised. The cash drawer, hidden behind a *Cash McCall Private Eye* poster, was still there.

"I don't know," Tessie said.

"Vandals," the policeman said.

Matthew came in late, as usual. Tessie tried to see surprise in his face, or his eyes, at the mess, but he was impassive. He set about cleaning up, steering clear of the cop. As he swept up the glass, Tessie saw, or imagined she saw that he was looking very pale, and shortly after the policeman left, he put down his broom and collapsed against the wall, and Tessie had to put him in her car and drive to the emergency entrance of the Bronx Hospital, and she stayed there until someone saw him.

"Bleeding ulcers," the doctor said.

"So young," Tessie said. The doctor said they are getting them younger and younger these days. "Strain of survival."

Matthew's mother came. She was younger than Tessie expected, a beautiful girl, with thick, reddish hair twisted in a bun. She was wearing sunglasses, which she left on when she went over to the screened-in bed they had put Matthew in, and Tessie could hear her speaking angrily to him. Then she came from behind the screen, sat on the bench along the wall, and cried behind the sunglasses. Tessie tried to talk with her, but she spoke very little English, or so pretended. Tessie was relieved when Gloria Muñoz arrived.

"I think the mother blames him for getting sick," Tessie told her.

"There was a robbery last night," Mrs. Muñoz said. "A furniture store on Jerome Avenue was broken into. Your place was broken into. Now Mita is speaking."

254

"Oh, cut it," Tessie said. "You're talking to me now. His own mother thinks he is guilty solely on the basis of his getting a bellyache? That is pure superstition and plain ignorance and you know it. It's her own son, for godsakes."

"That's why she cries," Gloria said. "She doesn't lie to herself, but she cries."

"I'm not lying to myself," Tessie said.

Mrs. Muñoz touched Tessie's arm gently. "She appreciates your concern for her son. But the police found some stolen property from the furniture store in her house this morning. A lamp. He and two others. Drunk, hit the furniture store first, then tore up your place, they figure."

Tessie was shocked. "Jesus Christ," she said. "I gave him a key."

Gloria Muñoz laughed then. "She took his away," she said. "So who is the ignorant one?"

Tessie thought it out clearly.

Tessie, think how partial you are to fiction, she told herself.

Fictions about boys who are going bad.

Fictions about boys going bad being saved.

Being saved by a wonderful woman.

Many times the boy, wicked to the core.

The boy, wicked to the core (because of no

fault of his own, remember), or victimized by a small serpent entwined around his insides giving him a sour breath and a nasty eye (according to the fairy tales)

The boy, wicked to the core, though beautiful to the eye (

Wait a minute, wicked to the core is one story

Wicked on the outside crying on the inside is another, and would explain beautiful to the eye, if that's what you buy.

) So, he did some wicked things. He only robbed, cheated, tore the streamers off an old woman's hat, there you go again. Tore the eyes out of an old woman's face, you mean. Face it. But the serpent was eating his *kishkes,* you have to understand. Now, here you go, connecting the serpent eating his *kishkes* with remorse. Scared to be bad doesn't equal good, does it?

The boy is wicked on the outside only because of the stale bread and the crooked living quarters made of matchsticks and wet ashes, both of which put him in a bad temper and made him steal and beat up on old women.

Along comes a woman, tough right through (because of the *tsouris* she has always had to bear) and nobody's fool.

They have a lot in common, these two. In this fiction. Yes? Name one thing, Tessie. All right, so they have nothing in common, that is just as good. Despite their having nothing in common ... you see? Despite their having nothing in command, they find they have the most important thing in common, their humanity. Hers (in the shape of washcloth, soap, toothbrush, grindstone, and spelling book) is going to help him clean up his act and get to work, and his (shaped like that nonexistent thing, a nonoffensive weapon) is going to protect her from the other boys, wicked to the core, and from being alone.

In the end, it was the key that did the trick. "He didn't have to break in," she said. "He had his own key."

"Oh, please, Tessie," Victory said. "How can you be such a fool. I always thought you were so cynical."

"Gloria Muñoz is the cynic, sweetheart," Tessie said.

Gloria, who had just come into the store, didn't mind hearing that, she said. "You bet your ass," she said. "Nothing is going to convince me he didn't break into your store."

Still, Tessie fought back, and defended Matthew as innocent. "Maybe not of the furniture store," she told Gloria. "But of tearing up my joint, I would suspect you first. And the furniture store, maybe he went along, but believe me, he didn't want to."

"And the lamp they found in his house? Stolen goods?" Gloria said.

"Peer pressure," Tessie said. "How could he say no to his friends?"

"You can trust someone who mugged your friend?" she said.

Victory looked alarmed. "Oh," she whispered, "I never said it was him for sure. I wouldn't want to accuse anyone without being sure."

"Bullshit," Gloria said. "You wouldn't be so scared if you weren't sure."

"Gloria, you think you know everything?" Tessie said.

Gloria laughed. "Only what you don't know," she said. "And what about you? Didn't you say you thought he once stole your *garbage?*"

Tessie waved that away. "Oh, how can I tell? He sees me, he sees a generic old lady; I see him, I see a generic P.R."

Never mind, Gloria said. She was there to keep an eye on the boy.

"Don't need you," Tessie said.

"That's okay," Gloria said.

She came at ten o'clock every morning, and left when Tessie locked up for the night. In between, at first, she paced the aisles, expectantly, and Matthew avoided her as much as he could. Tessie called her "the store dick" and "the floor-walker" and on the third day stopped off at the five-and-ten and bought her a play policeman's hat.

"As long as I'm here . . ." she said, and Tessie handed her a stack of books to put away.

When a salesman came, she stood behind Tessie as she ordered, listening to everything.

"You got a line of Spanish books?" she asked him.

"Do you mind?" Tessie said.

But the salesman had already flipped the pages of his order book to the back, where he showed Tessie (turning just slightly to include Gloria) a small listing of books. Tessie ended up ordering half a dozen books with titles like *Anima, Viva Cortolena, Anna y Dinero, Ahi, Ahi.*

"Business is gonna boom," Gloria said, chopping her hands in the air at Tessie.

Tessie had to laugh.

There was a narrow alley behind the store, where the garbage trucks backed in, and behind it was a chain-link fence and an empty lot. Once a house had stood on that lot, owned by the O'Neill sisters. It had been a wooden house, empty for many years before it finally burned to the ground in an arson fire ten years ago. A lilac bush leaned against the fence, which was sagging into Tessie's part of the yard, and if she left the back door open a crack, she could smell the sweet, faint scent of lilacs. The more the fence sagged, the more it pulled the lilac bush with it, and this year Tessie could see exposed roots, and the flowers were reaching so far into the yard that every time the garbage truck backed in, it cut some down. She thought of the lilac bush as hers.

She took Matthew with her to the hardware store, which had stocked, for the last fifteen years, a single lawn mower and one redwood tub under a flowered, hand-lettered sign: "Summerize Your Home." She knew she would get the tub for a good price if Manny, the owner, survived the shock of someone actually wanting to buy it.

"It's rotted over here," Tessie pointed out, picking at the dried, slatted wood.

She paid ten dollars for it and several large bags of soil. Matthew staggered under the weight of the tub, and Tessie dragged the soil along the ground, and eventually they got the supplies back to the store.

Gloria had found a small shovel in the basement, and Tessie and Matthew set about digging up the lilac bush while Gloria minded the counter.

It was hard work. They dug a wide, deep

trench, looking for the bottom of the root system, but no matter how wide or deep they dug, the roots just went on and on. Tessie quit from time to time, but Matthew worked steadily. When it was time to go home, Matthew took a book on gardening from the shelf.

". . . bring it back tomorrow," he said.

Tessie looked at Gloria as if to say, See?

The next day he came to work with a large shovel.

"Where'd you steal that?" Gloria said, but he hardly seemed to notice. He went straight outside, and began to work on the lilac bush.

"I know what I'm doing now," he said. "You got to take it out at the root, yeah, but sometimes when the root gets this big, you got to cut."

"Are you sure?" Tessie said. "How do you know where to cut?"

With care, he sawed at the thick, tangled root of the plant. "It's got to be small enough to fit in the tub, don't it?"

He had taken his shirt off, and Tessie couldn't help noticing how thin his chest was; she could count the ribs. His stomach was concave. As if aware of her attention, he rubbed his stomach.

"Are you all right?" she said.

He frowned. "Yeah," he said.

261

But she noticed he slowed his work, and his body seemed too careful again, and stooped, and afraid. Soon he sat down on the edge of the wall and lit a cigarette.

"Matthew," she said. Her voice was, in her own ears, softer than she had ever heard it to be, but not softer than she sometimes meant it to be. She spoke slowly and cautiously, so she could stop at any time. She told him how she felt about Mita, the truth.

"I don't know whether you believe me or not," she said to him when she was finished.

"Yeah, I do," he said, and went back to work.

"The stupidest thing you could have done," Gloria Muñoz said to her. But without conviction, Tessie thought.

It occurred to Tessie she never told Louise the facts of life.

Tessie didn't like meetings. You got people together they acted different, talked differently, looked different from the way they ordinarily did.

Flynn, for instance, her neighbor Flynn for the last twenty years, who banged on the ceiling with a broom handle if a pin dropped, now started calling her "the esteemed Mrs. Goodman." That steamed Tessie right there.

And Beadie Kesselman grew an English accent all of a sudden. "Mah apahtment is in disrepaih." Last night at the incinerator it was: "Look at this dreck. I got roaches coming out of my ears."

And other things. Morton, the landlord, was wearing his business suit, to impress everyone with the fact that he was important enough to wear a business suit to work, even though everyone knew he was only an exterminator, and also to show that he considered this occasion important enough not to wear his filthy corduroy pants which everyone knew by heart, which stank, but now the business suit stank too, like sour pot roast. And Beadie smelled like fried onions, which she cooked every night, and there were cigarettes and mothballs and Flynn, of course, like Flynn's Bar and Grill.

Even though Mr. Hirsch had been told about the meeting, he thought he was on his way to throw out the garbage and got invited in on the spur of the moment, so he kept saying, "What a nice little get-together, what a pleasant surprise."

It was Tessie who had arranged this and it was Gloria who had talked her into it. Hate it or not, something had to be done. The muggings were epidemic; the break-ins were increasing; a six-year-old girl had been caught in the crossfire of a drug dispute and lay paralyzed.

"Acción Locale needs a stick up their ass," Gloria had said. "They're asleep at the wheel. The same ten, fifteen of them sitting around filing papers and looking important. There's no action in 'Acción.' They need some new blood."

Now, looking around, Tessie wondered whether this new blood was a little thin.

She had posted notices in all the buildings and in the windows of stores up and down the streets, but beside the handful of *alte cockers* who showed up (because they lived in the building and coffee and cake were promised), only six of the new young people who were moving into the neighborhood came, and even counting herself and Gloria, who hadn't shown up yet, it was not what you would call an impressive showing.

Since Morton was supposed to be president of this Neighborhood Association (which he formed about the same time he bought the business suit and the building they lived in), he called the meeting to order.

"Please, people," he said in his whiny voice. "*Sha.*" Nobody listened. He turned to Tessie.

"How many teas, how many coffees," she called out, to get everyone's attention. It did. "Raise your hands, I'll count while Morton tells

264

you why we are here."

Morton couldn't tell, because he didn't exactly know, but it made him feel like a big shot to stand up there facing everyone, and you could smell him less when he was in front of the open window.

"You know," he said, "the Puerto Ricans have their own association. They meet once a week. God bless them, it's wonderful. That's what makes America. I understand they are doing a very excellent and fine job. Now, *this* association was formed a long time ago, before some of these new residents were even born, I might add, and I would like to think we are still a going operation."

Beadie Kesselman snorted. "Morton, what kind of going operation? We never even had one meeting. This is our first meeting persay, unless you count during the blackout we gave candles out in the lobby, but that wasn't a meeting persay, so this is our first meeting."

"What's your point?" Flynn shouted.

"Excuse me," Beadie said, "my point is, don't give ourselves medals if this is only our first meeting. *Farshteist?*"

"Talk English, we got a melting pot here," Morton said.

"No wonder we don't have meetings, we can't even discuss about how many meetings we had

265

without getting into an argument," Beadie said.

Tessie was embarrassed in front of the young people, but Gloria, who had just come in, was grinning.

Everyone was talking at once. Beadie wanted to discuss building repairs, which was her way of getting Morton's attention. Poor Miss Carter kept interrupting to talk about neighborhood cleanliness. Finally, it was Flynn who prevailed, by repeating the words *safety first* so many times he finally cut through the noise.

"The esteemed Mrs. Goodman called this meeting, so let her talk first," he said.

Tessie thanked him, and said she thought the first order of business should be protecting people from getting mugged every time they left their apartments.

One of the young people suggested a resident patrol. "We can go in pairs, like auxiliary police," he said.

Beadie Kesselman objected on the grounds that her feet swelled up and she couldn't walk around too much. "Especially in hot weather," she added.

Morton laughed, and asked Beadie if her feet were a hundred percent perfect would she consider walking around the neighborhood after six o'clock at night with a billy club, and she said of course not, you think I'm crazy, and he said then why give these people the impression that if it were not for your feet you would be for it, and she said if the answer is no, what difference did it make why it was no? No is no, no?

Tessie heard one of the young people whisper, "This is ridiculous." They were shaking their heads, sorry and amused, not even angry. She was sorry she had called this meeting. Taking care of herself, which sometimes seemed easy and sometimes impossible, was at least serious. This was a joke.

Flynn claimed he would go out there alone. He was an ex-cop. He was also very slow on his feet from varicose veins, and a disease that made him fall asleep right in the middle of a card game or driving or god knows what. He had a disability pension. Gonzalez said he would go with him. Morton looked for a moment as though he were going to sign up as the third musketeer, but then said nothing.

One of the young women raised her hand, and in a soft voice suggested "safe" houses, places, shops, or apartments that would be open for help or shelter at assigned times. They would all take turns.

"I'm no flower child who is going to let every Tom, Dick, and Harry inside my house," someone said, and people groaned and said, "Oh, please," but Tessie noticed no one picked up the suggestion.

Flynn suggested getting the police to put on a heavier concentration of men, and everyone laughed.

Gloria suggested forming a liaison with the Puerto Rican Local Action Committee.

"What for?" Morton said. "And why, may I ask, should we give the new organization the benefit of our long existence?"

Gonzalez stood up. "I am the secretary-treasurer of Acción Locale," he said with stiff dignity, "and we don't need you." He was about to say more, but then seemed to realize that Morton was, after all, his employer, and he sat down abruptly.

Mr. Hirsch raised his hand, and then stood up and told a longish story about his wife, Raisa, God rest her, when she was alive, waking up one morning and finding the gold earrings she had been wearing when she went to sleep (and which he had given her) were gone, and they tore off the sheets, shook them out, and the blankets, emptied pillowcases and turned the mattress, looked under the bed, but the earrings were gone, completely, and he bought her new earrings, and six months later Raisa woke up one morning and what do you think was in the palm of her hand? The earrings. He looked around him and laid his palm out, as if to show the assembled how he held the truth there for them to see.

Everyone was at a loss.

"What's your point, Hyman?" someone finally said, but it was too late. The story seemed to have washed everything else out of people's minds and they sat there, contemplating it, or nothing, and the meeting was over.

"We should meet again," Morton said. "Tonight we laid the groundwork, so to speak."

Tessie stood at the door and shooed them out, saying, "Go, go, go," as they went. When someone tried to thank her for her hospitality, she said, "Never mind."

The young people didn't leave.

"Look," one of them said to her kindly, "what can you older people do?" Tessie appreciated not being called a "senior." "You shouldn't blame yourselves. You weren't prepared for something like this."

"Pogroms," Morton said.

Tessie laughed. Morton was born in this country. "The closest you ever got to a pogrom is when you exterminated the ants in your own bathtub," she said. "Do me a favor, Morton."

Some of the young people wanted to continue talking, and they stayed on. Flynn stayed, and Gloria and one or two others. The one who had spoken to Tessie earlier said, "What we have here is two low-power groups: the Puerto Ricans and the elderly. What we have to do is figure out a way to make them stronger."

"Join the two groups together, number one," Tessie said.

"Forget it," Gloria said. "They don't want it. They look at us, they see 'spic.'"

"Now hold on," Morton said.

One of the other young people, a shy young woman, spoke up. "Mrs. Muñoz is doing some interesting work through cultural channels, and since the crime is largely from the young segment of her community, it might be interesting to hear what she has to say."

Gloria talked about her séances, and the way she used strong spirits like Mita to discourage antisocial behavior. She was documenting it for a paper.

"That's all well and good," Morton said. "But we are civilized people. What are we supposed to do, make voodoo dolls?"

"On the other hand, it works," someone else said.

"It's behaviorism," the shy young woman explained.

"Who cares?" Morton said. "It isn't

changing their behavior yet, is it? They're still mugging and breaking in."

"Not the ones who come to me," Gloria said. Her color was high, and she was on her feet.

Then everyone began to talk at once, and it was just about that time Tessie came up with the plan, which she credited to Morton, because of his mention of voodoo dolls, though it was credited to her when the article appeared in the *New York Post* two weeks later:

Blond Grandma Dolls It Up in Bronx!

A group of feisty senior citizens, led by bookstore owner and grandmother Esther Goodman, joined with the Acción Locale to declare war on the "punks and hoods" recently terrorizing the residents of the section of the Bronx popularly known as the Wilds. Mrs. Goodman's group and the Acción Locale, in cooperation with their local precinct, have displayed photographic blow-ups of known offenders in all neighborhood shops and buildings. "We stick a colored pin in the picture, like a voodoo doll," says Mrs. Goodman. "If they are behaving themselves, the pin is blue. If they are engaging in unruly behavior, the pin is yellow. If they are armed and dangerous, the pin is red. And they can't

271

tear the pictures down because that would be admitting their guilt." . . .

Tessie had a rogue's gallery strung across the width of her store, which Matthew, of all people, rigged up.

News traveled, and the store was crowded with the curious, come to see. Tessie marked down a selection of books and put them on a stand near the door so everyone had to pass by it when they came in.

Gloria was still skeptical, but she was willing to go along. "It's good for business, at least, and the publicity can't hurt the neighborhood."

"Never mind," Tessie said. "Flynn looked it up in the police station; violent crime is down fifty percent during daytime hours since we started."

Gloria shrugged. "So everybody does night work. Tessie, think. If someone is armed and dangerous, what does he care if you stick a pin in his picture."

But, little by little, more merchants joined in. Joe Figueroa of Hum's Chinese hung the pictures vertically, and Temple Emeth Torah (whose Torah scrolls were stolen last year) hung them from right to left, which was the same as left to right in this case, it occurred to Tessie, since they could be read in either direction.

272

"It looks like a street fair," Gloria said.

Tessie agreed. There was a liveliness about the streets, and people were talking to one another.

Eventually Gloria came around enough to say, "Well, it couldn't hurt, could it?"

Louise complained that Matthew was taking it as a big joke. He insisted his picture be included among the known offenders, even though Tessie considered him reformed. He kept a supply of blue pins, and marked his picture of himself, wherever he went.

But finally, it was Gloria who was right. Night crime increased, and a rash of break-ins, like a tactical offensive, Flynn said, brought morale, and finally the pictures, down.

"What's the point?" most of the shopkeepers said.

"But at least," Gloria said, "it was great for business."

Louise was very angry. She was out of her mind, as a matter of fact, since she found out that Tessie intended to let Matthew move into the basement of the store.

"It will be good for his independence," Tessie said.

273

Russell was so outraged his Senior Citizen Appreciation smile cracked, and he said, "This is the craziest thing of all the crazy things you have ever done."

Gloria called her six kinds of fool. "Look, even if he is the good kid you say he is, still he has those friends, peer pressure. You would be setting him up."

All Tessie said was, "I know what I am doing."

Matthew said, "They think you're crazy trusting me." He didn't sound so sure, either.

"I'm not trusting you, I'm trusting myself," she said. "There is a difference. You think I would trust you?" she said. "I *got* you, now. Anything happens, I go straight to you. You have no choice, you have to be honest. Anyone steals anything, breaks in here, you get blamed for it, with your record. So you'll be my night watchman, too." She tapped her head. "Smart?"

Matthew, who was shaking a bag of loam mixed with plant food around the lilac tree, let his hands slip, so he flicked some dirt on the front of her dress.

"You are crazy," he said, but he looked a little relieved.

Louise walked in one day, took him by the collar, in the back, and pulled him upright, and

274

then she turned him around, and with her hands on his shoulders pushed him against the shelves. She grabbed a handful of hair, she grabbed his chin, she shook his shoulders, as if she didn't know what to grab first.

"You just watch it, you little rat," she said. "You just watch it with my mother."

"Both crazy," he said.

July 4 in the suburbs with Louise is a large lawn party that begins with Russell getting drunk on martinis.

("I have to talk to you," he whispered to Tessie.

"Me?" she said.

"Louise is seeing someone," he said.

Tessie couldn't believe it. "Louise? My Louise? Screwing around?"

Russell was annoyed. "Of course not," he said. "She is seeing a psychologist."

Tessie was disappointed.

"She is trying to establish her identity," he said. "What a cliché." He did not understand, he said.

Tessie told him not to be ridiculous. Of course he understood. With his education? The cliché was to pretend he didn't understand. "You're just frightened," she said.

He denied he was frightened. He denied he understood. He denied he wanted Tessie to stroke his bald head and comfort him and take his part against her own daughter, and he denied he was feeling sick, and then he threw up on the grass. That he couldn't deny, Tessie thought, and felt sorry for him for the first time since he misdiagnosed his own blood test and thought he had leukemia.

"Go lie down," she said.)

and ends with Tessie and Louise weaving about the lawn.

. . . *into the night with my shovel, digging for diamonds in the black snow,* she sang to herself.

"Stop waving that thing, you'll hurt yourself. They're only fireflies."

The air was so hot you could touch it, so dark you felt you could hold it in your hands, and Tessie and Louise were so drunk they bumped into it and sat down.

"Are you all right?" Tessie said to Louise.

She had never seen her daughter drunk before. She had never seen Russell drunk, either. Louise drunk was only less sober. Was this as far as she could go? The edges were off her *r*'s. Her serious precision had given way to intoxicated precision. She gathered her lips in, searched for the perfect word at the bottom of her glass.

"Demise. Downfall. Daddy's downfall," she said. "What was I saying?"

"You won't get any air out there," Russell

276

called to them from the upstairs window. "It's too hot."

"Shut up," Louise called to him.

"Louise, I'm shocked," Tessie said, sounding unshocked.

"I drank too much," Louise said.

"You didn't eat anything all day," Tessie said, providing her with an excuse, but then taking it back. Sadly. "It's me. I'm not good for you," she sighed. "I make you nervous. I don't know why, but I make you nervous."

"You zon't," Louise said.

"I do," Tessie said.

Louise pinched off a small piece of air. "Just a little," she said. "You always wanted me to rebel."

Tessie found an orange in her hand, which she faintly remembered taking from the large fruit bowl in the dining room. Absently, she began peeling it. "Remember the July fourth that pretty red-haired girl in your class got killed, hit by a car?" Tessie said. Then, "I did not."

"Yes, you did. What girl? Except you wanted me to rebel *your* rebellion, not my own."

"She was walking on the traffic island in the middle of University Avenue and a car jumped the curb, that's right, I remember."

"I did rebel, that's the funny thing. But not

277

the way you wanted. I rebelled by marrying a geriatrist." She giggled.

"Are you blaming that on me?"

"How could I blame it on you? You weren't even driving in those days."

"What does that have to do with your being upset with me?"

"I'm not upset with you, I'm upset with Russell."

"What did Russell do?"

"Russell takes after you," Louise said. "He bosses me."

"How can Russell take after me?" Tessie said. "*You're* my blood."

"It's Daddy's fault," Louise said. "I take after him."

"Oh, no, no, no," Tessie said. "Don't blame your father. Your father was just your father." She handed a section of the orange to Louise. "They're seedless," she said.

Louise chewed suspiciously nonetheless, as if looking for bones. "Well, you can't hog all the blame," she said.

"He was just a quiet man," Tessie said. "That's all."

"His downfall — my downfall was in not talking back to you."

Tessie sighed, dropped the orange in her lap, and brushed her hands off, as if there were crumbs. "What can I tell you?" she said.

"Nothing," Louise said. "Not a goddamn thing."

There was a while of silence, and then Tessie said, "This was a good talk."

"Mmmmmm," Louise said, and laid her head against Tessie's shoulder.

And July 5 in the Wilds begins with a man crazy from too much gin and sun tossing a baby out of a fourth-floor window into the alley, where it survives on a pile of soft green Hefty bags, which the Sanitation Department has not picked up all weekend.

It ends with Tessie coming home from Louise's (anxious to get home, driving out of that too-neat suburb past flat ranch houses with their roofs pulled down over their windows like thugs. The heat made the roads look wet in front of her, and the air shimmered with it. The Cross Bronx Expressway was backed up two miles because a portion of road had buckled, and traffic was narrowed to one lane. When she finally reached the Jerome Avenue exit, it was after twelve. She went straight to the store) to find the front door wide open, the lilac bush torn out of its barrel, and Matthew (she went downstairs, shouting, angry, saying, For chrissakes, someone could walk away with the store,

279

if I have told you once I have told you —
groping along the basement wall for the lights,
seeing a sprawled body on the basement floor,
saying to herself, Oh, no, I'm seeing things
again, then seeing it plain) dead.

It was no accident. Matthew had been stabbed
repeatedly. The police believed it was the same
group who had been doing the other robberies.
Tessie knew it was not. Look how the place was
ransacked, they said. Look how nothing was
taken, again, she said. A falling out among
thieves, Russell thought. No, Tessie said. She
didn't believe it.

"Well," Victory said, her head shaking slightly,
as if it had come loose, "there's one less of them,
one less . . ." She looked at Gloria and didn't
finish.

"Little savage," Louise said, crying. "I thought
he was so tough."

Tessie held her head in her hands.

"There is no last death," Gloria said. "There is
always one more. That's what everyone is afraid
of."

"Aha," Tessie said. "Answer me this."

They were in Gloria's apartment. It was similar to Tessie's (did she buy all this stuff second-
hand from one of us? Tessie wondered) except
for the large crucifix above the bed, and the one

in the hallway, which Tessie tried not to look at. Gloria offered to conduct a séance, and summon Barney's spirit, so Tessie could ask him what was hidden in the store. Tessie declined. "But I'll take a cup of coffee," she said. "Answer me this. If you think people get paid back for the bad things they do, with knives in their *kishkes* and devils cracking their heads open, wouldn't it also be true that people who do good things get rewarded? Wouldn't it work out that way?"

Gloria looked suspicious, but said yes.

"So tell me please, sweetheart, how come I'm poor and you're poor, and what's-his-name there, who sells drugs under the El, he has a limousine take him to the courthouse, where they give him brewed coffee while he waits for his lawyer to get him out? This coffee is terrible."

"He'll get his," Gloria said.

"Maybe he will, but it isn't going to be because of any spirits. And getting his isn't the same as you and me getting ours. I'm still waiting to hear about rewards for being good. I know already about the bad. And don't tell me I'm going to get Brownie points in some afterlife, either."

"You have to believe something," Gloria said.

"Aha," Tessie said. "This, what you are talking about, is not real belief. This is emergency belief. Anyway, didn't you once tell me you didn't believe in it yourself? So now you're changing your mind?"

Gloria considered. "Well, I do and I don't," she said. "I've been educated not to, but it's hard to resist. You see things you can't explain. On the anniversary of my grandmother's death, a taxi brought her ghost to my mother's door."

Tessie laughed. "A taxi? Why not a bus? Did she also give the driver a tip?"

Gloria smiled. "The details are fuzzy," she said. "But believe me, I believe that it happened. Or . . . well, at least I believe my mother believed in it."

"There's a big difference," Tessie said.

"Yes, I suppose there is. I think it isn't spirits I believe in as much as the possibility of spirits. I'm open to it."

Tessie shook her head. "I only believe in what I can touch, see, hear, and smell. And taste. A bird in the hand," she said.

"But Tessie, without some guiding spirit, how can you live? If there is no rhyme or reason to believe in, what's the point? How can you stand it?"

Tessie shrugged. "I don't know. I think you have to accept that nothing is for sure, no matter how hard you pray, or plead, or wish. You just continue to do what you do, and take your chances. Who knew I would end up here, in this pickle? Would it do any good if I decided to blame some powerful clump of air? I am still the only one who can get me out."

"But your getting 'in this pickle' as you put it, that wasn't your doing. Did you make your husband die? Did you make his money disappear? Maybe it all happened for a reason."

"And maybe not," Tessie said. "Face it, Gloria, part of life is accidental. A big part. Sometimes there just aren't reasons for things. It can be a big mistake to try and equal everything out. Like if someone gets cancer, do you have to blame them because they smoked or ate bacon and so forth? I know someone who didn't do any of these things and died a terrible cancer death. Maybe right by where he lived was one of those what-do-you-call-it, holes in the sky and he got violet rays. Accident. Should I then make up that some big shot in the sky knew he was evil and the cancer was deserved? This is supposed to make me feel better?"

"Ozone layer," Gloria said. "I don't know, Tessie. I still think you are wrong."

"Go ahead, sweetheart, think. You got the brains for it."

"Why do you like her so much?" Victory asked.

"She doesn't talk heart talk all the time," Tessie said. "Sometimes she talks brain talk."

"You sound like a man," Victory said.

Gloria had told Tessie that she thought in her native language, and had to translate in her head before she spoke, so people would understand her, and it was often a hardship. Tessie felt that she, too, had had to do this all her life, to be understood.

"We have a lot in common," she told Victory.

Russell and Louise were relieved that Tessie didn't go into what Russell called "a tailspin" as a result of Matthew's death.

"It isn't as if he was my child," Tessie said.

Louise was glad she knew the difference, she said.

As a matter of fact, when the sadness over Matthew lifted, it seemed to lift Tessie with it. She felt as if she had suddenly broken through the surface of still water, in which she had been submerged. She would like, she thought, to take a trip somewhere with blue skies and clear water.

She was filled with energy, and decided to redecorate her apartment. She accompanied herself with long medleys of songs she had thought she'd forgotten. The songs were connected by pulleys to the dust-mop strings, the tips of her fingers, the ends of picture wires, and she had only to reach up and remove a picture from the wall, or tug a nail out, or swipe the floor with a mop to get the song to unwind from the skein inside her. If she was stuck on a lyric, a good whack on the sofa cushion shook it loose, and if she couldn't decide where to move the big chair, the rhythm of the song (ta-da-da O-ver there) told her. Xavier Cugat's *"Cuanto le Gusta"* had thirteen *le gustas*, which coincided perfectly with the number of knickknacks she threw in a box and packed away. When Carmen Miranda sang it back in the forties, she wore fruit on her head. Tessie said "banana break" and stopped to see what she accomplished. She pushed the furniture against the wall, as if she needed space to dance.

When the Widows come, Pearl, the decorator, stands in the doorway and flings her arm wide open, then closes them around Tessie without actually hugging her, leaving a pad of air between her circled arms and Tessie's body. Then she steps back.

"Oh, oh, my," she says, surveying the room. "Oh, Tessie, look what you have done."

It sounds more like something you would say to an untrained dog than to someone who has just created a Bloomingdale's room, Tessie

285

thinks, but thanks her nevertheless.

"Do *you* like it?" Pearl says.

"Of course I like it," Tessie says. "Why else would I have done it?"

"Well," Pearl says comfortingly, "as long as you like it. If you like it, that's what counts. I think it is great, a great . . . beginning."

Tessie has thought of it as all done.

When Victory and Helen arrive, Victory says, "What happened here?"

"I'm getting ready for *Life*," she says. "They're coming to take pictures."

Victory purses her lips, and her head trembles in the constant gesture of denial which all of them have noticed, and which she refuses to see a doctor about. The gesture, at this moment, suits her mood, which is sour, because Tessie has invited Gloria to join them. ("Why?" Victory had asked. "For a séance," Tessie had said. "I'm not coming," Victory had said.)

When Gloria arrives they are talking about redecorating and how good it is for the nerves.

"Like buying a new hat, but on a bigger scale," Helen says.

Pearl is redecorating her house, to suit her new husband-to-be. Freddy is not the type for Modern, she says. He is more Colonial. Tessie suspects this means she is afraid he will spill things on the clear surfaces, crack the mirrors,

286

or spill ashes on the white rug.

Pearl gives Gloria, who is all in white, the once-over, and then says she is also redoing herself. She has an appointment at Elizabeth Arden.

"For what?" Tessie asks.

"The works," Pearl says. "New hair color, new cut, new makeup, and then they give you advice on what clothes to wear to go with it. The works."

"You're making a big mistake," Helen says. "What if he doesn't like the new you? He fell for you the way you are."

"He'll like it," she says. There is strain around her eyes. "He better."

There is a pause, while everyone tries to figure out, Tessie thinks, how to worm the rest out of her. There is no need. She begins to cry.

"He dumped you?" Helen says. Triumphantly? No, wistfully.

"He did not," Pearl says. "You would be the first to know. He did not." But it is, she admits, between the lines.

"Maybe he's just getting cold feet," Victory says.

"That's not it," Pearl says miserably. "He says he is haunted by Mel, by my love for Mel. He says everywhere in my house, Mel is there. That's why I'm redecorating. Now he started with me, he says when he looks at me all he can think is 'Mrs. Mel Perlstein, picking up one-hundred-percent pima cotton shirts once a week.' It's affecting our . . ." She peeks at Helen. "He can't even . . ."

Gloria, who has been sitting quietly, says, "In other words he can't get it up, and he's blaming it on you."

Uh-oh, Tessie thinks.

But maybe the bluntness shocks it out of Pearl: "Yes," she says. "Exactly. Poor thing."

"Poor thing?" Gloria says. "Are you kidding? *He's* got a poor thing, that's what. There he is with his poor thing, hanging between his legs like a big marshmallow, and he's blaming you. Wonderful."

Helen snorts "Marshmallow" and begins to laugh nervously, and Pearl says "What a picture" and laughs, and even Victory smiles. "Men," Victory says.

"I had the same thing with my third husband," Gloria says.

"Third?" Helen says. "How many have you had? All told."

"Total? Three," Gloria says crisply, as if she is answering an arithmetic problem. "First one died, second one died, third one divorced."

"So what happened with the third?" Helen asks.

288

"Same thing as with Pearl," Gloria says. "He couldn't perform, and he said it was my fault. Well, to be specific, he said it was the ghost of my dead husband that was turning him soft."

"So what did you do?"

"Oh, I tried everything," Gloria says. "I bought a new bed. I bought new sheets. I bought new, sexy, nightgowns."

"And . . . ?"

"*Nada*. Nothing. He just kept on insisting Carlo's ghost was dirtying our marriage bed."

"Dirtying?" Helen says.

"Dirtying," Gloria confirms. "Can you believe it?"

"So what finally happened?" Pearl says.

"What finally happened," Gloria says, "I got mad one night and told him to show me exactly where the ghost of Carlo was dirtying our marriage bed, and he said, 'Right here,' where he was lying at the time, and I went and got a bottle of Fantastik and sprayed the bastard from head to toe and told him that ought to clean it up."

"He left?" Pearl says.

"I threw him out," Gloria corrects.

There is a collective sigh of satisfaction.

"Are you ever sorry?" Pearl says.

"Only that I got rid of a perfectly good mattress," Gloria says, and everyone laughs.

Tessie had been worried about Gloria, how the others would take to her. Now she settles back and relaxes. Leave it to Gloria, she thinks.

"Are we really going to do this séance thing?" Helen asks.

In answer Gloria rises and begins opening the bridge table which Tessie had leaning against the wall. "As soon as I set up," she says. She covers the table with a white cloth, and carefully places a bridge chair at each corner, and a fifth one centered between two corners.

"Don't mind me," she says. "Go on talking."

"Men," Pearl says, picking up Victory's last word.

"They think they know everything," Helen says. "Did I ever tell you about the time Mel kept insisting that nobody made gefilte fish like his mother's gefilte fish? So I got the recipe from her, but he said no, it wasn't quite right."

"Maybe his mother left something out," Victory says.

They continue to watch Gloria as they talk. She is setting candles in the center of the table.

"No, it was just like his mother's, believe me," Helen says. "I tried again. And again. I even talked his mother into giving me some of hers and not telling him and, sure enough, when I served it to him, he said it wasn't as good as hers. Well, by that time, it was driving me crazy.

So I went out and bought a jar of Mother's Gefilte Fish, and I poured it into a pot, and put some carrots in, and boiled it a little, and then I smeared the walls with some of the juice, so the kitchen would smell like I had cooked it all day. I buried the jar in the bottom of the garbage pail. And wouldn't you know, he took one taste and said that's it, it was exactly like his mother's."

Gloria dims the lights.

"Did I ever tell you the time I poisoned Irwin?" Pearl says quickly. "I was soaking the plastic orange juice pitcher in lemony dish soap, on the counter. He took a glass, didn't even look at what was inside, because you know, when Irwin was thirsty Irwin was thirsty, and he poured and drank the whole thing down before I could stop him."

"Oh my god," Victory says, "he must've gotten so sick."

Pearl laughs. "Like a dog," she says.

Gloria sits down in the fifth chair and folds her hands on top of a book she has placed on the table.

Victory tries to start another story. "When George . . . ," she says, "when George . . . ," but she can't seem to concentrate. They are all watching Gloria. "Do we have to do this?" Victory says, plaintively.

"Come on, Vicki," Helen says. "It's something different."

When they are all seated around the table, Gloria lights the candles.

"Do we close our eyes?" Pearl says.

"Not yet."

Tessie closes hers nevertheless. She does not believe in any of this, yet she is eager to begin, and excited. Gloria's "possibility of spirits" spreads inside her like a slow smile.

"What do we do now?" Helen says.

"Sit quietly," Gloria says, gently. She explains that they are going to read from a book — "Not the Catholic Bible?" Victory says, alarmed. "No," Gloria assures her — which Tessie has selected. It is *The Complete Short Stories of Mark Twain*, because it was one of Barney's favorites. Where the book falls open is very significant, she says. She turns the book toward Tessie, who opens the book at page 16.

" 'Niagara Falls is a most enjoyable place of resort. The hotels are excellent, and the prices not at all exorbitant,' " she reads.

"Oh my god, I have the chills," Helen says. "Is that where you went on your honeymoon?"

It wasn't, Tessie says.

She opens it again, to page 150, which is the middle of a conversation between two men with Englishy names. On her third try, she hits page

466, which says, "The spirits went away to fetch him," which, Tessie thinks, is at least in the ballpark. Gloria asks everyone to clear their minds of everything else, and concentrate on Barney's spirit.

"Close our eyes?" Pearl says, again, and this time Gloria nods.

"What are we supposed to feel?" Helen says.

Gloria says, "Shhh."

After a few moments, Gloria says softly, "Hold hands."

Tessie reaches to her left, and takes Gloria's hand in hers. She weaves her fingers between Victory's on her right, thinking that in all these years she has never touched her friend's hand before. Eyes closed, she listens to the slight rustle as Helen reaches to grasp Victory and Pearl, Pearl's rings clicking as she slides her hands to Helen and to Gloria on the other side.

We've never been together for this long without talking, she thinks, and then pulls her mind toward the space the silence makes, concentrates on it. *Silence* draws into *Barney* and back into *silence*; holding tightly to her friends' hands she feels safe; silence settles into peace.

NONFICTION

NATURE

PUZZLES

There was another vision.

I had another vision, but this time it wasn't a vision. It was a sight, and it shook me like an earthquake had hit the Bronx. It is still in my eyes, like sand, I try rubbing it sometimes, to get it out. It turned my hair gray (well, my hair has been gray for some time, but after this happened I stopped coloring it). It even changed my voice.

I am not one of those people who tell you about some terrible catastrophe just to let you know how it affected *her*. Like those mothers who refer to their sons' skiing accidents as look-what-he-did-to-me, while the son is lying somewhere in the Alps with two broken legs and a fractured thing, or the wives who say what-aggravation-he-gave-me-getting-that-triple-bypass.

Did I say I wasn't one of those people? Well, I am. How can I not be? Those people are usually women, wives and mothers, who don't go skiing or get bypasses, but do have sons and husbands. So what else should we say? How else are we supposed to view things? Not only that, how about the catastrophes in which the main person is dead and gone; who else is there to do the feeling but the bystanders?

One Sunday afternoon, late in September, at about two o'clock, my friend Helen called me. I was cleaning closets at the time.

I love cleaning closets all the time, but cleaning closets in the fall is especially enjoyable. You work up a sweat and open all the windows wide, and in comes that sweet autumn smell of rotting leaves and apples (though God knows how I get that in the Bronx, maybe I only imagine it from memories of when Barney and I used to drive upstate to a farm off the Garden State Parkway on the border between New York and New Jersey to buy apples, fresh cider, the best doughnuts in the world), and everything summer goes away, and everything winter comes out, looking interesting again, if not exactly new.

I had found an old poncho I once made out of two of Louise's old baby blankets (long disuse had either brought out its essential ugliness or I had been temporarily insane when I made it; it went on the rummage pile), a Lily Daché hat from the fifties (which I didn't remember owning but which when I tried it on looked gorgeous if it ever came back into style, so I decided to save it for one more year), several army blankets which still had the smell of damp wood cabins from Louise's camping days, and a metal gadget that was either a car jack or some kind of giant shoehorn, I couldn't figure out which. Then there was the crumbling bride-and-groom statuette from Louise's wedding cake, which I put on a give-Louise pile, along with some of Barney's old track medals (for the baby when he was old enough) and a half-finished cross-stitched tablecloth.

A manila envelope of old pictures fell out of a box, all over the floor, and I spent a wonderful hour or so going through them.

There was a series taken at West Point, when we were very young. We had taken a ride there one autumn: Barney and me posing on a hill, Barney and me posing in front of the administration building, Barney and me sitting under a tree. Very imaginative. In every picture Barney was staring down at me, except the one where I was sitting on a wall. In that one, he was staring up at me. And in every picture I was staring straight at the camera, so you began to wonder who the picture taker was. There was one with my back to the camera and my arms reaching up around Barney's neck, and there was a big grin on his face. I wondered what I was up to, or what I could have been saying, in that one. Then there was a picture of Barney and me with another couple, and I couldn't for the life of me remember their names. So I tried a little trick I learned from Barney, I call it lifting my foot off the mental pedal, and sure enough the names came to me: Teddy and Edith Something. Ease up. Rothman. I guess Barney never knew he taught me that trick: it was years after West Point, but still, we were young. He was removing the stain from the old oak bookshelves, when we first bought the store. I remember he used some really strong stuff, he had to go to a marine supply store to get it — they used it on the hulls of ships — and he slopped it on and then just let it sit there. I was always in a hurry to scrape it and go on to the next shelf, but Barney used to say, "Let time do the work for you," and he would take a walk around the block, or go have a cup of tea, and sure enough, when he came back the thick gray paste had turned into currant jelly, mixed with all the old stains, and it almost slid right off. I helped, and if I was pressing too hard, he would come up behind me and put his arms around me from the back (nice chill) and put his big hands over mine and make me loosen my grip, and go easy. "Easy, easy, let up a little," he said. "Don't press so hard." You know, I used that trick for everything through the years: rust stains on the bathroom tile, crusts on pots and pans, even this whole business of being a widow, finally.

There were pictures of Victory and George as a young couple, of Louise as a baby; George and Barney and the four of us together. I decided then (as I must have decided every closet-cleaning day for the last million years) to get a nice album and put the pictures in it. Then I went back to work.

Then Helen called.

You know Helen. Always leaning on you, hard. The minute I heard her voice I said to myself, "Tessie, duck," because she was aiming something at me for sure. I was in for it, and I wanted to get out of it, but then she started to cry, which is very unlike Helen, and, I admit, that threw me.

She said, Did I have a minute? What could I say?

"Tell me one thing," she said. "Why doesn't anyone like me?"

That wasn't one, it was two. The first one was, "Does anybody like me?" which I couldn't answer because how could I lie, Helen is no fool, and how could I tell her the truth?

I stalled for time while I wracked my brain for a complimentary way of saying a person is selfish and obnoxious.

"Why are you asking?" I said.

She said it was because of Victory.

I said to myself, Uh-oh. Ever since Pearl had announced her marriage plans, Helen had been trying to drive a wedge between Victory and me. She'd call Victory and say, "Tessie said this" and then call me and say, "Victory said that."

She had called Victory, she said, to go shopping with her.

"I notice you didn't call me," I said, just to put her on the defensive.

She said that was because she knew how peculiar I could be sometimes, which was a reference to my friendship with Gloria, which was still a source of jealousy to my old friends.

Victory turned her down, she said.

While this was surprising, considering what a fanatic shopper Victory was, it didn't seem particularly alarming. "So what's the big deal?" I said.

"She hung up on me," Helen said. "Right in the middle of a sentence."

I asked her to tell me the sentence, because Helen could come up with some doozies. She had certain remarks which Victory and I called her "pickled herrings" because they were salty, and they repeated on you hours after she said them.

It was nothing, Helen said, nothing more than what would Victory be doing over the weekend.

"Be honest," Helen said. "Is she angry at me for something I did? What did I do? Did she tell you anything?"

I said I didn't know, and then, after several "Are you sure's" and "Really, I'm sure's," just to get her off the telephone, I promised I would call Victory and find out. And, feeling like Helen had me right where she wanted me, I called.

Now, here is a perfect example of someone being so caught up in their own feelings that they don't even notice someone else's. The minute I heard Victory's voice on the phone I knew something was wrong, and it wasn't with Helen. I asked her if she had been crying and she said she didn't know. I asked her if she had a cold. She said she didn't know. She sounded like she was in a trance. How can a person not know if they are sick? I asked her if she was all right, and she said she thought so, she didn't know.

I asked her if she wanted me to come over there.

She said she didn't know.

"Well, should I come?" I said.

"I think so," she said.

Again I said, "Are you all right?" and this time she said, "I don't think so." Those were her last words, and then she hung up on me.

I called Helen back and told her something was wrong, and to meet me on the corner in front of Victory's house.

"But I'm not dressed," she said, so I said, "Forget about it, Helen," which is the way you have to handle her. She said she would be there. Who needed her? I guess I did. I guess I was thinking about all the books I had read, scenes in which you help them walk off the effects of whatever it is they had taken, and I wanted someone along to make the black coffee. Or help me lift Victory. Victory is big.

She had had the blues for a long time. Oh, a long time.

Victory lived three blocks from my house in a building even older than mine. On the second floor. I got there before Helen, and I went straight up. I tapped quietly, trying not to attract attention. I put my face against the door and called her.

I tried to hear her calling me, but all I heard was a kind of throbbing sound, like a machine, or a heartbeat. I said to myself then, She probably went out somewhere, but even as I was running down the stairs to see if I could find her, I knew she hadn't gone anywhere. I remembered the old burglar game I used to play with Louise: run out in the street rather than be locked in with danger. I wished Victory had run out, but I knew she hadn't.

Helen finally turned up, and we went down to my store and called Victory's telephone number from there. Her line was busy.

Then we went back to the building. As soon as we stepped into the lobby, Helen got a dizzy spell and had to sit down. There had once been a nice wrought-iron bench with red velvet cushions in the lobby, I was thinking, but it was stolen in 1952. Those are the strange things you think of in the middle of emergencies. So Helen had to sit down on the steps, and in the middle of her dizzy spell she was concerned about keeping her skirt clean, so we rummaged around for a clean hanky to put under her bony behind. Those are the strange things you do to prevent facing things. But then (you would think Helen was busy enough staying clean and being dizzy) the superintendent came along, and Helen opened up her big mouth and told him something was wrong. I told her to shut up, but it was too late, and he went running up to Victory's apartment, and banged on the door and then he came down and said there was a funny smell up there, and he was going to call the police.

The banging brought out all the neighbors, of course, which was what I didn't want to happen, and they all clustered around Victory's door.

She'll be so embarrassed, I thought, yet knew it might not matter to her anymore.

I wanted to get in there first. Just in case she was in an awkward position, an unpleasant position was the way I put it to myself, knowing I could be clearer even then.

"I should have your key," I said. I must have said that to her a hundred times, because it's important to give your key to someone just in case, but she never gave it to me.

There is a red fire-alarm box on every other floor, with a small hammer on a chain and a little hatchet inside. I broke the glass door with the hammer and took out the hatchet and tried to break down Victory's door.

I was very calm. But the super thought I was hysterical, and he started shouting at me, what the hell was I doing and so forth, and Helen started yelling at him to leave me alone (not that she cared, she just wanted to get into the act), and then some man put his hand on her shoulder to calm her and she began screaming at him, and the super was pulling my arm, and two women neighbors started pulling at him. Of course, it was all foolish. The hatchet was tiny and the door was one of those old-fashioned, heavy wooden ones, so I wasn't even making a dent. Then the super knocked the hatchet out of my hand and I grabbed for the knob just to hold on, and it turned. It had been open all the time. And there we were in Victory's apartment, just as the police came running up the stairs.

There was a strong smell of something, and the super shouted "Gas," so the cops and he ran into the kitchen. I went straight to the bedroom, to Victory. She was asleep with her good robe on, and toilet paper wrapped around her freshly done hairdo to protect it from getting messed up by the pillow. The minute I saw her I knew what the smell was. It wasn't gas from the oven. It was as if she told me, in her high, baby-lady voice, "Tessie, do you really think I would let strangers into my house without cleaning up a little bit?" It was Noxon, which she used on the doorknobs and all metal appliances and sometimes even on silver (even though I told her it scratches silver), and Old English furniture polish, which she thought was better than Pride because it cost more, and Raid, which she would deny using to her death. The apartment was spotless.

Seconal. Saved up over a long time, in a little Tylenol bottle in her night table. It was probably the only thing Victory ever saved secretly for herself. She had never had a secret bank account, or even a secret money jar as a lot of us do. The throbbing I had heard was her dishwasher, running the last cycle.

"Hey, she's not supposed to have this," the super said, when he saw the gleaming pink baked enamel which had been George's last anniversary present to her. "It blows fuses."

They came to my house to mourn.

Pearl sat there, miserable, nibbling on sweets all night.

"Stop already," Helen said.

"I can't help it," Pearl said. "I'm bingeing. That's how I express my upset."

Helen kept forking her fingers through her hair, and saying "Why, why?" until it got me sick.

I was wondering why myself, but not as if there were no reason in the world. Not as if this was Queen Elizabeth who had had everything to live for. I just wondered which of all the whys.

Recently, her brother had moved his business to New Jersey, offering to relocate Victory, but she had refused. "It was not having a job anymore," Pearl sobbed.

Someone said it was the last mugging. Someone else said it was the Parkinson's that she didn't want to face. She never got over George's death, Helen said. Or the child's.

"I never wrote to her," her poor son, Mark, said. He had flown in from Arizona. I put my arm around him and tried to explain that it wasn't him, which both soothed him and hurt him, I think.

Finally, when I got good and sick of Helen's whys I said, "I'll tell you why. I think she put an end to what was no longer there. Just finished it off. Like turning off the oven after the turkey is cooked."

Of course, Helen looked shocked. She also looked haggard. I didn't believe she was either. The haggard came from no lipstick and haggard eye shadow. The shocked was pure phony.

"Don't look so shocked," I said.

She said I was being unfair to Victory, saying she was a nothing.

I would be unfair to Victory if I lied, I said.

Victory had once said — when Mark moved out of the house, I think it was, after the big fight with George — that a part of her went with him. When her baby girl died in infancy she had said the same thing. When George died, that's what she said again. And when they closed down the plant and told Victory she no longer had a place to spend her days, she said it. If Victory was fourths, she was all gone. Even if she was fifths, there hadn't been much left. Three rooms of furniture, a slot in the beauty-parlor appointment book.

"And us," Helen said. "What about us, her friends?"

I told her not to make me laugh. If someone came along who delivered the dry cleaning, you would leave her like that. I didn't say what I would do, because I didn't know. I said excuse me to Pearl, who was marrying the dry-cleaning man. Never mind, Pearl said. I happen to agree.

"I don't like what you are saying," Helen said.

"Listen, honey," I told her, "I've been around the block twice, so why should I care what you like?"

And then, of course, I should have known it, her eyes filled up with tears and she said she couldn't understand my brutality.

"Victory lived for her family," she said. Closed her eyes and laid her head back, like she was getting a hair rinse and it was oh, so good. "Lived for her family."

Oh, the sound of those words.

Then she snapped her head forward and attacked me. You, Tessie Goodman, who Victory was bigger than because she lived for her family, and gave them everything she had.

I wanted to kill Helen. I felt strong enough to lift her and throw her right out the window; if I had had the little red hatchet there God knows where I would have planted it first. She was praising Victory for letting herself get chipped away to nothing, taking away her own life.

I told her to get out.

Everyone was stunned.

"Go on," I said. "Go."

Then she got very quiet and said, Why, what did I mean, and tried to back down, to show everyone how reasonable she was trying to be, but I just didn't care. I said, "Because, Helen, that's why."

"It's grief," she said.

"Yes, that too," I said, and then I made her leave.

And I didn't do it for Victory, or for Victory's memory, or even for Helen's own good. I did it for myself.

Oh, Victory, would that little trick of easing up on the mental pedal have helped? Or was the pedal broken from lack of use?

You never opened the windows, because you didn't want to let the soot in. Remember when we were girls, how you loved the autumn, always wanting George to throw you in the leaves? I should have told you about the smell outside that day, I should have told you to open the windows wide. But then, it never would have cut through the Noxon and the Old English and the Raid.

I sent Mark one of the pictures of his mother I had found the day she died. She was standing in front of the 1954 Pontiac George had just bought, squinting a little bit into the sun, so it looked like she was smiling, and she had her arm flung over the hood, like a pinup girl. I happen to remember, though you can't see the rag, that she was in the middle of waxing the car when George snapped it.

Two weeks after Victory's death, Louise and Russell decided I was depressed and needed some company. So they were going to leave my older grandchild with me while they went away to some medical convention, at the Concord Hotel in Kiamesha Lake, New York. It occurred to me that it might have been better for my depression if they had sent me to the Concord Hotel and kept my granddaughter for themselves, but I didn't say so. I suspected that they were having troubles of their own and wanted some time to be alone.

"Sibboan will be thrilled," Louise said, the tense of her remark telling me they hadn't yet

312

had the nerve to broach it to her.

"She *is* thrilled," Russell (who is nothing if not sharp) corrected her with a frown.

They were in my kitchen for a change, having stopped off to see me on their way to somewhere (a transparent way of saying they were checking up to see that I hadn't decided to take Victory's hint and check out).

Louise didn't say a thing, but I noticed that she had started taking whatever was bothering her out on the English muffin crumbs. She captured one with her finger and dropped it into the ashtray, got some more, crushed them, you and you and you, into the ashtray with you. She lit up another cigarette.

"A health-food addict who smokes," Russell said.

"Don't start, Russ," she said.

To defend her, I lit up, too. I smoke maybe once a year.

"The two of you," he said. "You know," he said to me, "it is very risky for a woman of your age."

I told him to take off his white coat, I wasn't one of his patients, I was his mother-in-law. (I wasn't really mad at him, I just wanted to deflect his anger from Louise. Anyway, he expects that sort of thing from me. I think he even likes it.)

313

"Mother," Louise said.

"No, no, your mother's right, Lou," he said. (See, they were practically friends again.)

I told him not to be so understanding, I didn't appreciate it (I kind of like it, too).

"What do you mean by that?" he said.

"I don't like to be patronized," I said.

"Oh God, how did I get myself into this?" he said. Right where I wanted him. Would Louise pick up a pointer or two?

"Never mind," I said. "Let's drop it." (Never too much of a good thing.) "When am I going to get Sebby?"

I wasn't sure, as a matter of fact, if I really wanted her. I suspected wanting her came under the heading of I-want-it-because-I-can't-have-it, since it was the first time Russell and Louise were trusting me with their precious and they were plenty leery, especially since, as Russell so sweetly put it, I had gotten myself "involved with the ethnics." I'll put the maracas in a safe place and lock up the chili powder, I told them, but they were not amused. They wanted the grandmother-granddaughter re-union jamboree to take place in their house.

"No," I said.

"But, Mother . . . ," Louise said, "the neighborhood." She whispered as though the neighborhood might overhear and get insulted.

"Louise," I said. "You grew up in the neighborhood."

There it was again, they were reluctant, so my desires began working overtime and I was imagining something like the first moments between Anastasia and the Czarina when I heard Louise say "Yes," while Russell said, dryly, "Just try to keep her in one piece for a week, will you?"

"Russell," Louise warned.

"Lou," Russell said, "there's no harm in saying."

And I stood there with a stupid smile on my face, wondering what in the world I was going to do with the child for eight whole days.

The child, as it turned out, was not much thrilled. She came into the apartment reluctantly, like Eloise leaving the Plaza, I told her. She smiled wanly at that.

"Give Gram the cake," Louise said quickly, and pushed her at me.

She handed me the cake box nicely enough, but there was no repeat of the smile, and as Russell and Louise made a quick exit, I began to think it was going to be a long week.

"They need it," she said to me, as soon as the door closed behind them.

I like my granddaughter very much. She is as clever and heartless as most children, as well as endlessly observant of the conditions of old age without yet being an initiate of its euphemisms. That first day she held her nose when she came into my bedroom.

"Mothballs," I told her.

"My other grandmother smells like that, too," she said. She said she hoped I wouldn't get decrepit like her other grandmother, and asked if her grandfather was decrepit before he died. I think she was up to D in the dictionary, which she read all the time, she said. I raised my eyebrows when she said it, and she said if I didn't believe her, to say so. I liked her very much.

The first day we settled the matter of our names. She requested that I not call her Sebby, but Sibboan, and I requested that she forget about Gram which made me sound like a measuring cup. She could either call me Grandma (provided it was said clearly), Tessie, or Mrs. Goodman. I threw the last one in as a joke, but was relieved when she chose Tessie.

I asked her what she wanted to do for the week. I suggested the Bronx Zoo, the Botanical Gardens, the Jarmel Mansion, but she said she wanted to experience life. This apparently consisted of eating all the foods Louise deprived her of, which included anything that didn't look like it had been left for or by squirrels. It also consisted of "hanging out" in my bookstore, which around her house, I gathered, had the reputation of a cross between the Casbah and the Snake Pit.

We fed all the squirrel food Louise had brought (trail mix and granola) to the pigeons and jays that have come to nest lately in the big tree in the empty lot outside my bedroom window. Then I took her down Burnside to the old A & P. I showed her the exact spot where her mother had gotten caught shoplifting (she had been nine), the one and only time in her life she had ever done anything unlawful. Sibboan's eyes widened. "Really?" she said. "What did she take?"

"A box of All-Bran," I said, and we both laughed.

We filled the cart with frozen blintzes, frozen potato pancakes, frozen pizza, frozen fish sticks, all of which, I assured her, were just as good as having these things prepared from scratch by a mediocre cook, which I was. At first she was disappointed. What about the great, greasy pot roasts I used to make that her father said you could taste for days? I told her to look up *myth* in the dictionary, and meanwhile just forget it, the kitchen was closed.

Finally, she was won over by the rich array of preservatives listed on each box, which she read to me with scandalized delight.

When she stepped into the bookstore, I could see she was Barney's true heir. She entered as if it was the one place she belonged. It was all over her face. Her hand reached out for books. She was quick at putting them away on the shelves, quick at taking one down, quick at coming across something she had always wanted to read. She came across something she had always wanted to read on the average of once a minute, I think, that first day. And she read, curled up anywhere, with such a watchful look on her face, that I sensed books were as alive to her as people were, and as capable, in her mind, of surprising her at any minute, not necessarily pleasantly. She was very much on her guard, and yet very much in love, like a woman with a dangerous man.

She had a strongly developed sense of the peculiar, and an intense interest in crime and perversion, which she invariably called "something a little bit wrong." It was part fear, I was sure, instilled in her by her parents, and also part imagination or desire for adventure. In any case, she spent many happy hours that week, creeping up on some of my oldest customers and following them around the store, suspecting them of getting ready to shoplift, or who knows what. One afternoon Flynn came in, and fell asleep in front of my one blank wall in the whole store, while he was inspecting some patching job I had done on a splintering shelf. There he stood, motionless for at least five minutes, staring (his eyes don't close when he gets one of his spells) at a piece of wood and the cement behind it, while Sibboan stood, brow furrowed and eyes shining, fascinated, behind him.

"Something is a little bit wrong with that man," she said to me, and was impressed when I was able to introduce him as a personal friend.

If it weren't for this highly developed sense of "something a little bit wrong" I might not be alive today. Now that sounds like high drama, but it is literal fact. I am not, for once, exaggerating. I have no need to. My life has taken a decidedly dramatic turn without any extra help from me.

Thursday. Gloria, who had been working in the store with me for a while, had taken the afternoon off to do some shopping. I sent Sibboan across the street to McDonald's to get some of their apple turnovers with the fake apple filling–mucilage, she called it–and milk. I was doing some work downstairs, so I locked the door, giving her my key, before I went down.

M. H. Ross entered by the front door, using the key he had held in his pocket most of his life. It was the oldest key to the store that there was, and the O'Neill sisters had given it to him on his tenth birthday as a pledge of trust for their only nephew, who even then was showing signs of being a little nuts. He was absolutely noiseless, of that I am sure. It wasn't the noise that I heard, it was just that feeling which I had gotten so many times before, of someone's presence. There is a solid moment before something happens, not a noise, not a smell, nothing you can touch or hear, when you know for certain something is about to occur. It felt like cold air, which it might have been, slipping down the stairs even more quickly than he. I didn't place him right away, but I knew he was someone I had seen a long time ago, or had known. Now, that happens to me a lot, and half the time it isn't someone I know at all, but just the shape of a head, or a way of nodding or blinking, and my mind is paying respects to a memory I didn't even know I had. And sometimes I think it isn't the faces or the shapes I know, but the expressions I remember. This was an expression of either watchfulness or vagueness, and it came to me that I had seen it on the face of Fritzie O'Neill, and then I knew who the man was.

People don't usually think about their actions while they are performing them, but right then it seemed suddenly as if my actions were laid out in a row alongside my thoughts, so everything was twice as slow: thought, action, thought, action, crawling. There he was, I thought, then I looked and saw him, where? In a place he isn't supposed to be, I thought. I stepped back against the wall; where are my hands? I thought; here on my face, and I put them there. He was pale, and his whole face and hair seemed to twinkle, like someone on a television set with bad reception and it was like that, far away and with the sound turned off. The twinkling was melted snow, it had begun to snow, it fell off his hair and from his nose and eyelashes so it looked as though he were crying or had just come out of the shower, and he was shivering. No sound, except his teeth chattering as he came toward me. Blinked and stopped. Put his hand to his chest as though he had a sudden pain, moved toward me again, stopped again, moved, until he was close enough for me to see that he had no eyelashes. He put his hand on his chest again, pledging allegiance. Or like a squirrel in danger, the stillness, the hand, the blinking eyes. I said his name, Neil.

"I never touched a thing," he said.

I had not heard Neil O'Neill's voice for thirty years. I remembered it. It seemed to come from his top teeth and he moved his tongue as if he was pushing the sounds out.

"I never touched a thing," he repeated. "Don't touch, don't touch, they used to say it all the time, so much, about everything, I used to put my hands in the air all day long." He put his hands in the air as if he was surrendering to me, except flattened against his right palm, secured by his thumb, was a kitchen knife with a black handle.

"They made me feel like a thief the way they said it, and I never touched a penny. I never touched a thing."

When he sold the store to us, in the forties, he had been barely twenty, pale and quiet. "I thought you were going to become a priest, Neil," I said.

He just shook his head.

"What are you doing?" I said. I whispered.

He looked puzzled at the question. I began to understand that he didn't completely know I was there; or saw me on that little television screen behind his eyes, so that I was very remote to him. Maybe he sensed me, only sensed me as I had sensed his presence all those times.

"Why did you come back here?" I said.

"They must have hid it somewhere, they must have buried it," he said. "Fritzie said she buried it somewhere and if I would go away it would be for me."

He closed his eyes and put his hands in front of him, so that the knife handle almost touched me, but the blade grazed his arm. He didn't seem to feel it. I recognized the pose as a comic-book cartoon of someone trying to contact the dead.

"What are you looking for, Neil? I'll help you find it."

He opened his eyes and looked annoyed, as if I had disturbed his sleep. "You know," he said. "The money. The treasure. My payment. My portion."

"Aren't we all," I said, because aren't we?

"Where is it?" he said. "I looked everywhere. The smaller one, Nellie, wanted to hide it away in the ground, underneath the pipes. I caught her with a little pick trying to crack the floor, she tried to pretend she was picking up a teaspoon. But the next day Fritzie had a better idea. Not in the wall, not in the mattress. Now do you know?"

All I kept thinking was Sibboan, and wanting her to somehow not be able to get back in, so she would be safe. If I could keep Neil talking, maybe I could figure out what to do.

"I think I know," I said. I didn't have the least idea.

"I knew it," he said. "She knew, she knew." He said this to the knife.

"Show me," he said, and put the knife against my cheek. I walked, not knowing where I was going, carefully feeling the cool knife against my face. I walked him to the stairs, maybe I could get him upstairs.

"No," he said, as if he had heard my mind. He made me turn around and walk back into the little room where I, and before that his aunts, had once slept. He pushed me onto the bed.

"Where is my prie-dieu?" he said.

I was extremely drowsy by this time; I felt I could have put my head down on the pillow and just gone to sleep. I had to struggle to think clearly, and yet I could feel my heart against my ribs.

I knew at once what he meant. It was a small wooden frame with a lower ledge for kneeling and an upper one for a book, presumably a Bible. It had been there when we bought the store. I had seen it over the years, and had told Barney a hundred times to throw it away. I had seen it again, months ago, when I was combing the store for my own treasure, but I could not remember whether I had finally thrown it away myself. If it was still in the store and I could find it, maybe I had a chance.

A draft of air blew a picture off the shelf above him, and it tumbled and swooped like a bird. Neil dodged it as if it were aimed at him, and as he did he bumped his shoulder into the door frame, looking at the door frame as if it were a person who had hurt him, lifting his head up quickly and knocking it on the corner of a low-hanging shelf as he turned, lifting his hands up as if to ward off a blow. It was such a crazy scene of clumsiness I started to giggle to myself and then I couldn't hold it in, I pressed my hands on my mouth and tried, I just couldn't stop laughing at the sight of him, I finally just let loose and laughed and howled, even while he was cutting into the air with the knife, he wasn't really aiming it at me, but then he tripped and fell toward me and the knife touched my arm again and it felt warm and wet instead of cold, and that shut me up right away and I passed out cold.

When I woke, Joe Fig was there, standing over me, as they say in the crime stories, and my little Sibboan; Neil was sitting on the end of the bed, attached to it, I saw, with Joe's belt. I felt something had to be said, so I said,

"Where am I?" which seemed to satisfy everyone, and Joe said, "You're safe and sound," and I thought Jesus Christ, that's just what he's supposed to say, and Sibboan, who had seen Neil let himself into the store, said right then she thought there was something a little bit wrong about him, so she had told Joe. Neil said, very politely, "I'm very sorry, Mrs. Goodman. But do you know where my prie-dieu is?"

The police came, and they acted just the way crime books said they did, taking out a piece of paper to read Neil his rights, and even said to him, "We can do this in a friendly way, or . . . ," to which he replied (very sensibly, I thought), "Do I look like a public enemy?"

But they handcuffed him anyway, and pushed him to make him walk. I told them to stop and I went behind the mess near the cellar door and under some old shelves I found the prie-dieu he was looking for and gave it to him.

Weeks later, I got a thank-you note from wherever they were keeping him.

Dear Mrs. Goodman:
Neil really didn't want to buy your store. He only wanted what contained his portion and he is sorry for misleading you in any way. He thanks you sincerely for the prie-dieu but wishes you to know that the

treasure was not in it. Or it has been removed. He would respectfully request that you keep looking and if you find his treasure, that you be honest enough to keep it for him.

Very truly yours,
P. T. Ross

P.S. Neil did not mean to cut your arm.

"He didn't mean what he did to Mateo, either, I suppose."

—Gloria

"Does this mean no buyers?"

—Russell

"I never believed in those letters from the beginning."

—Louise

Do you believe this?

It snowed all fall and winter. The first Thursday in November, we had the big one.

I don't like snow. I am too old. But sometimes, I have to admit, when nothing else is doing, snow is not bad. It gets your mind off other things for a while, and then when you get back to them, they aren't so bad because you say, "Oh, well, I have such and such trouble, but at least it isn't snowing."

When you are in the middle of the snowstorm all sorts of things are suspended besides alternate-side-of-the-street parking. For instance, if you have a doctor's appointment. When I make a doctor's appointment, even if it is just for a checkup, I automatically get sick. I find a little lump I never noticed before (benign cyst at best, removal under general anesthesia in any case), or get that mysterious pain on the lower left side, which I am sure is nothing but will have to mention or else it will get worse, but which, once mentioned, gets so much better it isn't there and I can't describe it, and I feel like a fool until I leave the office, and then it comes back. So along comes a snowstorm so bad you have to cancel the doctor's appointment, and you are too busy to bother about little pains, and by late in the afternoon you are standing at the window looking out at cars sliding along and you notice the little lump is gone, and the pain (which you probably got from pressing at it all that time) went away.

And if you have sciatica, or rheumatism, it is all right in the snow. Everyone has sciatica in snowy weather and wants to talk about it.

There is nothing like a weather emergency to

make people friendly. It's neutral, you see, and nobody's fault. I have a theory about that. I'm not talking pestilence or floods, God forbid, but an honest-to-God bad storm could save a marriage. Think. How many times, think, do you stand by the window, waiting to catch a glimpse of that hero you married? As many times as it snowed last year, right? It is the law of diversion. Take for instance, the Zampels. Now, every time the Zampels started to have a knock-down drag-out fight, their little boy Rory would divert their attention by falling down the stairs or off his bicycle, or cut himself slicing an apple, and they would have to stop the fighting to take him to the doctor, and never finish the fight. It's the same principle. Of course, the kid ended up with scars, contusions, and a big indentation on his skull in the front and had to walk on crutches down the aisle at his parents' twenty-fifth reaffirmation-of-vows ceremony. How much easier it would have been on the little tyke if they had lived in California where the mud slides at least once a year, or somewhere down in the cyclone belt.

Snow is also good for the book business, because, aside from milk and bread, the biggest necessity is to not get stuck in the house with nothing to do and nothing to read.

That is my snowstorm theory.

It started late in the morning, about eleven, big, fat, lazy flakes that had covered the lilac tree in front of the store in less than fifteen minutes. I had to call Flynn to come over and help me drag the tree inside.

This might be a good time to say that Flynn is not as bad as I thought he was. Of course, he is no Barney, but then, Barney was no Barney either, was he? I have never met a strong man. Not even my father, whom I would rather call hard. But Flynn was kind, next to Barney, and Gonzalez, the kindest.

After we dragged the lilac bush in and I was brushing it off, Flynn went out to get us some hot coffee at the McDonald's. By the time he came back the whole street was white, and you could hear the plows breaking down under the Elevated, where part of the street is still cobblestone and the plows catch on the lumpy stone sections every minute or two.

Flynn said he had better go home, but I told him to stay awhile. Knowing how he falls asleep suddenly, I could just picture him standing in front of our building with his hand on the doorknob, snoozing away and frozen stiff.

So, for the next few hours, he helped me around the store, sweeping up, straightening displays.

People kept coming in, slamming the door,

stamping their feet all over the floor, excited by the storm, wanting to talk about how bad it was out there, what car had just spun out of control, how they almost slipped because the footing was so bad. I must have laid down two weeks' worth of old newspapers near the front door with all the in-and-out going on. We sold out of every single magazine I had, and I blessed Gloria for talking me into putting up a stand.

She stopped in, too, on her way to an emergency meeting of the Joint Neighborhood Associations, because of several of the old buildings being without heat. She didn't know if our building was among them, and Flynn and I decided we had better call and find out.

Morton, the landlord, was in Nassau for the week.

Gonzalez, the superintendent, had taken his wife to Puerto Rico. Gonzalez's mother-in-law, in whose care he had left the building, wasn't sure where the boiler was exactly, but with her teeth chattering, told us she was leaving for her sister's in New Rochelle in five minutes. Beadie Kesselman, who was on her way to her daughter's in Manhattan, stopped into the store to tell us that the building had no heat. She had knocked on Mr. Hirsch's door but there was no answer. She was concerned. So Flynn decided to go back to the house and see if Mr. Hirsch was all right. If there was nothing he could do about the boiler, he would come back with anyone who was stranded. I had plenty of heat.

Meanwhile, Gloria came back, and beat around the bush for a few minutes, and then came right out and asked me if I would keep the store open all night as an emergency shelter, and I said, Are you crazy, you have some kind of nerve, and all the other usual things you say when someone asks you something you can't refuse, and then I said she would have to stay too, to organize things, and she said she had planned to, just as soon as she got her boys home from school. Flynn came back with Mr. Hirsch, and another old man. I sent them downstairs, into the little bedroom. Mr. Hirsch's color looked bad.

Fifteen minutes later Gloria came in with two old women, and I thought Noah's Ark, and I told her to take them downstairs with the two old men, and bring me a pair of kangaroos, when in walked a young girl from the redevelopment group with her baby hanging in a pouch in front of her, and I thought to myself, I better not ask for anything else without thinking twice because my wishes are getting heard, and just as I thought that, in walked my son-in-law Russell, and I said, whoops, think again, because I sure didn't ask for him to show up here.

He looked terrible. His clothes were dripping wet, his face blotchy red, and the scared look in his eyes, which he usually hides by not looking straight at me, was so bright it looked like tears. He didn't even notice all the riffraff who were by this time drifting into my store with the look of permanent boarders.

"Where are your galoshes?" I said, but he didn't answer, he just looked down at his feet as though he didn't know he had them.

I asked him what the matter was, and he said nothing, which made me laugh, and when I did that, he started to cry.

It's a pitiful thing to see a man cry, they don't know how. He did it as if he was trying to imitate people he had heard or seen doing it, first ahuh-ahuh-ahuh, then a dry clicking in his throat, something like a cough, then holding his face in his hands, drywashing it. He gave up after a minute or two, but then he said to me, "It's happened. It's finally happened. Your daughter has left me," and tears finally started to drip from his eyes.

Strangely enough, I didn't feel like applauding.

There had been an argument, he said. I

asked what kind. Just an argument, he said. A theoretical argument.

"Russell," I said, trying to be patient, "what do you mean? Is Louise leaving you because you support vivisection? Is she throwing you out because you are hawkish on defense spending? Bullish on America? Because you oppose the E.R.A.?"

"I do not," he said.

Gloria came over. "Is this your son-in-law?"

"Yes."

"The doctor?"

"Yes."

"We need him," she said, and pulled him by the arm.

Someone I had never seen before, in terry-cloth mules, was feeling faint. "I get this sometimes when I'm in a strange place," she said, so I knew she wasn't a regular customer.

Russell took her pulse and listened to her heart.

"I feel better now," she said. She asked who I was. I didn't start with her.

"She threw me out," Russell said.

"Good for her," I said, because if he had wanted sympathy he would have gone home to his own mother. "You probably deserved it. But call her and tell her you're here, safe and sound. She'll be worried."

He shook his head.

"She doesn't care anymore," he said. "She doesn't need me anymore."

Was this pitiful?

"Do you hear yourself?" I said.

"She wants her own checking account."

"What's wrong with that?"

"Nothing," he said. "Except, I offered to give her her own checking account a year ago, and she said no. I offered to start her off with five hundred dollars, but no. She wants to pay her own car insurance, too." He said this last as if that clinched it.

"So what?" Gloria said.

He looked blankly at her for a minute, trying to place her, but then answered her.

"So, it implies she doesn't trust me. It implies she is getting ready to manage without me."

Flynn, who had fallen asleep against the counter, snorted in his sleep; it was the obvious comment. It made Russell jump.

"Otherwise, why would she be doing this?"

"Ask her," I told him.

"I did," he said. "She said I am trying to sap her strength. She said I am the only person in her life who makes her feel as though her intelligence is like skin lesions, to cure or cover up."

335

"Skin lesions?" Gloria said. "Jesus."

"My wife used to be a nurse," he said, as if that explained it.

I reminded him she was pre-med when they had met.

"Oh, and because of me I suppose she didn't finish? Isn't that a little bit of a cliché?"

The whole thing was, I told him. He was. And yet it was.

Of course, though I was tempted to say yes, it was because of him my daughter didn't fulfill her plans, I couldn't. It wasn't fair. It wasn't true. It would have been like blaming Barney for dying.

Anyway, Louise had it wrong. Russell treated *everyone* as though their intelligence was skin lesions.

"Are you having an affair?" I said.

"Are you crazy?" he said. Then: "There is a dress in her closet she claims she has never worn because I am supposed to have told her I didn't like it." He said he rested his case.

Flynn, who had just awakened, said, Let her wear it.

"That's not the point," Gloria said disgustedly.

Russell put up a finger. "That's what Louise said, too."

The phone rang. It was Louise. She sounded

slightly nasal, but all right otherwise. "Is he there?" she said, and when I told her he was, she said, "I thought so. I knew he would go running to you."

I asked her if she blamed me for that, and she said, Oh, no, if there had to be another woman she was glad it was her own mother, and she laughed, so I laughed, but I wasn't so sure it was funny.

I asked her if there *was* another woman, if he was having an affair, and she said, "Are you crazy?" just the way he had.

Then what was going on, I asked her, and she told me to mind my own business, and I said to her, Listen, honey, your husband is going totally crazy. He is sitting among uneducated ethnics, treating them without a fee, talking to them like they are his equals, airing his dirty linen in public, so never mind about my business, *your* business is everybody's business tonight. And then she really started to laugh, not bitterly, just the way someone can, seeing the ridiculous side of it, and I did too, and she kept saying "Poor Russy" between laughs, and I knew everything was going to be all right, and I said to myself, See, my snowstorm theory of saving marriages works. And then Russell popped up, as if he had just thought of something brilliant, and said out loud, "She's premenstrual."

Gloria screamed, *What?* and I told him to shut up, but Louise had stopped laughing on the other end, and she screamed, *What?* and the damned fool kept shouting it as if he had struck oil or discovered gold, and of course Louise heard, and started screaming, *What? What what you sonofabitch?* and Russell heard her and screamed, *You're premenstrual* into the phone, which got everyone's attention, and turned Flynn brick red in the face, he walked away, and Gloria said "Fuck you" and walked away, and Louise hung up so hard it nearly broke my eardrum, and that was the end of the reconciliation.

I told him to go to the other side of the store, out of my sight, which was as close as I could come to saying "Get out" because I would be damned if I would send him out in the storm for someone to feel sorry for.

The store filled up. Two young couples with five children between them came in and asked if this was the temporary shelter, and Gloria said yes and then walked away fast before I could ask her how the word was spreading so fast.

"How did you hear of us?" I said to the next batch of people, amusing myself by making it sound like I was one of those exclusive restaurant people and they had just stepped in to see if we had a table.

"The sign in the basement," they said.

"You put up signs," I said to Gloria. "I thought this was just a temporary, emergency measure."

"Well . . . ," she said.

"What if they steal my books?" I said.

She patted my shoulder. "Don't get nervous. Do they look like readers?"

"What does a reader look like?"

"His eyes are open."

I had to admit she was right. Most of the people had brought blankets, their own pillows, sleeping bags, and were trying to go to sleep. Too bad, in a way, I thought. It would have been a good way to build up a clientele, after all. So I made an announcement, everyone was welcome to help themselves to anything on the shelves, I would accept money, deposits, or I.O.U.'s under these special circumstances. But there were few takers. The store was warm, and I began to feel drowsy, too.

It was getting dark. There is something sneaky about nighttime snow, it's quiet, the way it infects everything around it with quiet, cars, footsteps, dimming its whiteness to night-gray, and the streetlights to the paleness of a fifteen-watt closet bulb, no wonder you stand and watch it for hours, you don't want to turn your back on it. I don't know how long I stood there, but the backs of my legs were tired, and I looked around for something to sit on. All the chairs were taken. And when I went downstairs, there was no room, either. Mr. Hirsch was fast asleep in my bed, and even the desk chair was occupied.

I sat on the steps for a while, resting my head against the wall. I thought of Victory, how she would have scolded me, letting all those strangers in, not because she really objected, but just to register herself with me. And I thought of Barney, how it might have been me, carping, saying to him, "Who do you think you are, the Red Cross?" when all along I loved him for it, and here I am, I thought, and then I awoke uncomfortable and stiff, thinking, Here I am, I had better go someplace else and get some rest.

I went over to the window, I remembered the old rocking chair Barney had put there so many years ago, finally of some use. I tried to maneuver it out, but finally I had to climb in. It felt strange to be so visible to whoever went by, but of course, the few people who passed didn't notice me. Too intent on their own purpose, and I could cross and uncross my legs and no one cared. When I woke it was 3:00 A.M. and

340

the window was halfway covered with snow and it was coming down faster now, not thick, lazy flakes, but a thin, quick, slanted fall, like exclamation points aiming at the window where I sat. My left hand, which had fallen asleep, felt dead; I couldn't even lift it off the old book cabinet where it rested. I lifted it with my right hand and let it fall back again. The old book cabinet. I wondered if the knobs were real brass. I rubbed one, to see if it would shine, and to work my fingers a little. The door fell open, and inside I saw two stacks of books. Oh, Barney, I thought, will it ever end? But then, in the dim light, I watched my own hand as it came alive, reaching into the cabinet for the topmost book, and I watched myself as I made out the faded gold lettering on the spine: G. de. B. Almost as it had appeared in the ledger: G.d.B. The mysterious expenditure: a book, what else? And where else but here, safe as a purloined letter, under my nose?

I lifted the book and read the ornate script surrounded by gold curls all over the front cover: *Georges-Louis Marie Leclerc, Comte de Buffon. Histoire Naturelle des Oiseaux.* Vol. I.

By that time I was wide awake. I examined the books more carefully. There were two stacks of them, where I had watched Barney put them all these years, behind the little doors of the cabinet. I counted. There were ten in all. They were all by the same French author, and they all seemed to be natural history books, all about birds. Very pretty pictures, too, I thought. I opened the first one, the cover thick between my still-sleepy fingers. Some dust flew, but inside the book was clean, and pale white. Brown, slanted script, from a thick-pointed but fluid pen, said: *"Pour ma chère Geneviève, le plus bel oiseau de toute la nature,"* and it was signed, "Georges."

The treasure, Barney's treasure, had been found.

Fishman says I am not rich.

Janet, the expert who researched the books for me, says I am rich beyond words to own such a set, but they shouldn't net me more than forty thousand or so. All the plates are hand-colored, and there are more than a thousand in these ten books alone. This Buffon fellow was some terrific painter. I understand he did other animals besides birds, but my Barney just stuck with the one thing.

Still, to pay $20,000 for one book. Was he crazy? I asked her.

Fishman says yes, unless he had had a buyer in mind, which, since no one has turned up, he didn't.

But Janet says no, since the complete set was

bound uniformly (you should have seen it, hand-tooled leather, enough gold to cap teeth, once we saw what was under all that dust and grime). The minute Barney got the final book of the set, it got more valuable, for two reasons: first of all, that book was the one with the inscription in it. Second, it proved for sure that it was the first-edition set that had once belonged to Buffon himself, and which he gave to his mistress (they call it an "association copy" because it was inscribed to someone closely associated with him). Unfortunately, the mistress didn't know a good thing when she saw one, and she had sold the books off, one by one — which is why Barney bought them one by one — they were scattered.

"He never told you?" Fishman said.

"That's the way some collectors are," Janet said.

"That's the way Barney was," I said.

My possession of the set does give me what Fishman calls assets, which is supposed to make me feel more secure, but doesn't, because assets don't buy me even a new toilet seat. I can take a loan out and buy a new toilet seat, Fishman says, showing a sense of humor for once. He has begun showing the sense of humor since he is courting me, which is since my financial picture has improved.

Flynn, my downstairs neighbor, is courting me, too, but his motive is more basic: he needs someone to keep him awake. Trouble is, Flynn puts me to sleep.

My standing in the book business has improved since the discovery of the Buffon collection, and I have been notified of my future listing in a small but exclusive newsletter of antiquarian dealers. I have listed the store as "Barney's Books," even though I have changed the name over the door. The honor is Barney's, after all.

Also, who needs it? Business is good now, the books are flying right out the door.

And the browser came back.

He was not the man I thought he was, nor the other, nor the other.

His hair was more nickel-plated than birch silver this time, with an unhealthy green tinge to it, and there were bags under his eyes. He looked like he needed some looking after. He wore, or carried, a tweed cabbie's hat with a little button on top, smoked a pipe, and swung a carved wooden cane, though he had no limp. What does that tell you? Props.

He came in one day during the January thaw, on an unseasonably sunny, warm afternoon, when everything was melting and the sound of cracking ice was everywhere, so when I first heard the tapping on the window, I didn't look up at once. I had to hear it three more times before I took notice. I recognized him even through the drippy, half-fogged window, holding one hand, curved in scout fashion against the window as if he was peering beyond, smiling at me. I was surprised to see him. You know, I am not the waving type ordinarily, but I gave him a little one.

He came right in then, and stood, stamping his feet on the rubber mat, looking very pleased. He said, "Long time no see."

What a wit, I thought, but I said hello back. Then he looked down at the hat in his hands, put it on, tipped it and took it off again, which I thought was very cute.

I said how have you been, and he said he had had pneumonia, very bad, and thanked me for inquiring.

"You look a little sickly," I said.

He complimented me on being very direct.

He said he had been wanting to come back and talk to me ever since our conversation some months ago, but then he had gotten sick. Did I remember the conversation? he asked.

Sure I did. I had thought he was M. H. Ross, wanting to buy my store.

"I'm not selling," I told him. "No kidding

345

this time. The place is turning into a gold mine."

"Well," he said, sighing. "That's that." No harm in trying, or something like that.

"No harm," I said.

He played with his hat. He tapped his cane. Could he propose something else to me, he wanted to know.

That was the kind of line Pearl would have loved; she'd have used a ten-foot pole to reach the innuendo, or made one up.

"What did you have in mind?" I asked.

Would I agree to have dinner with him?

Boy, he made it sound like a trip to the Orient. No big deal. Sure, I said.

He looked a little surprised, as if he had expected he might have to coax me or something, which made me a little sorry I had said yes so fast. He asked me when, and I told him Saturday night.

During the week I had second thoughts, but he hadn't given me his telephone number. Otherwise I would have canceled. Not that I was nervous. I wasn't. But there was something.

Louise made a terrible fuss about it. I was sorry I had even told her. She made me go out and buy a new dress, and we argued in the dressing room of B. Altman's about which dress looked better, and then she hugged me and said wasn't it great, wasn't it just like the old days, which it was absolutely *not* like, believe me, everything was different, but she is going through a difficult time so for once I didn't contradict her. She cries easily since she left Russell, but she laughs easily, too. I think she might be on to something.

I finally ended up with a gypsy-type dress, with a lot of green wild berries around the hemline on a black background, and the only trouble was, it made me look a lot younger than I am. And a lot younger than he. He was wearing a tweed jacket, but had left the cane at home. He was puffing on a pipe like crazy. He seemed a little nervous. He looked very English, I told him. I noticed his speech was a little affected, like he was trying to sound English, too. He curled the *o* in *home*, in a ridiculous way.

"Where is *hoem*?" he repeated. He repeated every question I asked him. "Why, right here." So then I had to clarify that I meant his original home.

"My original *hoem*?" he said, and I thought at this rate the basic facts could take all night.

"My original *hoem* is England," he said, which fitted with the English theme; but somehow I didn't believe him.

We went to Roma, a nice Italian place on Central Avenue in White Plains.

My stomach was not a hundred percent, so I said I hope they had something plain.

"Something plain?" he said. "That is excellent restaurant strategy, you know. If you are courting a client, never order something messy or difficult. Always get something plain."

I said he sounded like a very methodical man.

"A methodical man? In a way," he said. "In a haphazard way."

I said, "It occurs to me I know nothing about you except for your name" (which was Ben Harry). I didn't make a joke or comment about the two first names, it seemed to obvious, so after a while he brought it up, saying I was the first woman who hadn't, somehow implying that thousands of women had paid verbal attention to his name.

"Well, listen," I said. "Tessie has class."

He nearly split his sides over this little bit of mouth, letting out a long chain of Tessie's which ended with I'm beautiful. For a minute he turned into Arnold Barnett right before my eyes, and I knew I couldn't trust him. The thought passed so quickly, I don't even think I realized I had thought it.

The waiter brought the menus. I said the

food looked expensive. He said, waving his hand, what did it matter. He said in some of the finer restaurants in Europe, the ladies' copy of the menu did not have the prices listed.

"I'll shield my eyes," I told him.

He asked me if I liked travel. He said it that way, without the "to" so it sounded like a sport. I told him I had never.

"Ahhh," he said, regretfully. "When you travel you become a missile." He said miss-syle. "You can be a discus and throw yourself into the trip and catch the wind of it as you go by. Or, you can be a grapnel, a small anchor, flung somewhere to cling fast. Or, you can be simply a ball that rolls along and rolls along and just about comes to a stop" — he was acting this out with the bowl of his pipe on the tablecloth — "when it reaches an incline and picks up speed . . . and so on."

The miss-syle, or the discus, or whatever his hand was, ended up on top of mine, and, surprisingly, his hands were icy cold. I had the feeling he had said this little speech before.

Did my husband travel, he wanted to know.

I said, "No, hardly ever."

His eyes sprang wide open at this, as if the news shocked him.

"He really hated it," I said.

"Hated," Ben said. He raised his eyebrows. "A strong word."

"Well," I said, feeling as if I were defending Barney, "he just wasn't comfortable if he didn't understand the language and was out of reach of his own pillow." (That was me, not Barney.) "Not that he was provincial," I said. "He wasn't. He had quite a broad view of the world. But he needed to be anchored."

Ben made a polite, sympathetic face, which made me realize I was talking bullshit. I said so.

He laughed. That's what he loved about me, he said, and again, I got that alarm: What does he want?

Oh, he had been everywhere, Greece blah, London blah blah, Paree, blah blah, and something about Museums of Natural History.

"Where would someone go on their first night in a strange city, if she didn't know anyone?" I asked, thinking that ought to carry us through the dessert.

He said some people go to churches, chess players drop in at their clubs (I could see he loved saying *club*), some people stayed at the telephone making whatever contacts they could, and some go to bed early, which is the most primitive refuge, but the surest. He, he said, nodding his head at me, takes a lovely lady to dinner.

"I would go to a bookstore," I said.

When I said that, he reddened, and then paled.

"Really," he said, which, considering all the wit and wisdom that had been flying, sounded pretty lame. "To a bookstore, hmmm?" Then he seemed to recover, somewhat. "Well," he said. "I too like bookstores, as you know. As a matter of fact, I have a little surprise for you."

Here it comes, I thought.

"I have a little bookstore of my own," he said.

I gave him a *really*. "A little bookstore of your own, hmm."

And what did that have to do with me? I didn't say anything, figuring he would tell me what he wanted to more quickly without the games.

"In Chicago," he said.

"The windy city," I said.

"I call it 'Call me Ahab,'" he said.

"Isn't that 'Ishmael'?" I said.

"I don't know, my son named it," he said.

I asked him what he was doing in New York all winter if his bookstore was back in Chicago. He said he didn't really run it anymore, he let his sons do that, and he just traveled.

What kind of bookstore was it? I asked.

He flushed again.

"Antiquarian?"

He paled.

Despite that, when we got home, I invited him in. You ask why? Challenge, to solve the puzzle, because it was the wrong thing to do; that's me. I offered coffee. When we got into the house, he said he would prefer, if I didn't mind, a nightcap.

"In my house a nightcap is a pointed flannel hat with a pompom on it," I said. "Talk English. You want a drink?"

I poured him a shot of Pinch and I took one.

He was puffing on his pipe, sending up short, thick signals, until the whole living room where we stood was clouded. Under the cover of the smoke, he made a grab for me. I was expecting it.

He patted me all over, as if he was searching for something. We kissed. No flavor, I thought. No zip. He kissed me again, this time tipping me all the way backward, as if by acrobatics he could make himself taste good. I thought, "When we are dancing and you're dangerously near me / I get ideas, I get ideas." An old favorite. I opened my eyes and saw him looking beyond me, around my living room.

I pushed him away and said, "They're not here, Harry." At first he tried to pretend he didn't know what I meant.

"What?" he said, trying to look muddled, puzzled. He looked ridiculous.

And even if he was a good kisser, I told him, enough was enough, and he would have to pay full price.

"For what?" he said. Still trying.

"Don't make me laugh," I said. "For the Buffon."

I thought he would faint dead away.

"You know?"

"Where have you been?" I asked him.

He was backing into the armchair. "I've been sick," he said.

"You look it," I said.

I told him not to sit down.

He said he would have made me a fair offer, that he was a man of honor, on his sacred word.

Man of honor? Sacred word? Searching my shop, hoping to find the books before I knew they were there, or what they were? And if he had found them, I asked, what would he have considered "fair"? A dollar a book? Maybe six dollars a book?

Suddenly he was all business. He offered me twenty-five thousand for the whole set.

"Are you nuts?" I said. Barney had paid twenty for one book.

Barney overpaid, he said. He looked at his

fingernails when he said it, so I knew he was lying.

"The price just went up," I said. "Every time you lie to me, Mr. Man of Honor, the price goes up a little bit more." He started to argue, then started to tell me how incredible a woman he thought I was, but I held up my finger and said, "The price," and he shut up. I had the man by the balls.

Forty-five, he said, depending on the condition of the books.

"Sixty-five," I said, "if I decide to sell."

The negotiations took somewhat more than a month. He examined the books. He offered me forty-five thousand. I turned him down. He claimed there was browning and foxing (conditions of aging in books, when the pages are brown around the edges, and when they get little age spots like an old man's hand) in several of the earlier volumes. I said the only foxing was what he was trying to do, and then for a week I hung up on him every time he called.

We started all over again. He examined the books again, this time admitting they were in mint condition. He offered me fifty, and I could have taken it, except I felt like making him suffer a little, so I said no, and it dragged on a while longer.

Gloria accused me of liking him hanging around. And I suppose, in a way, I did. We ate together sometimes, and I liked having a man pay.

But then, one day, I said sixty, and he said, "Sold American" (like the old Philip Morris cigarette commercial), and I couldn't say no, so I said yes. After the deal was "cut," as he liked to put it (he was a businessman but definitely not a bookman, I told him), he asked me to marry him.

"We have an adversary relationship from the word 'go,'" he said.

I said I had had one of those and I thought I could live without another. I said I thought I preferred being the witty one of the pair, and he was too much competition for me. I said I was tempted, which I was, and that I kind of regretted saying no, which I did. But I didn't say, and that was the biggest reason of all, his kisses were not nutmeg, and his breath wasn't sweet. I didn't love him.

Then he offered to go partners with me in a bookshop he had looked at in San Diego. I told him to give me a little time, and I would let him know. He told me to take three weeks.

I did. I told him no, at the end of it. But meanwhile, I had put a down payment on the bookshop myself, because if Ben is anything,

he is a smart businessman, and if it was good
enough for him to buy, it was good enough for
me.

I had been thinking of California for a while
anyway, their services for senior citizens are
excellent and I have to look ahead to the day
when I begin to get old. I have always liked the
sound of the sea, and lately I have wanted to be
near water. When I told him about it, he burst
out laughing, and another of his long stream of
Tessie's, and told me how wonderful I was, and
that time I almost succumbed. I loved being
called wonderful, no doubt about it. But I
didn't succumb, nor to Flynn, nor to Fishman,
though I am taking Gloria Muñoz with me to
work in the store.

I have turned Tessie's Place over to Louise, in
joint ownership with Sibboan, to whom I have
sold my half for a dollar. Louise is running it
with her new boyfriend (who is worse than
Russell, but at least not a gerontologist), and I
am ready to go.

Last night, Louise and I had dinner. "Have
you any advice?" she said. I couldn't think of a
thing. But then, late, after I had gone to bed,
and maybe even after I had gone to sleep, I
thought, "Don't let anyone tell you that all you
need is love. It isn't love, it is possibilities
you need. At any age. Possibilities are the

essential," and I wrote it down so I wouldn't forget, and in the morning I called to tell her, and I read it off the paper to her, and she thanked me, but said she had been thinking of advice about the store.

So here I go, off to the Wilds of California. I am sitting here, looking out the window onto the filthy street, and across the Deegan, which carries cars up to Yonkers; and across the little strip of river beyond it are the hills of Washington Heights, like the backs of old green sheep, and it looks pretty there (though I know it's not), and off the water comes the smell of summer again. It seems to me that what I am seeing is everything I ever wanted, before I wanted more. I also notice that the fireflies are back.

THORNDIKE PRESS HOPES you have enjoyed this Large Print book. All our Large Print titles are designed for the easiest reading, and all our books are made to last. Other Thorndike Press Large Print books are available at your library, through selected bookstores, or directly from the publisher. For more information about current and upcoming titles, please call us, toll free, at 1-800-223-6121, or mail your name and address to:

THORNDIKE PRESS
P. O. BOX 159
THORNDIKE, MAINE 04986

There is no obligation, of course.